I0706313

Published by: Cinnabar Moth Publishing LLC
Santa Fe, New Mexico

Cover Design by: Ira Geneve

ISBN-13: 978-1-962308-03-8
Library of Congress Control Number: 2023949955

The Family that Finds Us

PHOENIX BLACKWOOD

Dedication:

To those of you who feel alone or too broken to be loved -- you're perfect. Keep fighting and love will come.

Content Notes:

The Family that Finds Us deals with many difficult topics that may be triggering for some readers.

Sexual assault
Drug use
Homophobia
Transphobia
Abuse
Explicit language
Alcoholism

Acknowledgments

This book wouldn't have been possible without the support of some and the passion of others, and they all deserve recognition now that the trilogy has come to a close. These books grew up with me, and everyone that's been in my inner circle at some point in my life have heard bits and pieces of this story, even in its earliest form, before it was a fully fledged series. Friends in high school read the awfully written screenplay that was very different, but still was the same story, just in a more primitive form. (I still have the screenplay. It's in a binder that will never again see the light of day.)

Things didn't really shape up into something actually readable until I was in my mid 20's, and that's where this first thanks comes in. Thank you, Kelly, for pushing me to write and coming to my house every week to write with me. Thank you for reading the chapters as they came to life, and I'm sorry for leaving you on that awful cliffhanger for so long. You were the first person that made me think, "Hey, I can do this. I can actually write a book."

Thank you, André, for listening to me every time I started to ramble about these characters, and being a sounding board for plot points and character development. Thank you so much for introducing me to Cinnabar Moth and pushing me to write a short story for them to show them what I could create. Thanks for being my writing buddy – we've got more short stories in us still! We're going to create great things together. Maybe one day we'll even co-author a book. You've done amazing things with your voice acting, and your passion really shines through – it's been so great to go on this journey with you.

I'd like to thank everyone at Cinnabar Moth Publishing for

believing in this story. Thank you, Kisstopher, especially, for loving these characters as much as I do. For someone to see the passion and big emotions that are behind characters like Theo, Alex, and Phee, is amazing and I'm so glad you took a chance on me. I'm going to miss these three, but there's more in store for you yet! Thank you so much for the encouragement and really believing that these stories can help people, and let people feel seen. It's all I ever wanted with these three.

Thank you, Theo, for starting it all. For being with me while I was growing up, while I was discovering myself. Thank you for going through the journey with me, and letting me explore my own identity through you. I'm sorry I put you through so much, but your story is powerful and you'll show people how great you are. You were my best friend when I had no one, you never rejected me, and you showed me what true strength was.

Thank you, Alex, for showing me that there's people who truly care. For having the patience and empathy that's so difficult to find in this world. You're a light in the dark, and you're the embodiment of who I wish I could be. You're caring and courageous at the same time – you know what you want and don't let people walk on you. A beautiful person, you've shown me how far a little empathy can get you, even if it has to be tough love sometimes.

And lastly, thank you, Phee. You've shown me how difficult relationships can still work, even when you feel like giving up. Sometimes a little distance is all that's needed. You're the most like me out of the three, a little ball of anxiety with big emotions that can be hard to contain. You'll take the world by storm, let your passion guide you.

Thank you, reader, for going on this journey of difficult circumstances and immense growth. I hope these stories helped you feel seen in who you are, or at least see the world from another point of view. Thank you for taking the time to read these stories, and giving these characters your time and love. You're worthy of all the love in the world, and I hope you find it, even if it's in the small things.

The small things are what really matter.

CHAPTER ONE

The day started off chaotic. I woke before my alarm to the clamoring of dishes in the kitchen. It was a wonder we had any left with how many my mother had broken over the years. I groaned and lifted my phone from the nightstand, turning it on to see it was 5:30 AM. An ungodly hour when no one should be awake, let alone drunk. Pulling myself from bed, I got dressed – skinny jeans and a t-shirt with some Converse – and cautiously opened my door to assess the situation outside.

The faucet was running, but the dishes were slamming in a way that didn't seem like normal washing. I peeked around the corner to see my mother pick up a plate with one hand and take a sponge to it before it slipped out of her hands back into the dirty dishwater. She growled as her stance swayed between her feet, and she leaned on the counter, wetting the front of her shirt. Carefully, I walked up behind her and took the sponge from her hand gently and picked up the plate that she'd dropped and began washing it for her. She staggered over to the kitchen table and plopped into a seat, leaning on the table and resting her face on its surface.

"Thank you, my preciou-ous-es son." She slurred her words as she spoke into the table, and I sighed inaudibly.

At least she wasn't angry-drunk. This was the drunk I could handle, the drunk I knew how to care for. I'd been doing it half my life, it would be strange if I weren't good at it by now. I finished the dishes and laid them out on the drying rack after wiping them dry with a kitchen towel, then sat down in the chair next to her at the table.

"Do you need anything, mom? Have you eaten? Drank anything?"

"Mmno." She rolled her face to look at me, her deep dark eyes glistening but not completely there.

I got a plastic cup from the cupboard and filled it with some ice water and handed it to her. Her hands shook as she tried to lift the cup from mine, so I helped her guide it to her mouth and take a couple sips, then set it back down on the table in front of her. I rummaged through the fridge to pull out some milk and went to the pantry for some cereal. Only, as lifted the milk to pour, I felt objects hit the side of the carton. I opened the cap to take a whiff and gagged; the milk was sour. Sighing, I dropped the carton into the trash and opened the barren fridge to search for another option.

"Eggs, mom?"

I lifted the carton to find three eggs left inside. Searching the pantry, I found bread, then looked it over to find that it was moldy. Into the trash it went with another sigh. I pulled a pan from the rack and turned on the stove. The stove clicked to life, and I set the pan atop the flame and dug some old, but at least still edible, butter from the door of the fridge. I dropped it in and then cracked the eggs on the counter and dropped the contents into the pan.

"Is there any money, mom? I can go shopping after school."

"I th-think there's some left on th-the EBT car-rd, Jeremy."

I left the eggs for a second to rummage through my mom's

purse for the card and managed to find it after digging through a bunch of wrappers and loose change. Sliding the card into my pocket, I returned to the stove and flipped the eggs. I pulled two plates from the drying rack and accompanied them with forks, putting two eggs on my mom's plate and one on my own. The plates clattered as I set them on the hard surface of the table, and my mom lifted her head slowly, picking up the fork and clumsily cutting into an egg. I sighed as I cut into mine, finishing it off quickly as I heard my alarm go off on my phone in my bedroom. I set the plate back into the sink and went to turn off the alarm. Getting together my homework I'd finished the night before, I stuffed it into my backpack and threw the bag onto my shoulders.

I went back into the kitchen to make sure the stove was turned off, then took my mother's empty plate and stuck it in the sink alongside mine. I helped my mom up from the table and guided her into her room. It was a mess. I hadn't been in here in days. There was laundry strewn across the bed and floor, empty boxes and wrappers of snacks, and a plethora of empty cans and bottles. I laid my mom down on the clear side of the bed and pulled the blankets over her.

"I'll help you clean up when I get home. Love you, mom."

"Mmrmph," was her response, face halfway in the pillow.

I closed the door behind me and then left the apartment, making sure to lock up. I waited for the bus to arrive in front of the apartment. A couple other kids from the building went to the same school, so there was a small crowd gathered outside the door and, as always, I did my best to blend in.

———

When I arrived at school, I skipped my locker and went straight for Theo's. They had their face buried inside, with Alex right next to them.

"Theo?" I asked quietly.

They jerked their head back from inside their locker, startled by my presence. Their look softened when they saw me. "Hey."

"Do you think Seth might be able to give me a ride to the grocery store after school? It's okay if not, I'll take the bus or something."

"I'll shoot him a text." They looked me up and down for a second, "Everything okay?"

"Yeah, my mom's just having a bad day. I took care of her this morning but there's almost no food in the house, I don't know when the last time she went shopping was, and she's not in shape to do it herself."

Theo gave me a solemn nod, then closed their locker. "Did you eat breakfast? Alex always has a spare granola bar or something."

"I had an egg, I'm okay."

"*An* egg?" Alex jumped in, pulling a granola bar from her bag, just as Theo had predicted. "Eat it." She handed me the bar and I gave her a half smile as I took it.

"Okay, mom."

She rolled her eyes and gave me a light shove. The warning bell rang, and we went our separate ways to our classes.

It was senior year, and things hadn't gotten much easier than they had been the past couple years. Theo and Alex were still constantly accosted in the hallways, teachers and school staff doing little to help the situation. I flew under the radar most days, keeping my head down and doing my best to blend in. Some days I wished that I had Theo's confidence to be who I really was, which was vastly different from the person that I showed to the world.

Ever since we'd gone to Harriet's party last year, and Alex had dressed me in a bunch of feminine clothes, I'd had this constant feeling gnawing at me that my true self was vastly different than

I'd ever imagined. I hadn't talked to anyone about it. I couldn't tell my mom. She'd reacted poorly when I came out as gay; I had no idea how she'd react to this. I couldn't come out at school, or what little peace I had would be destroyed by the same bullies roaming the halls. I knew Theo and Alex would be supportive, but I think part of me was afraid to say anything out loud. As if by not saying anything, it wasn't real, and I wouldn't have to deal with it. It was a lie that I told myself constantly, that pushing away my true self was best for everyone, including me. Someday I'd let it out, but today was not that day. And neither was tomorrow, or the next day.

Right now, I had a test to ace. My grades were one of the only things that I was proud of, and I wanted to keep them that way. After the test, I had a meeting with my advisor to start planning my senior project, which I was at a loss for. I'd thought about it all summer, and still had no idea what to do. I'd been hoping that the idea would just come to me, but no matter how hard I thought I seemed to draw a blank. I knew I wanted to do photography, as it was my favorite medium and I'd always felt a connection with the camera, but I had no idea what my subject matter would be, what purpose it would serve.

I found myself wandering and thinking about it during the test, and shook my head to try and focus. *One thing at a time, Jeremy.* God, I was starting to dislike that name. I finished the test, taking a little more time than I usually did to go over the things I'd answered while my mind was roaming. Then, as the bell rang, I took off towards my advising teacher's office. She was the school's main art teacher — there were two, but she taught the photography classes, so it was natural that I'd be assigned to her.

Upon entering the empty classroom, I was greeted by her warm smile. She was a small woman, a few inches shorter than me with short curly hair and glasses that framed her face as if they were made for her. She made her way over and hugged me, letting out a sigh.

"Jeremy, I've missed you! How was your summer?"

Theo had their English teacher to back them, and I had this lovely woman, Miss Erickson, or rather Clare as she preferred to be called. She always introduced herself by her first name to her classes. It made her seem more down to earth, making herself more of an equal with the students. A lot of teachers felt that using their first name was a sign of disrespect from the students, but Clare might've been one of the most respected teachers in the whole school. I didn't know a single person who would intentionally disrespect her.

I hugged her back. "It's been okay."

She ended the embrace and held me at arm's length. "Just okay? Nothing new and exciting? Surely you did something to keep yourself occupied this summer."

I sighed and sat down on a stool next to Clare's desk. "Honestly, I was mostly taking care of my mom. I worked a few odd jobs to get some money for a new camera, though!" I'd almost forgotten. I rummaged through my backpack and pulled out my prized possession, a digital camera with a shiny new lens and all the features I'd need for my senior project.

"Ooh, what a beauty! Let me see." She took the camera gently in her hands and turned it over. The casing had a few scuffs and scratches – I'd only had enough money to buy a second-hand camera, but it was still beautiful to me. Clare appreciated this too, smiling as she held it up to her face and focused the lens with her hands. "It's a good one!"

She handed it back to me and I cradled it in my lap. Sitting down at her desk, she turned to me. "So let's talk shop, kiddo.

What do you want to do for your senior project?"

My eyes wavered and darted to the floor, I felt bad that I hadn't come prepared. "I'm… not really sure. I thought about it all summer, but I could never come up with anything. I know I want to do photography, but I have no idea what my subject matter should be."

Clare pressed her hands against her face, in what most would interpret as a scowl but was actually just her thinking face. "Hmm… well, don't worry too much, you still have a good amount of time, but you should settle on something soon."

"I know, I was hoping maybe you'd have some ideas?"

"That's not really something I can decide for you, Jer, the project should be personal to you, not me."

I bowed my head. "Yeah, I get it."

"What's something that's really important to you right now?"

Keeping my head above water. Doing the complicated dance of life with my mother. Not letting anyone see what was really going on with me.

"I don't really know."

"C'mon, you've gotta give me something better than that. What do you really care about?"

"My friends, I guess."

"Start there, think about what parts of your friendship are really important. You'll find something to capture, I know it."

I nodded slowly. "Okay."

"You don't seem convinced."

"It's just that I thought a lot about things, and I don't really know what I can share that wouldn't be too personal."

"You can't be afraid of getting too personal, personal is what makes art."

"But it's not just my story to tell, you know? Plus, I'm not sure it's one I can tell."

"Pull out the parts that are your story, then tell it. No matter how personal it gets, the beauty is in the details. That's where power and meaning comes from. You can't be scared of it, that's what will ruin it."

"What if I am scared? Like, all the time?"

"Then you've got to push through it to the other side. Everything's so much more manageable once you tell that story. Getting it out there is half the battle."

I looked down, scuffing my shoe on the floor. This was shaping up to be something I didn't think I could handle. Tell a personal story, about myself? I couldn't even admit to myself what was gnawing at me all the time. I nodded at her, a little more convincingly this time, wanting to get out of the conversation.

"Think about it, Jer. We can check in again next week, and I hope you have an idea by then so we can start planning."

"Okay." I stood up from the stool and gave Clare what I hoped was a reassuring smile as I waved and walked out the door.

I flew through the rest of my classes that day, meeting up with Theo and Alex for lunch, where Theo told me that Seth would give me a ride after school. I realized that I should've just texted him myself instead of asking Theo – he was out of school and taking a gap year to decide between cooking and music as his career path. We all knew it would be cooking, except for him, apparently. My mind hadn't been the most focused in the morning, so I'd defaulted to asking the person I had actual contact with. Either way, the outcome was me standing in front of the school, scuffing my Converse against the ground as Seth pulled up to the front of the building. I hopped in the front seat, tossing my bag in the back.

Seth shot me a smile and a nod. "What store are we hitting up?"

"Uh, the cheap one on Main? If that's okay? Aren't we picking up Theo and Alex, too? I didn't see them when I was waiting."

"Nah, they took the bus. Theo wasn't feeling well and wanted to go straight home. Main it is."

I sighed and leaned back into the seat. Seth and I were closer than most people realized – all the times I was over and Theo and Alex were holed up in their room, I'd hang out with Seth in the living room. When he cooked, I became somewhat like his sous-chef. I'd learned some fancy knife work and knew how to tell when things needed the occasional stir or flip.

He also knew what it was like to be a guy who liked guys. Although he'd been going out with his girlfriend Rachel since last year, that didn't negate the fact that he was bisexual and had dated guys in the past. We talked a lot about celebrity crushes and found we had similar taste in men a lot of the time – tall, beefy guys. Dark eyes that you could lose yourself in.

"How's senior year shaping up?" Seth broke into my thoughts, and I blinked a couple times before I had an answer.

"We just got in what, like a week ago?"

Seth chuckled. "Feels like forever for me, now that I'm not going."

I rolled my eyes. "Yeah, how's freedom taste?"

"Like a new risotto recipe every day." He grinned.

"Maybe you'd be able to find some kind of food to make from the scraps left in my house and I wouldn't have to go shopping."

"Damn, that bad?"

I nodded.

"Mom angry drunk? You okay?"

"She's more sad and clumsy drunk lately, I'm fine. She hasn't done anything to me in a while, I'm mostly just taking care of her."

"It's still tough, you shouldn't have to be the parent."

"It is what it is." I shrugged, picking at my cuticles.

"You wanna hang out after we get your house situated? Take your mind off things for a bit? I've got a new co-op game we can try out."

Damn, that sounded nice. "Can we do it tomorrow? The house is a mess, I've gotta clean up and take care of my mom if she's anything like she was this morning."

"Sure thing, you want help? I don't mind cleaning."

"No thanks, I don't want her freaking out because I brought someone into the house. I appreciate the offer, though."

"No problem, let me know if you do want the help."

We pulled into the parking lot of the grocery store, and I felt around my pocket for the EBT card to be sure it was still there. Getting out of the car, I shut the door and shook out my shoulders a little, realizing I was carrying a tension that I hadn't noticed. Seth got out as well and walked with me to get a cart.

"You don't have to shop with me, I don't mind if you just wait in the car."

"Nah, I'll keep you company. I should pick up a couple things for the dinner I want to make anyway."

I nodded, and we stepped inside the store. Near the entrance was the produce section – this store wasn't known for its quality, so you had to pick through most of the fruit to find anything that looked good enough to eat. I dug up some bananas that were still green and some apples with only a few bruises and deposited them into the main part of the cart.

Seth picked up some mostly brown bananas and I gave him a questioning look before he answered my silent question. "Banana bread. Theo and I were going to experiment and make it, you know, *good.*"

I snickered and nodded. "Save me a piece."

"Sure will."

We made our way through the store. I mostly picked up the cheapest options for pantry and fridge staples – eggs, bread, rice, noodles, the list went on. Seth picked up a few more ingredients for whatever he had plans to cook tonight. We made our way to the registers, and I put the groceries up on the checkout belt, nervously turning the EBT card over in my hands. I had no idea how much money was left on it, my mom usually spent most of it in the beginning of the month, and we were at the very end of August. I just prayed that there was enough money to cover the groceries. I'd purposely shopped on the frugal side.

After scanning all my groceries and bagging everything up, I swiped the card and heard the terrible beep I'd been dreading.

"Looks like that only covers about half," the cashier said with a sympathetic smile.

I gulped, glancing at the groceries and trying to figure out what I could put back while still having enough to eat.

Seth placed a hand on my shoulder, soothing my panic a little. "Don't worry, I've got it."

"Are you sure?" I glanced up at him, not really wanting him to spend his money on me but needing it all the same.

"Yeah, don't worry about it. I got a job a couple days a week at a cafe and no bills to pay, I've just been throwing it in savings."

"Thank you." I sighed as he swiped his card to cover the last of my groceries.

Afterwards, he paid for his own bag of assorted food, and we walked back to the car. He threw his bag in the trunk while I put my bags in the back seat. We arrived at my apartment building shortly after, and he helped me bring the groceries up the stairs to my third-floor abode. Turning the key in the lock, I heard a crash inside and opened the door to see my mom in the living room, in a bathrobe, prancing around. She'd knocked the lamp on the end table over onto the floor, but didn't seem to notice or, at least, didn't care. She swayed back and forth as music was playing from the television mounted on the wall. Catching sight of me, she floated over and took my hand as I held the bags, trying not to drop them.

"Dance with me!"

I turned to look at Seth, who had a face that didn't know what to make of the situation. Stumbling forward, I stopped on my heels once I got my balance and my mom frowned when she was met with the resistance.

"Mom, what are you doing?"

"Having fun! You're too uptight Jeremy, you've got to let… let loose sometimes." Her speech held the familiar slur that was a regular part of her vernacular at this point.

I looked around the apartment to see that the situation had gotten worse since this morning. The mess was no longer contained to my mother's room. There were bottles and cans strewn about everywhere and everything was out of place, no doubt from my mom knocking into things.

Seth took a step inside to bring in the groceries that he was holding, then glanced over at me. "You sure you don't want my help?"

I nodded as my mom looked over at Seth, letting go of me and traipsing over to him. "Is this your boyfriend?" she asked, draping a hand over his shoulder.

His stance tensed up, not sure what to do with the contact.

"No, mom."

"You know, as much as I wish you'd bring a nice girl home, he's not bad looking," she went on as if she hadn't heard me.

Seth's face flushed red as he slowly took her hand off her shoulder. I put the bags down and walked over, escorting him out the door. "Thank you so much, for everything. Sorry about this." My embarrassment knew no bounds.

He gave me a weak smile as he backed out the door. "Don't worry about it. I'll see you tomorrow."

I gave him a nod as he turned to walk back down the stairs, then shut the door and locked it. As I turned around, I found my mom rummaging through the bags on the floor.

"You didn't get any snacks?"

"No, mom, I just got the essentials. There wasn't a lot of money left on the card. Seth had to pay for half of it. I can make you a sandwich or something if you want."

"Oh, my lovely boy." A cringe rang through my body at the word boy. "Would you? Make me a pb&j?"

"Sure, mom."

I gathered up the bags and brought them all to the kitchen in two trips. I pulled out the bread and some peanut butter, then dug the jelly out of the fridge. The kitchen was a mess, despite me doing the dishes this morning. The drying rack was still full, the remnants of breakfast still untouched in the sink. Newspaper leaflets were strewn about the table, everything was out of place. I sighed as I cleared off a spot on the counter and put a napkin down to spread peanut butter and jelly onto the bread.

My mom clapped as I brought the sandwich to her, and she immediately took a bite, then with her mouth full, "Thank you! Such a precious boy!" Another cringe.

I turned back to the kitchen and pulled a garbage bag out of the cupboard. I threw away old, moldy food from both the fridge and pantry, along with stuff that had so much freezer burn it wasn't identifiable anymore. With the bag half full, I set to cleaning the shelves everywhere and then put the new food away in its places. I turned to the table and put the couple cups there in the sink and balled up the newspaper and threw it in the trash bag. Washing the dishes came next, and I put away the dry ones from earlier. Afterwards, I tidied up and put everything in its place, then moved onto the living room.

Starting with the lamp that, miraculously, wasn't broken, I cleaned up the end table and then picked up all the bottles and cans that were strewn about the table and floor. Mom was sitting on the couch enjoying her sandwich as messily as a toddler while I picked up everything she'd knocked out of place. It wasn't too bad once I got all the bottles and cans picked up, so then I set to sweeping both the kitchen and the living room. In reality, I was procrastinating the true beast: my mother's room.

After the kitchen and living room were clean, I had a full heavy-duty garbage bag and would undoubtedly fill another after the next task. Inhaling deeply, I opened the door to my mother's room and the stench hit me in the face. The smell of stale beer and old food mixed with dirty laundry and someone who hadn't showered in at least a week. I began trying to clear off the bedside table, throwing away empty wine bottles and beer cans. Once that was clean, I pulled out the laundry basket and picked up all the clothes that were on the floor. I'd bring those down to laundry after. After taking one look at the bed, I decided to strip it and put on clean sheets and blankets. I gathered the remainder of the bottles and cans and brought the dirty dishes to the kitchen for another round of washing. I pulled the vacuum from the linen closet, then listened to the crunching sound it made as it sucked up unidentifiable foodstuffs and debris from the carpet.

The bedroom sufficiently clean, I moved on to her bathroom. That wasn't too bad, and I laid out a fresh towel and clean change of pajamas on the sink counter. Going back into the living room, I found my mom curled up on the couch with the napkin from her sandwich still clutched in her hand.

"Mom, get up, you've gotta take a shower."

"I don't feel like it, I'll do it later."

"You haven't showered in over a week. I put out fresh clothes and towels, all you have to do is get in. Take a bath if you want. You'll feel better after, then you can go to sleep. I cleaned your room and your bed is all made up."

"Ugh." She grunted as she pushed herself up from the couch, and I guided her into the bathroom.

I turned the faucet on for her, then left her to shower as I picked up the bags of trash and her overfilled laundry basket. I threw the bags in the dumpster, then headed for the apartment's communal laundry room, dumping half my mother's clothes into a free washer and adding a little extra detergent to counteract the smell coming from them. The washer clicked and roared to life with a rush of water, and I sighed and leaned against the machine to put my hands over my face. I was exhausted and had no idea how long I'd been cleaning. It was dark out now, but I still had to stay up to wait for the laundry to finish, which would at least be one more load.

After trudging back up the stairs and locking the door behind me, I went to my mom's bathroom and knocked on the door. "You okay, mom?"

"I'm… I'm fine," came faintly from the other side of the door. The water was splashing as if it was coming in contact with something other than the floor of the tub, which was a promising sign.

I went into my room to take my own shower, feeling dirty and sweaty from all the cleaning I'd done. I grabbed a pair of leggings and an oversized t-shirt to change into, then turned on the shower in the main bathroom of the apartment. I let the water wash over me, warm and soothing. Standing under the stream, I got lightheaded and guided myself to the floor of the shower before I fell. I'd forgotten to eat. A problem I'd have to solve when I got out. I leaned my head against the wall of the shower and closed my eyes, letting the steam and heat of the water overtake me.

My mom had been like this for years now. It had started off slow, getting drunk a couple nights of the week after work. Her moods were unpredictable. Some days she'd be giddy and messy, others she'd be angry and downright aggressive and hateful. I hated to say it, but I preferred the way she was today. She was drunk out of her mind, but not violent. More like a child needing to be taken care of. That I could do, I'd been doing it half my life. The drunk I didn't like was when she took her rage and grief out on me, because I was the only person left in her life. Everyone else had left as she became more and more of an alcoholic. She'd isolated herself from friends, estranged herself from family. It was just me, and so it was my job to take care of her. Child protective services never got involved because I never told anyone what was going on. I kept all the bruises hidden, masked how exhausted I was at school by chugging energy drinks between classes.

She'd made this hell for both of us. I was just biding my time until I could escape and move on, but at the same time I worried about her. Who would take care of her when I was gone? I felt a loyalty, a responsibility, to take care of her. She was my mother, after all. I wouldn't be here without her. I did still love her, despite everything she'd done. I believed that she loved me too, even though her actions didn't always show it.

Slowly, I opened my eyes to the water and pulled a bar of soap from the shelf and started cleaning myself so I could get out. My shower thoughts always wandered into anxiety, and I didn't want to listen to it right now. I made quick work of it and then got out and dried myself off, putting on the clean clothes I'd selected.

I made my way out to the kitchen and made myself a sandwich, went to check on the laundry and switch it over while I was eating it, then checked on my mom, who was asleep in her bed. Her hair was damp, which meant she'd at least gotten in the shower. A small victory. Returning to my room, I dug homework out of my backpack and set to work as my eyes grew blurry with sleepiness.

CHAPTER TWO

I didn't know when I fell asleep, but I awoke with a start when my alarm went off. My homework was still scattered across my bed, a pencil still clutched in my hand. I scrambled to get everything into my backpack, then grabbed the laundry and brought it back up to the apartment. I set the basket in the living room and checked on my mom, who was still sleeping, before rushing down the stairs to wait at the bus stop. I pulled my long black hair into a top bun, as I hadn't had time to brush through it, then kept my eyes on the ground, not wanting to make eye contact with anyone waiting at the stop. Staying under the radar was how I survived.

My first class was homeroom, thankfully, so I had time to finish up the homework I'd fallen asleep on. After that, my classes were a blur. I was still exhausted and aching from all the work I'd done yesterday, caretaking really taking a toll on my mind and body. It was frustrating, I should've been used to it by now. Sometimes, though, it just got to be too much. I didn't retain much information from any of my classes, and as if on autopilot hopped on the bus with Theo and Alex.

I still wanted to try out that new game with Seth, but a nap was really calling my name. Theo knew it too. They walked me straight into the guest bedroom and pulled an extra blanket out of the closet, handing it to me with a wordless but sympathetic smile. I kicked off my shoes, then curled up on the bed as Theo left the room. All of Alex's stuff was in here, but she rarely actually used the room, always holed up with Theo in theirs. I stayed in the room more than she did. I stared at the shelves with their assorted novels and textbooks from past school years, until my eyes closed of their own will and I was off to sleep.

I awoke to a knock on the door, jumping up quickly before realizing where I was. At home, banging on the door meant my mom was on a rampage and it was time to get out. Here, it was simply Seth cracking the door open to tell me he'd made dinner. I crawled out of bed, stretching out my back and cracking my neck a couple times before exiting the room and plopping down on a stool next to Theo.

"Have a good nap?" they asked.

"Yeah, I feel a little better now." I gave them a faint smile.

"We're still on for that game, yeah?" Seth nodded at me as he dished out the food – chicken parm with spinach, apparently.

"Hell yeah," I said, digging a fork into a piece of cheesy chicken.

We all ate in silence, too busy enjoying the food to make conversation. Alex finished first, as always, and started washing her dish, collecting Seth's shortly after. We all had our roles here – Seth cooked, Alex did the dishes, Theo put the leftovers away. I usually helped Seth cook, that was my job, but I'd slept through it.

Once I was finished, Alex grabbed my dish and Seth tapped me on the shoulder to follow him into the living room. He pulled a game case from the console under the television, put the disk in the gaming system, then handed me the case to look at. It was a cool space-ish, sci-fi looking game, where you played collecting resources from the galaxies. Think Minecraft, but in space, with a more artistic style. It looked like a soothing, laid-back adventure as Seth sat down next to me and handed me a controller. We started playing and fell into a rhythm quickly. He harvested food and resources while I started wrangling strange-looking alien animals. All in all, it was pretty cool.

"How's your mom doing?" Seth broke the silence we'd fallen into.

"Okay, I got her to take a shower last night and cleaned the whole house, that's why I was so tired."

"Damn, even just from the living room that seemed like a big job."

"The living room was the easiest part," I scoffed. "You should've seen her bedroom."

"Yikes."

"Yeah," I muttered.

We fell back into silence as we played on, creating our own little homestead on a planet with purple and blue foliage covering the ground. My favorite part by far were these horse-adjacent looking animals that could fly, with wings that looked like fins. The light gravity on the planet let them swim effortlessly through the sky, and you could ride them all the way to the edge of the atmosphere. This, of course, made them very difficult to contain, regular fencing being useless. I created a closed-in building for them with a glass ceiling to let the light in so that the grass would continue to grow, then filled it with far too many of the horse creatures. I attached a name to each one, getting less and less creative with each one.

"Harold? Seriously, Jer?" Seth chuckled.

"I'm running out of names! You try naming twenty horses."

"You don't *have* to name them."

"But all the other ones have names! I don't want him to feel left out."

"They're pixels, Jer."

"Let me care for my pixels in peace, then." He rolled his eyes, and I shoved him playfully with my elbow while capturing another horse creature we didn't need. This one was Gerald.

———

It was dark as Seth pulled up to my apartment building, then waved as I got out of the car and walked inside. It was a little later than I'd meant to come home. I still had some homework to finish up and *really* needed to start brainstorming on my senior project. My stance froze when I heard a crash inside as I put my key in the door. I sighed, mom was probably dancing in the living room again, knocking things over and undoing all the work I'd done yesterday.

"God fucking damn it!" left her mouth as I opened the door to see a plate full of rice shattered on the floor.

She looked up at me, and I saw the fire in her eyes. This wasn't loopy, giddy drunk anymore. This was angry drunk. My posture shrank as she stared daggers in my direction.

"Where… where have you been? Its fucking late!" She growled.

"I was at Theo and Seth's," I muttered, trying to beeline it to my room as quickly as possible to avoid my mother's wrath that I knew was coming.

I stopped short as a glass of water flew at the wall just inches in front of my face, shattering on contact. A glance in my mother's direction showed her shaking as her expression scrunched her face.

"You think you can just traipse around with these boys? You soil our family name! You're such a disgrace. Can't believe your dad, leaving me alone here with you."

She lunged at me, and I ran the rest of the way to my room,

shutting and locking the door behind me as I leaned against it and felt her pound at the other side. Tears stung at my face. Most of the time, I didn't let my mother's words bother me, but when it came to my sexuality, it hurt in a different way. She'd hit me when she was sober when I first came out, so part of me believed these words, even though she was drunk out of her mind. It felt like she hated me, despised who I was. Just like everyone would at school.

The pounding on the door stopped after a few minutes, and I heard footsteps shuffle away and a growl leave my mother's throat. I sat there, back against the door, and let the tears fall silently. Someday I'd be out of here. Someday, I'd be surrounded by people who loved me for who I was. If only I could show the world who I really was. I was so scared. The inner argument that I had all the time started pinging around in my head.

What if I'm really a girl?

You're a fucking freak.

Tears blurred my vision as I pulled my phone from my pocket and tapped Theo's name in my contacts. I held the phone to my ear and listened to the phone dial. Theo picked up after the third ring.

"Hey, what's up? Didn't Seth just drop you off?"

"Yeah," I sniffled, "My mom's mean drunk."

"Shit, do you want me to tell him to turn around and get you?"

"No, I'm… I'm in my room with the door locked. I think getting out would be harder than just staying in here."

"Is there anything I can do?"

"I, uh… Theo? Can I ask you something personal?" My voice wavered.

"Shoot."

"How did you know you weren't a girl?"

"It was hard, Jer. 'Girl' always felt like a box I'd been shoved in that was full of spikes sticking out the walls. I had to be a certain way, but it was so uncomfortable. This girl I met in the hospital really helped me with it. She taught me about being non-binary and how I didn't have to stay in a box that hurt."

I sniffled again, a sob escaping my body.

"Jer, are you crying? What's this about?"

Without thinking, it slipped out of my mouth. "'Boy' is a box that hurts."

There was silence on the other end of the phone. I couldn't believe that I'd said it, it felt good and terrible at the same time to admit it. Saying it out loud made it real, I'd never said it before. Now it was out there, in the air between us, a silence ringing in my ears, screaming all the awful things I'd always thought about myself.

Theo cleared their throat. "Then don't stay in it. Get out Jer, it's the best thing you can do for yourself."

"I'm scared." My voice was so small, barely a whisper.

"That's okay. I was scared too."

"My mom will never understand."

"Fuck her, she treats you like shit anyway. I know you want her to accept you, but at a certain point you've got to let it go. It's not your fault she is the way she is. I know it's hard, and you want her love, but you've gotta turn to the people who actually treat you with love."

"Maybe I should wait, until I get out of here."

"That's up to you, whatever you feel the safest doing. But let us help you. Don't have us keep calling you something that hurts. Even if it's just at my house, we can make the changes so you feel good."

"Okay," I breathed, my tears subsiding a bit.

"Do you have a name you like?"

"No," I muttered. "I haven't let myself think about it. I've been too scared to even admit it to myself. Tonight it was just too much, so I called you."

"Is this the first time you've ever admitted it to yourself?"

"Yeah."

"That's a big step. Be proud of it."

"I don't know how."

"That's okay. When did you start feeling like this?"

"Something always felt wrong, but I guess it really started getting in my head the night of Harriet's party, when Alex dressed me in girl clothes. It felt so *right*. Like nothing I'd ever felt before."

"Do you think you're a girl? Or non-binary?"

"I think… I think…" It was so hard to say. My voice lowered even more, "I think I'm a girl." The tears returned.

"Okay. Jer?"

"Yeah?" My voice cracked.

"I'm proud of you, okay?"

More tears forced their way out, and I sobbed into the phone again.

"Are you sure you don't want Seth to come get you?"

"Yeah. I'll… I'll see you at school tomorrow. Can I come over after?"

"Of course."

I hung up the phone and dropped it at my feet, sobs overtaking my body. This was a deep, primal cry. One I rarely felt. Everything was coming down around me, and it was so overwhelming. Getting up from the floor, I freed my feet from their shoes and climbed into bed, wrapped myself into a cocoon of blankets and let the sobs overtake me. Fuck homework. Fuck my senior project. Fuck everything.

———

I emerged from my bed at the sound of my alarm and rubbed at my eyes, which still stung from crying the night before. There was a lightness to my shoulders, I felt a little better having talked to Theo. At the same, there was a gnawing in the pit of my stomach that I couldn't shake. Now it was out in the open, there was no escaping it. I couldn't keep pretending that it didn't exist.

I changed my clothes quickly, grabbed my backpack, and snuck out the door, tiptoeing to the exit, past my mom who was now passed out on the couch. I kept my head down, as always, until I got to school. As I approached Theo's locker, they turned to me and brought me into an embrace that I hadn't been expecting. Theo wasn't a touchy-feely person; a hug from them was almost unheard of. Here now, they squeezed me tight, and I buried my face in their neck, tears threatening to spill out again. I leaned into their arms, wrapping mine around their back and holding tight. After a few minutes, we let go and Theo held me at arm's length with their hands on my shoulders.

"How are you feeling?" they asked.

"Not great," I mumbled.

"Just get through school today, okay? We'll talk more at my house. It's going to be okay."

Theo took their hands off me as Alex approached and kissed them on the cheek.

"Hey," she breathed, then glanced at me. "Everything okay? You look a little rough, Jer."

"You didn't tell her?" I turned to Theo.

They shook their head, "Not my place."

"Tell me what?" She looked quizzically between the two of us.

My eyes immediately darted down to the floor, "I'll, uh, tell you later. At home."

"Okay," she accepted, then placed a hand on my shoulder. "You alright, though?"

"Kind of…" I muttered as the warning bell rang for classes.

"Alright, see you on the bus." She and Theo turned away towards their class as I turned in the opposite direction towards mine.

I kept my head down through all my classes, only speaking if spoken to. I did my best to catch up on homework during homeroom, and reluctantly turned in my half-done work for other classes. I'd never let things slip this far before. I was always on time with assignments, early, even. My grades could take this oversight, but at this rate I wasn't sure if I could keep up with everything. An anxiety rose within me, the same anxiety I got every time I felt I wasn't good enough. Like I was a failure. Like my mother's words were true, I was a disgrace. I should've died, not my dad.

I shook my head against the thought, then jumped as the final bell rang, dismissing us from classes. Getting on Theo's bus, I sat down across from them and Alex, trying to hold back tears. I managed to keep it all under wraps until we got off the bus. Walking across the threshold of the house, all my composure left me, and I started sobbing again. I dropped my backpack in the entrance and threw myself down on the couch, not knowing how to handle myself anymore.

Alex rushed to my side, placing a hand on my back. "Hey, what happened? What's wrong?"

Theo came and sat down on the coffee table in front of me, and I buried my face in my hands. I couldn't answer Alex's question, I couldn't get any coherent words out. So instead, we all just sat there. Alex rubbing my back, Theo waiting patiently and handing me the occasional tissue to get the snot off my face. I didn't know how long I was crying for, but it felt like an eternity.

Eventually, I stopped and grabbed a pillow from the couch and hugged it to my chest. Alex brushed the hair away from my face, tucking it behind my ear as I blew my nose into another tissue. Theo grabbed me a cup of water, and I took a few sips before placing it on the table and leaning back into the couch, exhausted.

"What's going on, Jer?" Alex asked again.

I glanced at Theo, then at Alex before letting the flood of words leave my mouth. "I think I'm trans and my mom hates me and she'll never understand and everyone would be better off if I was dead everything's too much I don't know what to do." I said without a single pause or breath taken.

Alex leaned back a little, still keeping her hand on my shoulder. "Woah, that's a lot."

I nodded, still clutching the pillow tightly to my chest.

"Is that what you were talking about this morning? That you're trans?"

Another nod. Then, I looked up at Theo. "Can we smoke?"

"Sure." They tapped me on the knee before getting up and ascending the stairs, Alex and I right behind them.

Theo shut and locked their door and opened their window before pulling a shoebox out of their dresser and hopping up onto their bed. Alex and I joined them as they made quick work of rolling a joint, handing it to me first. I lit it and breathed in, willing that lightheaded, relaxed feeling to wash over me. I blew the smoke out the window before handing the joint to Theo, who took a drag and then handed it to Alex, who still coughed with her whole body after taking the tiniest hit. I took a second, longer drag, then flopped back on the bed, staring up at the ceiling.

Soon, Alex joined me. "Okay, let's talk."

"I feel like… like I'm a girl." I fidgeted with my hands, wringing them together and pulling at my fingers.

Theo got up to put the box away, then lay between me and Alex.

"What do you want to do about it?"

"I don't know. I'm so scared, I know everyone will hate me."

"We'll never hate you, Jer," Alex cooed.

"My mom will. Everyone at school will," I muttered.

"You've only got what, another year with your mom? And the right people at school won't. Our friends won't. I'm sure Rachel would be happy to take a new trans girl under her wing," Alex added.

Rachel had made an incredible coming-out story. She'd stayed closeted at school for the majority of the time that we knew her, but once she got back together with Seth, she really came into herself. She stopped caring about the backlash at school and ditched her boy clothes and started wearing dresses and skirts. Of course, she got the backlash that we all did, but she was so strong about it. She could shut people down so quickly with her words that they'd be dumbfounded and stand there with their mouths hanging open as she walked away. There was a confidence about her. She knew she had a place where she'd always be accepted, and that let her laugh in the face of people who didn't follow suit. She had a strength that I didn't think I could ever replicate. I was so afraid to be me that I could barely admit things to myself.

"I… I don't know if I'm ready to do anything. I just wish I didn't feel so wrong. All the time, I just think about how right it felt when Alex dressed me for Harriet's party. I never would've chosen those clothes on my own, but they felt so *good*."

"Have you ever considered that you're just a boy that likes to wear feminine things? Maybe that's all there is to it," Alex asked.

"It's… It's more than just the clothes. When Theo talks about their dysphoria, I *get it*. Because I feel like that all the time. Things feel so wrong, my name has been bothering me lately, and every time someone calls me a boy it's like a dagger in the chest."

"Ah, I guess there is more going on there, then."

"Why don't we find you a name? Finding a new name was a huge turning point for me, and everything started to feel better afterwards," Theo said.

"I guess. Okay, yeah." I was apprehensive, but also anxious to find something to be called that didn't make the hair on the back of my neck stand on end.

Theo got up and grabbed their laptop from their desk, opening it as they sat back down between me and Alex. I sat up, dragging myself to the side of the bed so that my back was against the wall. Theo scooted back as well, leaning against the window pane.

"What kind of name do you want? Do you just want me to bring up a list of feminine names, or do you have anything in mind?"

"I just... Want it to be really different. I don't want it to sound similar to Jeremy."

Theo nodded. "Okay." They set to typing, pulling up a list of feminine names, then handed me the laptop.

I scrolled through, cringing at some and nodding at others. I liked Fiona, but something didn't feel quite right. "I think... I want a 'P' name," I muttered as I scrolled down quickly to get to the Ps. Then I found it: Phiona. A little unconventional, with the same ring that I'd liked about the F spelling of the name. I highlighted it and handed the computer back to Theo. "It could be 'Phee' for short."

Theo smiled, looking at the screen and then back at me. "Phee," they said, looking me in the eyes.

I couldn't help the smile that formed across my face and I felt butterflies in my stomach the instant they called me by the new name.

Theo nodded. "That's a good one, then. Sam did the same thing when I picked my new name, and I got the same funny look on my face."

"Shut up." I rolled my eyes, shoving them slightly.

Laughter came out of both of us, and they put a hand on my shoulder. "Seriously though, you like it, yeah?"

"Yeah." I stared down at my hands, wringing them together again. "I don't think I'm ready to come out at school, though."

"That's okay," Theo nodded at me, "We can just call you that here. You can take things as slow as you want."

Alex shot up from where she was lying down. "Does this mean I get to make you over? Even if it's just for at home." She clasped her hands together, looking at me hopefully.

"I don't have any money, Alex. I don't know how I'll get new clothes."

She waved her hands at me. "Don't worry about it! I've got a bunch saved from lifeguarding this summer. I'd let you pick from my closet, but we're definitely not the same size, you're a lot sleeker than me. Come on, let's look at some clothes." Alex pulled the laptop from Theo's hands and started typing and hit enter before handing it back to me. "That's my favorite site, it's got a ton of options, I'm sure you'll find something you like." Alex lay across Theo's lap to watch as I scrolled through the sections. "Put anything you like in the cart, we'll weed it down after."

"Okay," I said softly, adding a few things here and there. My style could be easily described as 'punk kid', and I was a little afraid of it looking too childish, but Alex didn't pass any judgment as I added items to the cart. She just smiled and nodded at me as Theo ran their hands through her hair. After about thirty minutes of browsing, I handed Alex the laptop with a cart full of items to pick through. To my surprise, she nodded at almost every single one and hit "purchase" before I could stop her.

"I didn't mean to get all of it!" I waved my hands in front of the screen.

She gave me a sly smile. "Tough. Consider it an early birthday present."

32

CHAPTER THREE

I awoke to a shift in weight in the bed as Alex got up and left the room. We'd fallen asleep watching movies the night before, and I'd never made it down to the bed in the guest bedroom. Theo's mattress was barely big enough for two, so we'd fallen asleep in a heap, sideways on the bed with our legs hanging off. I sat up and stretched, careful not to disturb Theo, who was still asleep with the laptop on their chest. I lifted up the laptop to put it away on their desk, and Theo stirred a little but didn't wake up. I made my way down to the kitchen in yesterday's clothes to find Seth cooking up a breakfast for all of us.

"Just in time, my sous chef." Seth handed me a spatula to stir up some mushrooms, peppers, and onions he had cooking.

He pulled some bacon from the pan and patted it dry with some paper towels, then cracked a few eggs into a bowl before adding them to the vegetables in my pan. The smells were intoxicating, and I breathed in deeply as Seth tossed in some seasoning.

"Keep stirring, pull that when the eggs are done." He nodded at me, then turned to attend to the toast that had just popped out of the toaster.

Listening to the sizzle, I stirred until the eggs were fluffy and slightly firm, then dumped a serving onto the four plates Seth had set out on the kitchen island. He divided up the bacon and toast, setting out some butter and jam as well. Alex joined us shortly after, eagerly grabbing a plate and sitting down at the island. I sat next to her, and Seth sat on the other side of the island.

"Theo's out cold," Alex said through a mouthful of food. "I think they fell asleep late last night."

"I'm surprised Dulce hasn't gotten them up, usually they're out early for a run," Seth added.

As if on cue, the three-legged chocolate lab padded down the stairs and started whining at the front door. Alex dropped her fork onto her plate and grabbed the leash that was hanging by the door.

"I'm just gonna let her out, don't want a mess in the house."

Seth and I nodded at her as she shut the door, and we ate in a silence that wouldn't normally be awkward, but my nerves were getting the better of me. Other than Theo, Seth was pretty much my best friend. It felt weird not telling him what we'd talked about last night. I knew he wouldn't react negatively, him being with Rachel and all, but telling him was still scary. I didn't want him to think of me differently, I still wanted to be his friend in the same way I was now. I didn't want our relationship to change or be awkward because I was a girl.

Seth had a sixth sense for things being off, having grown up with Theo and needing to intuit emotions from the smallest gestures. "What's up, Jer?"

"What?" I asked too quickly.

"You're fidgety. Your leg keeps bouncing and you're pushing around your food a lot more than you're eating it."

Damn, he was on top of things. "I... uh... there's something I have to tell you."

"What's that?"

"You have to promise our friendship won't be any different, okay? I don't want things to change."

"Alright, now you're making me nervous, man. Spill it."

I flinched at 'man'. "Promise."

He put his fork down and crossed his heart with his index finger. "Promise. Do we gotta hide a body?"

I rolled my eyes at him, "No… I'm… I'm…"

I couldn't get it out. My mouth went dry, and I could feel hot tears make their way into my eyes.

"Hey, it's okay. You can tell me anything." Seth reached across the island and put his hand on my arm lightly before moving it away.

I looked down at the counter, placing my hands on either side of my head and groaning. Was this going to be so hard every time? Did it ever get easier?

"I'm… a girl. Like Rachel."

"Oh, shit." Seth leaned back a little, looking me up and down. "How long have you felt like that?"

"A while. I never really knew how to put it into words, or what was going on. It kinda dawned on me the day of Harriet's party, and it's been eating at me ever since."

"Is there something else you want me to call you?" He didn't miss a beat.

"Phiona… Phee for short."

"Phee. I like it. It suits you."

"You can't tell anyone, okay? Only Theo and Alex know."

"No problem, ma—I mean, girl."

My cheeks flushed and I had to stifle a giggle. "That's going to take you a minute, isn't it?"

He shook his head. "I say it too much, regardless of gender. I call Alex 'man' all the time. It's a habit I gotta break."

"It's okay if you mess up, we've been friends for two years now? You never had to think about it before."

"So, are we keeping this under wraps from Monica, too? Or is home safe, and just outside we pretend you're a guy?"

"Home is safe. I'll tell Monica soon, it's okay if you call me 'Phee' around her."

He nodded. "Got it. Has Alex gone wild trying to make you over yet? She loves a good makeover."

I laughed a little. "She bought me a fuckton of clothes online last night, I'm sure she'll have a blast when they get here."

"She's gonna want to do your makeup so bad, too."

I nodded. "I'm glad she'll be able to teach me. I really liked it when she did my makeup for Harriet's party. Something simple, not too much."

The doorknob turned and Dulce came bounding inside as Alex unhooked the leash from her collar. Dulce ran straight back upstairs, and Alex plopped down on her stool, shoveling a forkful of food into her mouth. We both glanced at her and she caught the looks.

"What?" she asked.

"We were just… talking about you doing Phee's makeup," Seth said, waving his fork in the direction of my face.

"She told you?" She glanced at me, "I mean, you do want to use 'she/her', right? I just assumed."

"Yeah, I do." I nodded.

"Shoot! We didn't get you any makeup last night!" Alex's eyes widened.

"I still have the eyeliner and lipstick you gave me the night of

Harriet's party."

"That's good, your skin is already so perfect, you won't need much else. Maybe a little concealer for under your eyes. It would be nice for you to have options, though."

I shrugged. "It's okay, you already got me so much with the clothes. Thank you, by the way."

"Of course. I can't wait until they come in, you're gonna look so good in them."

I turned the key in the lock to my apartment, listening to the squeak of the hinges as the door swung open. I hadn't heard anything inside before I'd opened the door, so I held my breath to see what kind of state my mother would be in. My question was answered when I found her face down in the couch with the television playing softly. She was out cold, so I tiptoed past her to my room. Once I shut my door, I sighed in relief.

Tomorrow was the anniversary of my dad's death. She was always so much worse around this time, and it was a die roll to see what kind of mood she'd be in. It was always weighted towards angry, her grief getting the better of any other emotion. After all this time, she still mourned him like he'd died this year. It was a kind of love I didn't think she'd ever have for me. Or maybe she just couldn't express it towards me, having been hurt by it before. Either way, I couldn't help but be jealous of my father. Sure, he was dead, but he'd gotten the best parts of my mother. He took them with him when he died, and it wasn't fair. I didn't get to see those good parts anymore.

I dumped the contents of my backpack on my bed, plopping down and sorting through the papers and different assignments. I needed to catch up or my grades were going to start slipping.

After sorting through everything, I started systematically working on each assignment, late into the night, until they were all finished. Thankfully, tomorrow was Sunday, so I could sleep in. They weren't difficult, it just took time that it didn't feel like I had lately. Putting the final essay into my now neatly organized backpack, I lay back on the bed and sighed, closing my eyes. I had a meeting with Clare on Monday, and I needed to have something to bring her.

I got up and pulled a fresh change of clothes – leggings and an oversized t-shirt – from my dresser and quietly made my way to the bathroom. As I undressed, I stared at my body in the mirror until it began to fog up from the steam of the shower. I picked over each part. Too skinny, too many scars, gangly and awkward. I couldn't find an ounce of the femininity I wished I had. When I couldn't see myself in the mirror anymore, I took a deep breath and looked down. My chest, my arms, flat and lanky. Angular, not a curve in sight. Alex often joked about wishing she had my body, and what I wouldn't do to trade with her. Her body was perfect – beautiful curves, a round, heart-shaped face. What a horrible coincidence that we were both unhappy with our own bodies, wishing for each other's.

Why couldn't we find the beauty in our own bodies? I could so easily find the beauty in hers, and she could in mine. What if we could strive to find ourselves beautiful, not despite of, but in accordance with our bodies? I wanted to show people that they were beautiful, and maybe find the beauty in myself as well.

That was it. I knew what my senior project was going to be. Hopefully my friends would be game for it, as the photography was going to get *personal.* I hoped it wouldn't be asking too much.

I'd stepped into the shower through my thoughts and only recently noticed the warm water rush over me. I stared down at my body again, and instead of a critical eye I tried to find something I actually liked. Looking for what felt like an eternity, I did my best to keep my negative thoughts from consuming me. Then I landed on them. My hands. They were elegant. Long, slender fingers with a slight tinge of pink at the tips. My palms, smooth and soft. I'd always liked my hands, but I'd never really thought about it before. I turned them over and stared, a slight smile creeping onto my lips. Then, as I went to wash my hair, I realized that I really loved that part of myself as well. I could remember the day that Rachel told me she was jealous of my hair. I ran my hands through its thick, silky length and let the smile spread farther across my face. This felt so much better than picking myself apart like I always did.

Eventually, I pulled myself from the shower after washing up. I dried off, pulling on my clothes, then took the eyeliner and lipstick I had hidden in one of the drawers under the sink. Wiping down the mirror so that I could see myself, I applied the lipstick, easy enough. Then I took the eyeliner and made some real janky wings around my eyes. Shaking my head, I wiped them off to try again. After the third try, my eyes were irritated, and I decided to give up for the night. I'd have to have Alex teach me soon. I wiped the lipstick off as well and then gathered up my dirty clothes and towel and snuck back into my room, ready for sleep.

I jumped awake the next morning to banging on my door. This wasn't the soft knock of Seth telling me that breakfast was ready. This was an angry mother trying to draw me out. I curled deeper into bed, pulling the pillow over my face, willing her to leave me alone. Another bang on the door. I looked at the clock, it was barely eight AM. So much for sleeping in. I'd been up to nearly three in the morning the night before. The bangs came louder, rattling the door on its hinges and I was afraid she might break the whole thing down.

"Jeremy! I know you have to be awake in there! Answer me!"

Her speech wasn't slurred this time, maybe she'd run out of alcohol. She always seemed to have her ways of getting more, though. I got up and unlocked the door, still cautious even though I was pretty sure she wasn't drunk.

The door flew open as she banged on it again and I took a step back. "Did you have a girl over?!" she demanded.

"What? No, mom. No one was here."

"Then what is *this?*"

In her hands, she held the deep purple lipstick and eyeliner. *Shit.* I must've left them on the counter instead of putting them away in my tiredness last night. *Careless.* Not knowing how to play this off, I just blinked at her blankly, my mouth hanging slightly open.

"Answer me!"

"I—are you sure they're not yours, mom?"

"They were in *your* bathroom!"

Yeah, that was a pathetic attempt. Even her alcohol-addled brain wouldn't let that slip by her. I swallowed, hard.

"Tell me you weren't putting on makeup! It's bad enough you disgrace me with choosing boys. I won't have a cross-dresser as well!"

"I'm not a cross-dresser."

"Then what are you!?"

"A girl!" It slipped out before I could stop it, and I quickly covered my mouth with my hands, eyes wide and staring at her, waiting for the reaction.

She threw the makeup to the floor in front of her, and grabbed me by my shoulder, wordlessly dragging me into the kitchen. She was silent, but I could feel her rage fuming inside her body as she pulled a pair of scissors from a drawer.

"Mom, what are—" She forced my face over the sink, pinning me down.

I struggled against her, but she had an angry strength that I couldn't overpower. Then I heard it, the crunch of the scissors working their way through my beautiful, long hair.

"No!" I screamed, flailing against her as she pinned me down with one arm and cut with the other, lock after lock of black hair falling to the ground and into the sink.

Tears came next, as I fought the futile fight to get her to stop. I shrieked, begging for her to stop, but she just kept going, until there was nothing left. Just jagged tufts of hair sticking straight up from my scalp. She let go of me, throwing the scissors back into the drawer and slamming it shut without a word. She looked at me with the most haunting gaze I'd ever seen out of her, shook her head, and then walked into her room, slamming her door behind her. My knees grew weak, and I fell to the ground, clutching the discarded chunks of my hair that lay strewn about the floor. My wails could've been heard a block away. I'd found two things I liked about myself last night, and now one of them was gone.

Eventually, I dragged myself into my room, picking up my phone and texting Theo through my tears to come get me. Not even ten minutes later, there was a knock at the apartment door. I was still crying as I opened it to watch Theo's face morph in horror as they caught sight of me.

"Oh my god, Phee, what did she do?"

I shook my head, staring down at the floor as tears fell from my face. Theo wrapped their arms around me, and I choked out, "She was sober."

Theo rubbed my back for a minute, then guided me towards my room, "C'mon, get your stuff. You're gonna stay at my house."

I grabbed the discarded makeup from my floor and stuffed it into a duffel bag, along with a couple changes of clothes. Then, I grabbed my backpack and solemnly followed Theo out the door, locking it behind me.

Fuck my mother. Fucking fuck her. She'll never want me to be happy.

Theo took my bags and put them in the trunk of Seth's car, then opened the door for me to get in the back seat. Seth caught my reflection in the mirror, then did a double take and completely turned around to look at my tear-streaked face.

"What the *fuck* did she do?"

I shook my head, covering my face with my hands as Theo got in the passenger seat.

"Drive, Seth," they said softly. "Let's get her out of here."

Seth's gaze lingered on me for a second, then he turned to Theo for a brief moment before looking forward in his seat again and shifting the car into drive.

I never wanted to see my mother again. I wanted her to rot in that apartment, alone in the drunken stupor of grief and liquor of her own making.

CHAPTER FOUR

I pulled the hood of the sweatshirt I'd tossed on over my head, sniffling as tears still ran down my face. We sat in the living room, Theo sitting on the table in front of me and Seth to my right on the couch with a hand on my back.

"What happened?" Alex cooed as she descended the stairs, unaware of the state of my hair.

All she saw was how distraught I was, and she sat down on the couch, engulfing me in her arms. She was the mom friend, forever and always. She'd do everything in her power to make someone feel welcome and comforted. Her embrace was warm, and I leaned into her chest as the sobs came harder.

"Phee, what's wrong? Did your mom do something?"

I couldn't answer, my tears wetting the front of her shirt. She glanced between Theo and Seth, who could do nothing but give sympathetic glances

"She hasn't spoken since we got in the car, Al, it's bad," Theo said softly.

I leaned up for a second, then slowly lifted my hands to the hood of my sweatshirt. Then I pulled it down to reveal the choppy mess left in the aftermath of my mother's rage. Alex's eyes widened and she touched a spiky tuft of hair, her eyes scanning my head. She looked back at my face, then a look of rage I'd never expected to see on her overtook her expression.

"I'll fucking kill her."

I closed my eyes, pulling the hood back up and curling in on myself, pulling my knees close to my chest and burying my face in them. Alex placed a hand on my back and her tone lowered to a whisper. "Hey, I'm sorry. We can fix this, okay?"

"How?" I squeaked. "It's so short, we're going to have to buzz it." My voice cracked and the tears overtook the end of my sentence.

"We'll go to the hairdresser that does Theo's hair, I'm sure she'll be able to do something. I know it won't be like it was before, and I'm sorry for that. I'm so sorry she did this to you. It's not fair."

"Do you want to go now, Phee? We can go now," Theo asked softly, resting a hand on one of my knees.

"Okay," I managed.

———

We approached the salon, Alex leading me with a hand on my back and Theo in front of us, stealing glances back every couple seconds as if to see if I hadn't completely crumbled to the ground. Theo walked up to the front desk and asked the lady sitting there something before Alex and I were close enough to hear, so we only heard the salon manager's response.

"She's just on her lunch break, I'm pretty sure her next slot is free actually. Have a seat and I'll tell her you're here."

Theo nodded and guided us over to the chairs. On the table, there were a bunch of fashion magazines with different hairstyles, long ones that filled me with envy. The salon itself smelled of a mashup of fragrances, surely all from hair products. Some I liked, others made my nose wrinkle at the 'man' scent of them. I pulled the hood farther over my head, obscuring my vision. I didn't want to look at the world right now. I wanted to crawl into a hole and die.

Soon enough, I heard a smooth southern accent and peaked out from the hood to see a tattooed woman with short, bleached white hair.

"Theo! Back so soon? We just had an appointment the other week."

"It's… not for me. It's kind of an emergency, though."

Theo placed a hand on my shoulder and I reluctantly pulled down the hood, feeling the cold air hit the back of my neck.

The hairdresser walked up, running a hand through the awkward tufts of hair, "I'll say. It looks like someone went at this recklessly with kitchen scissors."

"That's exactly what happened," I muttered, too low for anyone to hear me.

"Come with me." The hairdresser nodded and waved us over to a salon chair with a sink behind it and set to washing. "What would you like?" she asked as I leaned back in the chair and the warm water rushed over my scalp.

"It… it was really long before and I loved it. I want that back, but I know you can't do that so just… something as feminine as you can make it."

The hairdresser glanced up at Theo and Alex, then asked softly, "What are your pronouns, hun?"

"She/her." The tears threatened to spill out from behind my eyes again.

"And your name?"

"Phee."

"That's a pretty name. How do you feel about color?"

"I like pink and purple."

She smiled. "I can definitely work with that."

After she was finished washing my hair, we went into a booth with a salon chair and she placed a smock around me as Theo and Alex stood by my side. She pulled out some bleach and started mixing it up before speaking again.

"Now, this might take a little while, because your hair's so dark. But don't worry, you're in good hands."

She applied the bleach, and I sat under a heated dryer as it developed, Theo and Alex wandering from the salon for a bit to go to a candy shop somewhere else in the mall. They'd promised to bring me back my favorites.

"What happened, if you don't mind me asking, hun? I know you didn't do this yourself." The hairdresser asked as she was checking over how the bleach was developing.

Something about this woman was so soothing and made me want to spill everything. Now I knew why Theo liked her so much.

"My mom cut it when I told her I was a girl." My lip quivered and I inhaled sharply to try and stop the tears from falling again.

"That's… that's unfair. I'm sorry. Was this your first time coming out?"

"No, I told Theo first, then Alex, and Theo's brother."

"How long have you felt like a girl?"

"A while. I've been in denial about it, I didn't want it to be true. I see how hard things are for Theo, and I didn't think I could handle it. I knew my mom would be awful. I didn't even really mean to tell her. She found makeup in my bathroom and started questioning me and it just slipped out, it was so foolish, I shouldn't have—" The words came spilling from me without any breaths in between, until the hairdresser stopped me.

"Woah there, slow down, hun. It's okay. There's no judgment

here. This is a safe place."

I took a deep breath in. This stranger's kindness was overwhelming, and the threat of crying snuck up on me again. "I just wish I could leave there and never go back."

"What's stopping you?" the hairdresser asked softly, pulling bits of tin foil out of my hair, then gestured for me to head back to the sink to wash the bleach out.

"She just... she needs someone to take care of her. I don't know what will happen to her if I leave." I sat down in the chair and leaned my head back into the sink.

"Your mom?"

"Yeah."

"Let me know if I'm overstepping but, hun, that's not really your job. You're the child. You shouldn't have to take care of her. She should be taking care of you, and frankly, treating you with a lot more love than this."

"I've just been doing it for so long. It feels like it's my job, even if it's not. Sometimes she's nice, but it flips on a switch so fast that I don't know what to do. She takes out all of her emotions on me and by drinking. It's the stuff she does when she's sober that really hurts, because it means she knew what she was doing and did it anyway."

"You're right, it's easier to forgive when a person isn't completely in control. But you shouldn't have to tolerate any behavior like this, even if she is drunk. It's abuse and it's not fair to you, you're well within your rights to leave."

"I know, and I want to hate her for this, I do hate her for this, but I still..."

"You love her at the same time?"

"Yeah." I sniffled as I sat up from the sink and we made our way back to the salon chair where the hairdresser started mixing up some pink and purple dyes.

"It's tough, but sometimes you have to break away from people, even if you love them. I can tell just from what you've told me that this isn't a sustainable relationship, something's got to change."

"I just have senior year left, and then I can go away to college. That's what I keep telling myself. Everything's just been so much harder since I realized I was a girl. I want to feel better on the inside but it's like no one wants me to."

"The world is a cruel place. Sometimes just being you is the fiercest act of defiance. It's worth it in the end, I promise. Don't let anyone tell you that you can't be who you are. Who you are is beautiful, and you can't let anyone stifle that, no matter how loud they are about it."

"I know why Theo likes you so much."

A smile danced across the hairdresser's face as she pulled out a pair of scissors. "I'm quite fond of Theo, too."

The woman brought me back to the sink to wash the extra dye out of my hair, then we went back to her salon chair for a final time as she set to cutting the awkward tufts into something resembling a decent haircut. I'd kept my back turned to the mirror this entire time, not wanting to face the reality of the state that my hair was in, so when Theo and Alex walked up their grins were a welcome reassurance.

The crunchy sound of the scissors snipping hair made me flinch, knowing that even more length was being cut away to make my hair look presentable. I sighed with relief when it finally subsided and the hairdresser pulled out a comb, some mousse, and a hairdryer to begin styling. Theo bounced on their heels excitedly as the hairdresser turned me around to face the mirror.

I brought my hands over my eyes and closed them at first, not ready to see how short my hair was. Alex's soft hands gently pulled mine down from my face, and I opened my eyes to see her between me and the mirror.

"You look hot as fuck, I promise. That purple eyeliner is gonna match even better now." She stepped out of the way, letting me see my reflection for the first time.

Tears stung at the back of my eyes at the shock of how short my hair was. It took me a minute to blink them back and process, but once I got past the length, I had to admit that I liked it. It was a cute pixie cut with pink that faded into a purple ombre on the sides. I sniffled, mourning my mid-back length bun that I'd had for years, but I had to admit that under the circumstances, this was really nice. I turned my head and brought my hands to my hair, still silky smooth to the touch.

Nodding, I got up and gave the hairdresser a hug, "Thank you."

"You're welcome, sweetie. Just think about what I said."

———————

We sat on a bench in the mall, each digging into bags of candy in our laps. Theo and Alex had gotten me a huge bag of all my favorites, and I was definitely eating my emotions in sugar. I picked apart a gummy shark with my teeth as Alex placed a gentle hand on my shoulder.

"You want some retail therapy? We still have to get you makeup for that full makeover," she asked softly.

"You shouldn't spend any more money on me, you've already spent so much with the clothes. I feel bad."

She waved a hand in the air. "I did nothing but work this summer, trust me, it's fine."

"You should save it. Not use it on me."

"But what if that's what I want to do with it? You're gonna

deny me spending on my truest desires?" She wrinkled her nose, pushing me lightly as I chewed my way through another gummy.

"Fine. But not too much, okay?"

"Hell yeah! I'm gonna make you look *so cute*." Alex hopped up from the bench.

Theo jumped at Alex's sudden movement, they'd been people watching while silently eating some chocolate candy out of their bag. Their eyes were a bit glazed over. They looked lost.

I glanced over at them before asking, "Theo, you okay?"

"Mm? Yeah." They turned to me, not meeting my eyes. If I didn't know better, I'd think that they were high.

Alex caught on, turning around and running her hand gently through Theo's hair. "You sure, T? Phee's right, you look out of it."

Theo leaned into Alex's touch, closing their eyes slightly. "Yeah. I took some of my meds before we left. They're kinda hitting me."

My mom's outbursts always triggered Theo, even when all they saw was the aftermath. They always tried so hard to be a good friend and push through it to help me that sometimes I forgot how much it affected them. This glazed-over, out of touch look meant they'd taken their as-needed anxiety medication. I felt a pang of guilt in my chest like a firework and knelt down in front of them.

"Do you want to go home? I'm sorry."

They put a hand on my shoulder, squinting through their glasses to try and focus their eyes. "No, it's okay. I'm fine. You've got nothing to be sorry for. Let Alex make you over and then we'll go and I'll take a nap."

They stood up, a little wobbly at first and Alex steadied them with an arm around their back. Blinking hard, they opened their eyes and leaned into Alex's shoulder.

"You sure, T?" Alex asked, brushing some stray hair from

their face.

"Mmyeah."

We walked together towards the mall's biggest makeup store, and Alex's eyes lit up like she was a kid in a candy store. Except, she already had the candy, and was ready for something more. Theo sat down on a bench facing the store and we left all our candy with them while Alex dragged me by the arm into the store.

"This is gonna be so much fun! We can match your hair with stuff, you're gonna be hot as fuck."

I was wary, unsure of my surroundings. I'd never been inside a makeup store, and I had no idea what half of these products were. Alex, however, knew exactly what she was doing and went straight for some naturally toned creams that came in plastic bottles.

"We've gotta get you a foundation, you're darker than me, you'd look ridiculous if I put mine on your face." She plucked a few sample bottles from the shelf and started comparing them to my skin, switching between a few until she found a shade that matched my skin tone.

My skin wasn't dark by any stretch of the imagination, but Alex was extremely fair so I could see how her foundation might make me look like a ghost. The matching made a little sense to me, although I wasn't really sure why you'd need to put more of the same color on your face. Did it make other colors stick better? Was it to hide blemishes? My skin was fairly smooth and I'd never had acne, so I wasn't really sure why I needed this. Nevertheless, I went along with it. She was the expert, after all. She'd been wearing makeup for years and had a number of looks that I admired, so whatever she needed to do the same on me I was happy to abide by.

Alex pulled me along to the next aisle, where she got a palette of natural tones in various shades. Next came the fun part, where I actually knew what things were – eyeshadow. We looked through a huge number of palettes, some with wide ranges of colors, until we finally settled on one that was mostly pink and purple shades with a few odd colors thrown in for contrast. A pale yellow, glittery silver, the works. She plucked a black eyeliner from another shelf without even double checking what it was, along with some mascara.

"We gotta get you the basics, these are the ones I use. Last is lipstick! You can get a few colors."

We walked over to a wall full of lipsticks and lip glosses, and I was in awe. There were so many choices. I already had the deep purple Alex had given me before, so I settled on a slightly reddish pink lip gloss that I could alternate with it. Alex picked out some makeup brushes and a few other miscellaneous items that I wasn't entirely sure what they were, but I didn't question it. She took our haul up to the registers, but not before shooing me away back towards Theo on their bench so that I wouldn't see the price.

Theo was slouched over on the bench with their hand in their candy bag, undoubtedly covered in chocolate. I knelt down in front of them again and took the bag gently, and they blinked to focus on me.

"Shit, was I sleeping?"

"Just about." I gave them a weak smile before helping them up and picking up mine and Alex's candy bags.

Alex met us with a full bag from the makeup store, then we turned to make our exit from the mall and start on the ten-minute walk home. I wasn't sure if Theo would last that long, but miraculously, they did. They turned their key in the door and immediately flopped down on the couch with a sigh, unable to keep their eyes open any longer. Alex pulled their shoes off and covered them with a blanket, kissing them in the forehead as she removed their glasses and set them on the coffee table. I locked the door behind us as Alex came bounding up to me with the bag of makeup we'd acquired.

"Go get the stuff you already have, I'm going to teach you some things." She was eager, a bounce in her step.

I rummaged through the duffel bag I'd dropped on the floor of the guest room, pulling out the eyeliner and lipstick. Staring at them in my hands, I flashed back to this morning. These were the reason my mom had cut my hair. If she hadn't found them, I'd still have my long, silky mane. I wanted to throw them, smash them into a million pieces, but at the same time they represented a part of me that I couldn't let go of. They were the femininity I'd been hiding for so long, my true self incarnate. My mom would've found out some other way, if not for this makeup. Maybe it would've been even worse if it happened another way.

Despite her best effort, my mother couldn't strip me of my femininity. It was a part of me, no matter how hard I'd tried to hide it from her, from the whole world, from myself. Deep down, I *wanted* this. I craved the feminine, I longed to be beautiful like all the girls with their perfect makeup and dresses, flowing long hair. I was still a girl, even with short hair. She couldn't dictate who I was, no matter how hard she tried.

I jumped at a gentle touch on my shoulder, not realizing that Alex had entered the room. "Hey, you okay?" she asked.

"Yeah," I stared down at the makeup in my hands, "I was just… thinking."

"C'mon." She tugged at my sleeve, "I've got a look you're gonna love."

I followed her, sitting down on the closed toilet lid in the downstairs bathroom. She carefully laid out each makeup accessory, including the two I'd had in my hands, on the edge of the sink.

"I'm gonna teach you how to do this, okay? As much as I love doing makeup, I know you're gonna want to do it for yourself too, so you won't need me all the time."

I nodded, watching as she took this egg-shaped sponge and put some of the foundation cream on it.

"This goes everywhere on your face, it just smooths everything out, makes your tone more even. Your skin is so nice you might be able to get away without it on some days if you don't feel like doing it." She patted the sponge against my face until the color was sufficiently blended in. Then, she took the palette of natural tones and a small but fluffy makeup brush. "This is to contour your face, I'll show you the places to put it so that it feminizes your face a little, but honestly, you've got a pretty androgynous face shape, so you won't need much."

"What are you talking about? I'm all angles."

"Girls have angles too! Not everyone is round-faced. Look at Theo. I mean, they're not a girl, but even before they started transitioning, they had a jawline that could kill."

"I just wish I was a bit softer everywhere, I wish I had your curves."

She rolled her eyes, brushing more makeup on my face. "And I'd give them to you if I could. I'd take your body in a heartbeat."

"Isn't it weird?" I asked.

"What?"

"That we can hate our bodies so much, but someone else can find it so beautiful at the same time."

"I think we've all got a lot of internalized self-hatred for our bodies because we grew up with them and absorbed every negative comment anyone ever had about them. Other people don't see that part. People see my wide hips and admire my hourglass shape, they don't think about the time in middle school when this kid said my ass was big enough to eat a whole globe."

I scoffed. "Seriously? Someone said that?"

She nodded. "And much more, too much to name. Now hold still, I'm about to do the eyeliner."

I held my breath as Alex uncapped the purple eyeliner and applied it to my eyelids, having done the eyeshadow while we were talking. She had fast hands. I wasn't really keeping up with everything she was doing. I was trying my best, but I think we both knew she'd have to show me this stuff again. Finishing off the look with some mascara, she gestured for me to get up and look in the mirror.

On first sight, I was stunned. I didn't even mind the short hair, my face had such a feminine touch. I glanced at Alex with tears in my eyes.

"That's me?"

"That's you." She smiled.

Tempted to touch my face to see if it was real, I leaned into the mirror instead. She'd put contour in all the right places, my eyes were perfectly upturned with the wing of eyeliner and shadows. I could easily be mistaken for a girl like this, even in the baggy hoodie and leggings I was wearing. Imagine if I'd been in a dress. I'd be *stunning*.

"Thank you," I breathed, staring at my reflection.

Alex patted me on the shoulder. "You're welcome. Now, let me grab an extra makeup bag I have so you have a place to put all this stuff."

CHAPTER FIVE

I arrived to school on Monday, my face wiped clean of makeup. I wasn't ready to come out at school, especially after my mother's reaction to me accidentally coming out to her. Enough people were already staring at my hair. I'd been so heartbroken that I hadn't considered what a statement the color would make. Theo patted me on the back as I tried to keep my head up, not shrink beneath the gazes of the other kids in the hallway.

That was, until Kyle and his group appeared in front of our lockers. He'd been a nuisance ever since Theo had come out, and targeted every queer kid that walked the hallways, no matter what consequences he got, which unfortunately were few and far between. The instant he caught sight of my hair he pointed at me and let out a booming laugh, enough to draw the attention of everyone who wasn't already looking.

Theo shoved by Kyle to get to their locker, while Alex and I hung back. Kyle didn't even acknowledge Theo, though. He made a beeline straight for me. He shoved me, laughing in my face.

"I always knew you were one of the queerdos. You hang around with them so much, it must've rubbed off. You like sucking dick?"

His hot breath blew in my face as he was inches away from me.

"Why, you want some? I wouldn't touch yours with a ten-foot pole," I snapped back at him. My patience for him was already gone.

His eyes widened and he pushed me again, harder, shoving me to the ground. Alex knelt at my side to shield me from the impact of a kick that was aimed for my chest. Before I knew it Theo was on top of him, yanking him back.

"Leave him the fuck alone," they spit in his ear.

Using the opportunity to get up, I staggered to my feet as Kyle's goons surrounded us. Seeing no way out, I lost it.

"Why are you so fucking obsessed with us? You say we're the ones that are gross, yet you're the ones that go around attacking people that are just trying to get through the day. Just leave us the fuck alone!"

Kyle wrenched from Theo's grip and grabbed me by the front of the shirt, bringing my face inches from his. "You're talking a big game for a pussy boy."

"You're the one who can't take a fucking hit. Always run away with your tail between your legs every time Theo shows you what's up."

He raised his fist, aimed directly for my face, when a swift punch to the gut knocked the wind out of him and he dropped my shirt, doubling over on himself.

I looked around, confused, as Theo was standing behind him still. The person who had delivered the punch was Alex, who was now standing there staring at her own fist as if she couldn't believe what she'd just done. Kyle's group backed up a step, and Theo took the chance to usher us out of the circle and we sprinted down the hallway. Once we were a few turns away from the scene, we slowed down a bit.

"That was a nice hit, Al. Just like I showed you," Theo praised her.

"It… it felt good, and it didn't, at the same time. I don't think I like hitting people."

"Hey, I don't like hitting people either. It's about survival, not a matter of liking it."

Alex nodded solemnly as we rounded the final corner to my classroom. I hadn't noticed that Theo and Alex had escorted me directly to class, instead of us splitting off a couple hallways ago like we usually did. They must've known that today would be hard.

Theo touched my arm lightly. "You okay, Jer? Do you need anything from us?"

I shook my head, feigning a smile as I turned into the classroom and waved goodbye.

Clare looked up from her desk and a huge smile graced her face. "Jeremy! Love the hair! What made you change it?"

Immediately, my eyes found the floor. "I… I just… wanted a change, I guess," I lied.

"Well, I like it! The color's so fun!"

I gave her a fake smile and sat down on a chair across from her desk, plopping my bag down next to me.

"So, have you put any more thought into your senior project?"

I looked up at her for the first time. "Yeah, I… I want to do photography on people's bodies and what makes them beautiful, all the parts of them that are beautiful. Even the parts of them that they don't see the beauty in. I can pair the photos with testimonies from each person, about what makes them insecure and what parts of them they do love."

"Wow, Jer. That's mighty personal. Will you be doing a self-portrait in this as well?"

"I… I hadn't really thought about it. I guess it would be hypocritical of me to ask people for something so personal and not do it myself, wouldn't it?"

"Maybe a little."

I sighed. "It's gonna be hard."

"No great artwork comes easily, Jer. I think this has the makings of something really special. Your artistic voice could show through a lot. Maybe start with close friends and work up to the self-portrait."

"I've gotta come up with some questions to ask first, I think. Find ones that will get at the heart of what I'm trying to do without being invasive."

"That's fair. Why don't you use this period to work on them? This is a solid starting point."

"Okay, yeah." I was happy to have something to focus on that wasn't my current situation. I pulled a blank notebook from my backpack and started writing, coming up with as many questions as I could and then weeding them down to the really important ones, then figuring out exactly how to phrase them. I ended up with:

What do you like most about your body? Why do you feel good about it?

What do you like least about your body? What has made you feel that way?

How do you see the beauty in other people's bodies?

I got up and handed the paper to Clare, who looked over it and handed it back to me.

"It's a good start, Jer. Maybe ask yourself those questions first, see how they feel."

I nodded, then jumped as the bell rang for the end of the period. Taking a deep breath, I tried to calm my frayed nerves. I needed a break from this, from *life*. Everything felt like so much. The weight of the world rested on my shoulders as I picked up my backpack and waved goodbye to Clare and walked out the door.

There was a rush of kids moving about the hallway, and I was swept up into the masses. I kept my head down, traveling with the flow to my next class. I ducked into my classroom before anyone really acknowledged my existence. If only it could always be so easy, I could fly under the radar and never be noticed again.

———

Our group met up at Best Boba after school. Our numbers had thinned significantly, some of us graduating. Rachel was away at college, and others had moved onto post-high-school jobs. Our group now consisted of me, Theo, Alex, Harriet, and Elliot. It was the beginning of the school year, so Harriet hadn't recruited any underclassmen yet. We were all seniors, it seemed pointless to me to bring more kids into a group that would fall apart in the next year. We'd all go our separate ways, probably lose contact and just be distant memories to each other.

Elliot glanced at me awkwardly from across the table. After Harriet's party, Elliot and I had taken a shot at dating. We'd lasted a whole year, but over last summer things began to fall apart. The spark was gone, and we just weren't into it anymore. Elliot constantly pried at why I wouldn't bring him to my apartment, and my situation was something I'd wanted to shield him from. That's where our breakdown in communication started, and it all went downhill from there. I started lying to him over silly little things and didn't even know why, things just slipped out before I really processed them. I felt awful for it, he didn't deserve a boyfriend who kept so many truths hidden. It wasn't that I didn't trust him, he was just so sweet and innocent in so many ways, I didn't want to tarnish him with my drama. Eventually, I knew I had to break it off, and he said that he'd seen it coming, but that didn't make him cry any less. We loved each other, but it wasn't right.

Today was the first time we'd seen each other in person since we broke up. We'd agreed to stay friends because we didn't want to lose each other completely, and we'd sent a few friendly texts back and forth that were cordial enough, but it was nothing like seeing each other in person. His face was flushed red, and he could barely look me in the eye. It had been two months, maybe too soon for a face-to-face meeting. A year wasn't anything to laugh at, it was a real relationship with a lot of wonderful and awful feelings, making up something beautiful that just kind of slowly crumbled to pieces in our hands. He was still mourning the loss, and in some ways I was too.

I was about to completely blow his mind. I was going to tell him and Harriet that I was a girl. I didn't know if he'd feel betrayed or relieved. But it had to be done, this was the safest place for me to come out other than Theo's house.

Harriet was glancing between me and Elliot, recognizing the awkwardness for what it was. Elliot must've told her. They were pretty close.

"You two okay, being here?" she asked.

"Yeah," Elliot's voice cracked.

I gave a little nod, picking at my cuticles instead of sipping on my bubble tea. Theo was leaning back casually in their chair as Alex looked between the group, trying to feel out the situation. This was nothing like our hangouts in previous years. Our group had been so much more lively, more carefree. There was something heavy about the current atmosphere.

"I… I have something to tell you two." I looked between Harriet and Elliot, trying to gauge their responses. Harriet just looked at me with wonder, waiting for me to go on. Elliot stared down at the table, not really acknowledging me. "I'm… I'm a girl." I swallowed hard, "My name is Phee and I want to use she/her pronouns, but not at school. I'm not ready for that yet."

"Ooh!" Harriet jumped up from her chair and engulfed me in a hug. "Hello, Phee."

Elliot's eyes grew wide, and he waited for Harriet to sit back down before shooting me in the heart with the question I should've been expecting. "Is that why you broke up with me?"

You could've heard a pin drop at the table, everyone fell so silent. I looked at Elliot, not blind to the tears in his eyes. He clearly wasn't over it yet. We weren't ready for this. I'd been his first partner, so he took it hard. He was mine as well, but I processed things very differently. I'd always been cold to painful emotions, not showing how they affected me for the most part.

"No, El. I didn't know, or at least I hadn't admitted it to myself, when we were together. It just really hit me a couple weeks ago. I've had these feelings for such a long time, and they made me pull away from everyone. I think it hurt our relationship, how distant I was with everything. You deserved better, and I couldn't do that for you."

"I wanted you to share those parts of yourself with me. I would've been there for you."

"I know, I'm sorry that I couldn't."

Elliot's gaze fell to the table, as his hands fidgeted with his cup of tea. This wasn't going to work. Us, together here. I wasn't going to take away his safe space.

"I should go." I stood from my seat, picking up my tea.

"No, stay!" Harriet, trying to keep the peace, put her hand on my shoulder, beckoning me to sit back down. "Tell us all about it now, please?"

I glanced at Elliot, whose gaze was fixated on his tea as he spoke, "It's okay, J–er, Phee. You don't have to leave. We said we'd make it work, right?"

Slowly, I lowered back down into my seat. "Okay, yeah."

Alex decided then was the time to try and break the tension. "Harriet, you've gotta see Phee when she's all made up! We got new clothes and makeup, she's gorgeous."

"Oh, I can't wait to see! Do you have any pictures? I was wondering about the hair, didn't think you'd go shorter with it, you seemed really attached to the length."

I froze, tears trying to force their way into my eyes at the reminder. "The hair wasn't my choice."

"What do you mean?"

"My mom cut it, when I told her I was a girl."

Harriet and Elliot's eyes grew wide.

"What the fuck?" Elliot muttered.

"I'm so sorry, Phee." Harriet's hand still hadn't left my shoulder.

"It's… I won't say it's all right. But Theo and Alex took me to Theo's hairdresser and she did a really good job with what she had left to work with." I ran a hand through my hair gingerly.

"You rock it, you know that? It's really good on you." Harriet smiled warmly.

"Ooh, here's a picture!" Alex held her phone out to Harriet.

It was a picture she'd taken yesterday, after she'd done my makeup. I glanced at it, my heart skipping a beat. Even with the shorter hair, I did look pretty feminine, and it was a good feeling to have the outside match the inside.

"You're gorgeous!" Harriet exclaimed.

"Wow." Elliot glanced between me and the picture, "Reminds me of how you were at the party."

I took it as a compliment, Harriet's party being the only place I'd ever really expressed my feminine side. "Thanks," I muttered. My cheeks flushed. I wasn't used to so much attention.

Theo, having abstained from the conversation with a pensive

look on their face this entire time, brought their hand down on the table firmly enough for us to all look in their direction. They glanced between us, then announced, "We've got to do something about Kyle. And his group. And all the teachers that treat us like shit."

"Theo, I feel like we've had this conversation before. What can we even do?"

"We've got to get more drastic. I know we've been reporting things and I fight off Kyle every day, but it's too much. Things will only keep getting worse. We're seniors now, we've got an influence over the underclassmen. We gather all the queer kids, all our allies—"

"All the underclassmen are scared. Kyle's a senior too, he's got just as much pull as we do on the student body, maybe more."

"—we stage a walkout." Theo kept going as if they hadn't heard Harriet, they were laser focused on this.

"What's that going to do besides get us in trouble? We're the minority here, I don't think there will be enough of us to really make a difference."

"I don't think we are. You said it yourself, everyone's underground. We start rallying people, get the few teachers that are on our side. We film Kyle the next time he harasses us and post it so we have evidence of bullying to build on. The principal will be forced to do something."

"I could show the pictures," I said softly, fidgeting with my tea.

"What pictures?" Harriet asked, and all eyes were on me.

"I've taken pictures of every mark Kyle's left on us. Elliot's broken nose, Alex's bruises, my bruises. I have them all saved, just in case we ever needed evidence."

"Damn," Harriet muttered. "That and video might actually be enough to get us somewhere."

"See? We've got to do this. I refuse to spend my senior year fighting. I'm tired." Theo leaned back in their chair again.

"Harriet, you and I could recruit people – you've already got a good handle on it, you could teach me and I'll help," Alex offered.

"We should all go to the good teachers together. It'll be more persuasive if there's more of us," Elliot added.

"Okay." Harriet conceded. "I'm in. What's senior year without a little ruckus, anyway?"

CHAPTER SIX

Theo was fired up when we got back to their house and immediately disappeared into their room to start writing a flier for the walkout, as well as an essay to the principal and a petition that we'd secretly pass around. When they got started on stuff like this, there was no stopping them, so it was best to leave them to their devices. Alex pulled out some homework to start on the coffee table in the living room, and I took my place next to Seth in the kitchen.

"What are we making tonight?" I asked, happy for the momentary distraction. It was so nice to focus on something that would result in a delicious meal and nothing else for a bit, I could see why Seth liked cooking so much.

"Chicken pot pie, and apple pie for dessert."

"Oh, I love apple pie."

"So does Theo, and it's gonna take something serious to get them to come eat with how they're holed up in their room writing. They forget about food when they're like this."

I snickered. He was right. They'd get such a hyperfocus that they'd forget to eat for an entire day if we let them.

Seth had already put chicken breasts in the oven to pre-cook them, and set to chopping up some vegetables while I started cutting up apples. I stole a couple pieces here and there, then tossed all the slices into a bowl and added sugar and cinnamon. Seth had already moved on to making the pie crusts, rolling out dough until it was large enough to cover the surface area of a pie tin. I pulled the chicken from the oven and started cutting it up, touching it and then jerking my hand away at the heat of it. I resorted to chopping it roughly with one hand with the knife, not holding it with the other.

Seth glanced over at me and snickered. "Baby."

"What? It's fucking hot."

He came over, putting his hand over mine on the knife and holding the chicken down with his other hand as I let go. Chopping like he wasn't touching a searing hot chicken breast that just came out of the oven, he glanced back at me with a sly smile.

I rolled my eyes and started filling one of the pie crusts with the apple slices and muttered, "Just because you're so dead inside you can't feel anything doesn't mean we all are."

Seth snorted playfully. "Bitch."

"Yes, I am, thank you," I shot back at him.

We both laughed, seamlessly traveling around each other in the kitchen until both pies were in the oven and baking. Seth set a timer, then flopped down on the couch next to Alex.

"Phee, wanna play our game?"

I looked between Alex and Seth, contemplating being a good student versus letting loose and having some fun, and chose the latter. "You bet," I said, plopping down on the other side of Alex, who had headphones in and barely noticed us as we turned the television on and grabbed our controllers.

We played until we heard Seth's timer go off, being tempted by the savory and sweet smells coming from the oven the whole time. Pulling the pies out of the oven, Seth set them on top of the stove to cool.

"Why don't you try and pry Theo from their writing?" he asked me.

I nodded, making my way up the stairs. One knock, no answer. Two knocks, still nothing. I cracked the door open to see Theo hunched over, furiously writing away in a notebook, crumpled paper all around them.

"Theo?" I asked.

Their head jerked up for a second, then back down to their writing. "What?"

"Dinner's ready. There's apple pie."

They sat up, looking at me with their piercingly golden eyes. "Apple pie?"

"Yeah."

"Fuck." They looked back at their notebook, then up at me again.

"Just a little break, T. You've gotta eat."

"Fine," they muttered, but not before picking up their notebook and pencil to bring it with them.

When we got downstairs, Alex was already seated on a stool at the kitchen island and Seth was dishing out the chicken pot pie, plates laid out for all of us. Theo and I sat down just as Seth put the pie down in the middle of the counter. Alex took a bite way too quickly, steam still coming off the forkful of food she'd put in her mouth.

"Fuck," she muttered, opening her mouth in an attempt to dissipate the heat.

Theo was already engrossed in their writing again before Seth could set a plate in front of them. When they didn't look up, Seth plopped the plate down right on top of their notebook.

"Fucking, Seth—" they started.

"Eat," he said firmly, nodding at the plate.

Theo rolled their eyes, but reluctantly picked up their fork and dug into the pie. They slid the notebook out from under their plate, handing it to Alex.

"Tell me what you think so far."

"Is it okay if I read it out loud? We can all weigh in," Alex suggested.

Taking a second to glance at all of us, Theo looked back at Alex. "Sure."

Alex cleared her throat before beginning, "Dear Principal Lewis, We, a portion of the student body, have some concerns we would like to address regarding our safety at school. Students who are members of the LGBTQ+ community have been unfairly targeted with bullying by other students and unfair, disrespectful treatment by some teachers. We would like to see consequences for these actions, because as of this date, nothing has been done regardless of our reports."

"In particular, Kyle Ritter and his group of friends have verbally abused and physically attacked LGBTQ+ members of the school on a daily basis, resulting in serious injury to some. We have attached photo evidence of these injuries. As of yet, he has not been disciplined for any of these instances of bullying and roams the halls looking for victims as though he is untouchable. In addition, there are numerous teachers who treat visibly LGBTQ+ students unfairly, refusing to use their proper names and pronouns, or calling them out with embarrassing information in a form of hazing."

"We implore you, Principal Lewis, to take action against these wrongdoings. Please make this school safe for its LGBTQ+ members, instead of the minefield that currently lies in front of us each day. It's exhausting. We're exhausted, and we need help. Any small step in the right direction would show good faith and give us some hope for the future. Hold a conference for the teachers explaining LGBTQ+ identities and their importance. We would even be willing to help educate and come up with a presentation. Discipline those who are involved in bullying. Let us live our lives in peace."

"Sincerely, Theo Venia, and a large portion of the student body. (Petition is attached)"

"That's really good, T," Seth nodded as he talked through a mouthful of food.

I took the notebook from Alex and looked it over quickly, then looked back up at Theo. "Yeah, it's got everything we need. I hope she hears it."

Theo nodded, taking the notebook back. "Now we've got to make a flier for the walkout. Because I really don't think this is going to get us anywhere on its own."

"You really think she can ignore this if we give her a petition and the pictures?" Alex asked.

"In my experience, people overlook these things. They don't care unless it's shoved in their face in a way that they can't ignore. So we're going to have to do that."

"Theo, you might hate this idea, but when we video Kyle harassing us, you shouldn't fight back. It'll prove the point even more. Do you think you can do that?" I looked at them warily.

They let out a slow sigh. "You're right. I'll try. We'll tape him tomorrow."

Tomorrow came all too soon. I awoke in the guest room of Theo's house. Tonight I'd go home and face my mother, but I did my best not to think about that. We had other things to attend to, harassment to expose. Wiggling into a pair of skinny jeans, I took in a deep breath, letting the room fall silent around me. There were sounds of movement upstairs, probably Theo getting ready while Alex slept until the last minute. The smell of cooking onions wafted into the room from the cracked door. My shoulders were heavy, like the weight of the world had come down on them. My chest was tight, holding in all of my anxieties. I pulled a t-shirt over my head and wandered out into the kitchen.

Seth was humming some tune, probably something he'd written, tossing some vegetables in a pan and cracking eggs into a bowl. He must've felt my presence, because he turned around with a smile.

"Hey. Omelets."

I weakly returned his smile and nodded as he dumped the vegetable mixture into the eggs before pouring a portion back into the pan. He stuck a lid on it and then pulled plates from the cupboard. I took them from him, laying them out on the island, then grabbed some cups and placed them next to the plates and set to making everyone's beverages. Coffee for Seth, tea for Theo, orange juice for Alex, milk for me.

I'd placed the last cups as Alex sleepily descended the stairs in her pajamas, hair frizzy and frantic. She rubbed her eyes and yawned before plopping down on her stool and downing half the glass of orange juice. She leaned on the counter lazily with her eyes closed, barely noticing as Seth slid a finished omelet onto her plate.

"You good, Alex?" I asked.

"Mm?" She opened one eye slightly. "Yeah. Theo and I were up late. They wouldn't stop writing. I fell asleep at like two. I don't even know if they slept." She lifted her fork slowly, as if it weighed at least ten pounds, before cutting a piece of her omelet and bringing it to her mouth.

"Damn, they're gonna be really on edge for today if they didn't sleep. How were they when you got up?" I fidgeted nervously, sitting down on my stool as Seth dished out another omelet.

"I dunno, they were in the shower when I woke up. Haven't seen them yet."

As if to answer my question, Theo descended the stairs. I took them in, assessing their posture, their face. They didn't look too bad, but the dark circles under their eyes had a tale to tell.

"Babe, did you sleep?" Alex asked, straightening to look at Theo as I had.

"Maybe an hour," they muttered.

Shit. That was going to make today really hard. I wasn't sure if they could keep their cool and not fight back on an hour of sleep. Their instincts kicked in a lot faster when they were tired, their brain didn't always have time to catch up.

Theo sat down, cutting into the fresh omelet that Seth had just served before taking a sip of their tea. They blinked hard, then rubbed at their eyes. I had a bad feeling about today, about everything. This needed to go off without a hitch, and I'd be damned if I had to deal with the aftermath of a fight and my mother on the same day.

I placed a hand gently on Theo's shoulder, "You gonna be okay for today? Maybe we should wait, record it some other time."

"I know how to take a hit, Phee."

"That's not what I'm afraid of." I turned them to look at me for a second.

Their eyes darted away from my face, and I knew they weren't sure how today was going to go either. They sighed and turned back to their food, cutting the already thoroughly cut-up omelet into smaller pieces. I glanced at Alex over Theo's head, and she had the same expression of worry that was plastered onto my face.

Alex ran her hand through Theo's hair. "Hey, maybe Phee's right. Maybe we should wait, a day when you've had a full night's sleep?"

"No," they growled, "We've gotta get the ball rolling. I want this video ready to go live by the time the principal gets the letter with the petition, so that if she doesn't act we can cite the video when we do the walkout."

"That'll all take a couple weeks at least, won't it? I'm sure we can do this another day, tomorrow, even. It doesn't have to be today. You need a good night's sleep to deal with this bullshit."

Theo shook their head adamantly. "No, I want to do this today. I won't fight back, I promise. I've got a good enough handle on things. It'll be fine."

Alex and I exchanged glances again, me biting my lip in apprehension.

"Stop looking at each other like that," Theo muttered. "I've done nothing but take hits my whole life, this isn't new."

We finished off our omelets, and Theo downed their cup of tea. I wasn't sure whether to be grateful or nervous about the caffeine in their system – it could wake them up and make them more aware, or get them more agitated. It was a crapshoot. Seth put the dishes in the sink and Alex, Theo and I filed out of the house, waiting for the bus outside. It came and we piled on, a somber mood between the group, like we were leading an animal to slaughter. Even if Theo didn't lose it and fight back, they were going to get hurt. Kyle was going to do something to them, and they were going to let it happen so that we'd have proof. Part of me almost wanted them to fight, give him what he deserved, but it wouldn't do any good, we'd just be in the same spot we were now.

The bus pulled up to the school, and we made our way through the hallways towards Theo's locker. I hung back and pulled out my phone, ready to hit record in an instant. As we approached Theo's locker, there was Kyle, as obsessed with us as ever. He had this infuriating smirk on his face that made *me* want to punch him, let alone Theo. Theo ignored him and put in their combination, and as they opened their locker, he slammed it shut just as quickly.

"What's the matter, don't want to talk to us today?" His tone was patronizing.

I hit record on my phone, trying to hold it inconspicuously so that he wouldn't realize he was being filmed, while still making sure that everything was in clear view.

"Fuck off, Kyle," Theo muttered as they put in their combination again.

"What's a carpet muncher like you gonna do about it, huh?" He pulled Theo away from their locker, then tried to shove them back into the lockers. They barely moved.

"Can you just leave me alone?" Their voice was tired, you could see it in their entire body how exhausted they were. Shoulders slumped forward slightly, legs swaying back and forth as Theo shifted their weight between their feet.

"Aw, you gonna cry, little bitch? No fight in you today?" Kyle shoved them harder, this time they had to take a step back and their back pressed up against the lockers.

I gulped, afraid of what was going to happen next. I kept recording, Alex at my side. She had a desperate look on her face. She didn't want to see this happen either. I could tell it was taking everything in her not to run in and intervene.

Theo didn't answer Kyle, only straightened their posture and glared him in the eye. That's when he spit right in their face, and you could see their hands twitch impulsively. They wiped the spit from their face. Every muscle in their body was tense, a protruding vein in their neck making a showing.

"You're making this too easy," Kyle snickered, then gave Theo a hard punch in the side of the head.

Theo fell to the ground, their body rag-dolled like there was no resistance to hitting the floor. That's when I knew there was something wrong. Kyle and his group started laughing and took turns kicking Theo. They weren't shielding their face, they were just lying on the ground as each impact shook their whole body.

They were unconscious.

Alex had already run to the group by the time I slid my phone into my pocket and started making a dash for them as well. The group had Theo completely surrounded, so it took Alex and I some serious effort to try and get past them and get to Theo. Alex hip-checked one kid so hard he fell over, and I took the opportunity to squeeze my lanky frame into the circle. I knelt down in front of Theo, shielding them from further kicks while I tried to wake them up.

"Theo, Theo! Hey!" I held them by the shoulders and shook them lightly. Their eyes flickered open and closed again, right as I took a kick to the middle of my back.

Alex had managed to shove her way into the circle as Kyle looked down and spit on both of us.

"Queerdos, the lot of you," he muttered, and strutted away, his group following close behind. In his mind, this was a tremendous victory. He was so full of himself.

I shook my head, turning my attention back to Theo. They were more important than getting frustrated over Kyle's ego. Alex lifted Theo so that they were sitting up against the lockers, and their eyes squinted open.

She leaned in to inspect the red mark on Theo's temple. "Babe, you okay?"

Theo's eyes didn't open more than a squint. "Did we get it?" came out before they coughed and pressed a hand to their ribs.

"We got everything, T," I said, pulling my phone from my pocket to show them.

CHAPTER SEVEN

Carefully, we managed to help Theo up and get them to the nurse. She took one look at the bruise already forming on their temple and turned to us.

"Were they unconscious?"

A solemn nod from the both of us, before Theo jumped in. "Only for a second. I'm fine, my head just hurts." They tried to stand up from the couch, a little wobbly.

"Nuh-uh." The nurse put a hand on their shoulder and lowered them back down on the couch. "A hit like that to the temple, better safe than sorry. I'll call your mother, you need to go to the hospital and get checked out."

Theo grumbled, but everyone could tell they weren't quite right. They were still squinting and kept blinking against the light.

"Was this Kyle again?" the nurse asked as she dialed the phone for Monica.

Alex and I both nodded, then exchanged glances. If we had the nurse on our side – the person who'd seen and cared for all these injuries, it might sway the principal. We waited until she was off the phone, then zeroed in on the task at hand.

"Miss, we're trying to do something about this," I said, my voice a little unsteady. "Theo wrote a letter to the principal, and we're trying to start a petition. Would you help?"

She nodded. "Any way I can. Don't get me wrong – I like you three – but I hate seeing you in my office so often. This isn't fair, what he's doing. It's bullying and abuse. If I had my way, he'd be catching charges."

At lunch, I kept obsessively checking my phone between bites of a cold-cut sandwich. Alex was across from me doing the same. We still hadn't heard anything from Theo, and the anticipation was eating away at us. Alex put her phone down and sighed, burying her face in her hands.

"We never should've done this. What if they're not okay?"

"It's Theo, they're always okay," I said, trying to soothe her but not really believing it myself. She shot me a look that said she wasn't buying it, and I put my sandwich down and leaned back. "I know, I know. I'm worried too."

We both jumped as Alex's phone buzzed on the table and she snatched it up. I studied her face as she read the text, looking for answers.

"Fuck, they have a concussion."

I leaned forward as she kept reading.

"They're out of school for a little bit and have to take it easy, but they'll be okay." She expelled the air she was holding in, then set her phone back down on the table, rubbing at her eyes. "I should've taken the hit. Why did we just assume Theo would do it?"

"You seriously think Theo could've held themself back if you got hit? It never would've worked otherwise, they're too protective of both of us."

"We should've at least had the argument. I can't believe we just let them do it." The guilt showed in her hands wringing together and her untouched food.

I reached over and put a hand on her shoulder. "Alex, they know we care about them. That's not up for debate."

Her phone buzzed again, a call this time. She answered it swiftly, putting the phone to her ear. "Hey, baby. How are you? We never should've let you—"

She squinted. I guess she needed to have the argument after the fact, for her conscience.

"I know, but we shouldn't have—"

A glance down at the floor.

"Okay. Okay, I love you too. I'll see you when I get home. You better rest."

She hung up the phone and turned back to me with a sigh.

"They said exactly what I said, didn't they?"

"Pretty much."

———

When we got back to Theo's house, Alex dropped her bag at the door and ran up the stairs. I glanced at Seth, who was on the couch playing a video game, and he gave me a subtle nod. Ascending the stairs, I poked my head into Theo's room. Alex was already sitting in the bed, arms wrapped around Theo with tears in her eyes.

"Allie, I'm fine," they muttered, though not pulling away from her embrace.

Alex ran a hand through Theo's hair, careful to avoid the now-darkened bruise on their temple. She kissed them on the top of their head and sniffled a bit before whispering, "We never should've let you get hurt."

Theo sighed and I sat down in their desk chair, rolling it closer to their bed. "How are you feeling?"

"My head is pounding, but otherwise I'm fine. I get dizzy when I stand up, so I've just been lying in bed watching movies and eating candy all day. I fell asleep like an hour ago." They gestured towards their laptop and the half-eaten bag of candy on the shelf lining their bed.

"Aren't you not supposed to look at screens if you have a concussion?" Alex's mom instincts were ever so strong.

"What am I supposed to do, stare at the walls all day? My head hurts too much to read." Theo scoffed. "It'll be fine."

Alex ran her hands along Theo's shoulders, still fighting back tears. When she felt guilty about something, she really couldn't let it go. If given the chance, she'd never let go of Theo again.

Theo tried to sit up, a little too quickly judging by the look on their face. They looked like they were about to say something, when all the color drained from their face. I knew the look from watching my mom for so long and rushed a trash can over to them just as they started to throw up. Luckily, I was fast enough and it didn't go anywhere but the trash. Alex pulled a water bottle from the top shelf and uncapped it, handing it to Theo. They rinsed their mouth out and spit into the trash can before taking a few sips.

"Fuck," they muttered, wiping their mouth with a tissue that Alex had supplied. "I didn't know that was going to happen."

Alex pulled Theo close to her chest as I took the bag out of the garbage can, careful not to spill anything as I tied it shut. I lumbered down the stairs with it and quickly put it in the garbage can outside, then came inside and washed my hands.

Seth looked up from his video game, "What's the rush?"

"Theo threw up. I didn't want to spill any."

"Oh, shit. How are they doing? They were really out of it earlier,

I didn't want to bother them."

"I think they're down for the count but fighting it, like they always do."

Seth nodded. "Maybe Alex can talk them into taking it easy."

"She's trying."

I pulled a new garbage bag from the cupboard and a fresh bottle of water from the fridge before ascending the stairs again. When I opened the door, Theo was squirming in Alex's arms.

"I've gotta… work on the petition…" Their attempts to wriggle free were half energy at best. They just didn't have it in them.

After putting the new bag in the trash and setting the bottle of water on the shelf, I picked up their laptop from the shelf and scooted the rolling chair over to the desk and set to work. "I'll do it, Theo. You rest, seriously. You need it."

They sighed, releasing the tension from their body and leaning into Alex's embrace. "Okay, okay. Fine." They closed their eyes and wrapped a hand around Alex's arm, and Alex continued rubbing their back with her free hand. Within minutes, their grip loosened as their body relaxed into sleep.

"God, why are they so impossible sometimes?" Alex muttered, exasperated.

"It's the fighter in them. They've had to fight so long to survive, they feel like they can never show any weakness. That's how you get picked off. I get it. I never let my mom see me cry if I can help it."

"They're safe here, though. They know that."

"It's a tough habit to break."

Alex fell silent and nodded as I pulled a micro USB cord out of the drawer of Theo's desk and plugged it into the laptop and began uploading the video I'd taken that morning. After it uploaded, I played it to be sure that the file came through okay.

Watching the scene back was almost gruesome. First the shove, then the spit. The twitch of Theo's hands, then the punch that knocked them out and left them vulnerable to the many kicks that landed before my phone went down and the video cut off as I ran towards the altercation. If this wasn't enough proof to spark an outrage, nothing would be. Our principal was in for a rude awakening if she didn't consider the petition.

"Shit, I should get pictures of the marks on Theo."

Alex nodded. "You're right, we'll get them when they wake up."

———

That was a longer wait than expected. So long, in fact, that Alex and I started to get really worried – they slept through the night and into the next day and were still sleeping when we got back from school. I'd thought that the "you can't go to sleep with a concussion or you'll never wake up" line wasn't real, but was starting to doubt myself and began falling down the rabbit hole of medical google while sitting at the kitchen island. I hadn't gone home like I'd planned to, I was too worried about Theo, even though I knew Alex wouldn't leave their side except for school.

Monica walked in the door just as I was scrolling through the "undetected brain bleeds" section of the page I was on, and I was thoroughly freaking out. It must've shown on my face, because Monica set her bag down on the counter and put a hand on my shoulder.

"What's wrong, Jeremy?" Her tone was soft.

My heart skipped a beat, realizing I still had to come out to her. Now wasn't the time. Instead, all my pent up worry just fell directly out of my mouth into the air around us. "Theo's been sleeping since yesterday afternoon, and I thought the not sleeping with a concussion thing was a myth but it's been so long, what if they're in a coma? What if they don't wake up? What if they have a brain bleed that didn't show up on the scans? What if we lose them forever?"

"Woah, slow down there. I looked at their scans myself, there's nothing there. It's pretty common for someone with a head injury to sleep longer than normal, they need the time to heal. I'll check on them, though."

I followed Monica up the stairs and waited in the hallway as she knocked on Theo's door. A weak "Come in," came from inside, Alex's voice. Theo was still out cold, and Alex sat up from being snuggled up against them. Monica knelt in front of the bed, placing a hand on Theo's shoulder.

"Theo, honey, wake up."

Nothing.

She nudged them a little as anxiety rose in my chest, threatening to spill out. Alex ran a hand through their hair. They still didn't move. Monica pulled what looked like a pen out of her pocket and clicked a button on the end of it, causing a light to come on. Gently, she opened one of Theo's eyes and shone the light into it. Theo immediately reacted, swatting the light away and squinting their eyes.

"Ow, Mom, what the fuck?" Their words were groggy, but coherent.

Alex and I audibly sighed with relief.

"You were sleeping for a really long time, hun. I was just checking on you." She placed a hand back on their shoulder, letting go when they tried to sit up.

"Woah, slow this time. I don't want you puking again," Alex warned.

Theo's face was already starting to pale, and they let themself drop back down onto the pillow and covered their face with their hands. They groaned as Alex reached for the water bottle I'd placed on the shelf the day before.

"Are you still dizzy?" Monica asked.

"Yeah," Theo muttered through their hands. "It's making me nauseous."

"Let me dig through the medicine cabinet, I think we have some dramamine." Monica left for a minute but returned quickly with a small box in her hand. She pulled a sheet of pills from the box and punched one out. "Here, take this. It'll help with the nausea."

Theo uncovered their face and squinted. "Why are the lights so bright?"

Alex took that as a cue to close the curtains, and I dimmed the desk light. Slowly, Alex helped Theo sit up, and Monica gave them the pill as Alex handed them the water. They blinked with the items in their hands for a minute before finally putting the pill in their mouth and washing it down with some water.

"You should take your meds, too. You slept through a couple doses," Monica reminded them.

Theo tried to turn towards the shelves behind them, but stopped halfway to cringe and try to blink away whatever was bothering them.

"Hey, I've got it." Alex placed a hand on their shoulder before pulling the pill sorter from their shelf and dumping a couple pills in their hand.

Theo took them, and their hands shook as they handed Alex back the water bottle. She placed it on the shelf and gently brushed her hand through the spiky tufts of Theo's hair.

"It's a pretty bad concussion," Monica said, standing up. "I'll check on you again later, maybe try and eat something once the dramamine kicks in and you're not too nauseated. I love you, sweetheart."

"Love you too, Mom." Theo sighed and leaned against Alex's shoulder, and she pulled them into her chest.

Monica left the room, closing the door behind her. I squinted to see in the dim light of the room, but didn't want to turn anything else on and bother Theo.

Theo ran a hand along Alex's arm, and without turning to me, asked, "How's the petition going?"

I opened up the laptop on Theo's desk to the blank document I'd started the day before. "I didn't get very far. I was working on the video last night mostly, making sure it was ready to go. Oh! We need to get pictures of the marks they left on you, more evidence. Do you think you're up to it? We can wait."

"No, no, we can do it now. Better to get the bruises when they're fresh, right?"

"We're gonna need the light."

"Okay." Theo preemptively squinted as Alex got up and turned the overhead light on.

I pulled out my camera and Theo turned their head to show the huge, dark bruise that covered their entire right temple, spreading down onto their cheek. I snapped a few pictures, and the more I looked at it, the worse it got.

"Damn, that's really bad."

"There's more." Theo lifted up their shirt to reveal their ribs, which had bruises spotted all along them. There was one particularly bad one on the right side of their ribs – I didn't even remember them being that bad when their ribs had actually been broken a couple years ago.

"Jesus." Alex gasped, tears filling her eyes as she put her hands over her mouth.

I set to taking a few close-up pictures of each bruise, then took one from slightly farther away so that it had Theo's face in it. They were squinting the whole time, and their hands shook while they held up their t-shirt.

Finally, I put my camera down and nodded at Alex. "Done."

She flipped the light off and Theo dropped their shirt and collapsed into Alex as soon as she was back on the bed. I plugged my camera into the laptop, uploading the pictures. I cropped them and then put them in the folder I'd started last night of all the other pictures I'd taken of Kyle's attacks. It was a huge folder at this point – close to fifty pictures. Elliot's broken nose, bruises on Alex's ribs, a busted lip of Theo's, the list went on and on. The fact that this level of brutality was going unpunished was simply baffling. I didn't understand how the higher ups in the school could get away with ignoring this.

Not anymore. Soon, there would be no ignoring us.

———

Walking through the threshold of my own apartment shouldn't have been as daunting as it was. I took a deep breath and turned the door handle slowly, creaking the door open and peeking through the crack. The apartment was yet again in a state of disarray, but my mother wasn't in sight. I opened the door and tiptoed into the living room, making a straight line to my room. I didn't want to confront my mother if I didn't have to.

"Jeremy!" the sing-song voice of my mother sailed from the kitchen as I swiftly walked by.

I was tempted to ignore it, lock myself away in my room and not come out until I had to go to school. Truthfully, it would've been pretty easy to do. But my mother's voice didn't sound angry, so it was better to have the confrontation while she was in a good mood. I dropped my bag in the hallway and slowly walked into the kitchen, my eyes glued to the floor, only glancing up to gauge my mother's expression.

It was one of pure delight. "Ooh, I love the colors!" she gently tussled my hair and I jerked back away from her.

I still hadn't forgiven her for what she'd done. I was still angry, still wanted my hair back. Usually I was quick to forgive, so she wasn't used to me showing the contempt that lived in my heart. Tears formed in her eyes, and I could smell the alcohol on her breath as she started talking.

"Honey, I'm s-so sorry for what I did. It was too far."

The apology was nice, but I still didn't believe it. I didn't say a word, staring at the floor as my mother squirmed in her own skin. Good. She should be the one uncomfortable for once, with the hell she'd made for me.

"Y-you know it's… sis a bad time of year for me."

"That's no excuse, mom."

Exasperated, she flopped down into one of the kitchen chairs. I stood there, avoiding eye contact the whole time. I didn't want to be here. How badly I wished to just stay at Theo's forever.

"Will you ever for-forgive me?"

I took the opportunity to test the waters. If this was going to explode again, it was better to happen when I was prepared. "Maybe if you can accept that I'm a girl."

She fell silent. I didn't find the hatred in her eyes that I expected, but a deep sadness that went down to her soul. We stood there staring at each other for a few minutes, and you could've cut the tension in the room with a knife. Was my mom trying to process, or was she hoping that if she waited long enough she'd have her son back?

"Who… who put these ideas in your head? Was it that boy you brought home the other day?"

"They're not 'ideas', mom. It's who I am. I've felt this way for a long time. I was never your son, so you can just forget that. I was pretending, being what everyone wanted me to be. I'm so tired of pretending. I want to be who I am, and I'm going to do it whether you like it or not."

"Jeremy—"

"It's Phiona!" I raised my voice, something I'd never done with my mother.

She sat there in stunned silence, any argument she had knocked out of her head by my shout. My face started getting hot and my vision blurred as tears tried to force their way out of my eyes.

"You only have to live with it for the rest of this school year. then I'll go to college and you never have to deal with me again." My voice wavered and cracked, and I turned and ran into my room, leaving my backpack in the hallway.

She couldn't see me cry. I'd shown her enough weakness lately, I wasn't going to give her more reasons to be disappointed in me. I heard soft footsteps on the carpet that paused when they got to the door of my room. I sat against the door after locking it, and tried to stifle the sobs that were coming out of me. I couldn't let her hear them. Not after I'd just told her off. The power of my words needed to sting, not be flushed away by my tears.

A soft knock came on the door, and I ignored it. I didn't want to deal with her right now, I sniffled and wiped at my nose with my sleeve.

"Jeremy, I still love you. You're still my son."

I could tell her intentions were good, but the blatant disregard for what I'd just told her rang much louder than the 'I love you'. I didn't answer, but buried my face in my hands. Eventually, the footsteps walked away from my door. I wiped my face, then cracked my door open to grab my backpack from the hallway and quickly retreated back inside my room.

Locking the door behind me, I dumped my backpack onto my bed. It held my schoolwork and homework assignments, but also the bag full of makeup that Alex had gotten me. I sat down on my bed and carefully took each product out of the makeup bag, one by one. Looking them over, I tried to remember what the steps were that Alex had hastily shown me. She'd worked so fast. I squinted to try and remember what went on first.

Using the mirror in the eyeshadow palette, I took the foundation – my best guess as a first step – and the weird egg-shaped sponge and applied it to my face. It covered the redness around my eyes and nose that had happened from my crying. Then, I took some eyeshadow. I wanted to go for a smoky effect, my favorite look of Alex's. I dabbed the smaller makeup brush into a deep purple, shading around my eyes.

Looking into the mirror, I shook my head. I looked like a purple panda. Grabbing the makeup wipes from my pile of stuff, I wiped at my eyes to try again. They were already irritated from crying, so the makeup wipe hurt, but I was determined to do this. I wanted to feel beautiful. After the eyeshadow was completely wiped off, I dabbed the brush into the same purple and tried again, this time using a lot less. It wasn't perfect by any stretch of the imagination, but it was better than my first attempt, so I went with it.

Next, I took out the darker shade of makeup and tried some contouring like Alex had shown me – making my nose thinner, emphasizing my cheekbones, rounding out my jawline. I'd taken my lesson from the eyeshadow and only used a little, and did pretty well for a first attempt. My hands shook as I held the eyeliner up to my face. This part was so precise, I was more afraid of messing up the eyeshadow than accidentally poking myself in the eye, but both were very real possibilities. Closing my eye lightly, I dragged the eyeliner along my lid in short strokes. Alex had done it in one long one, but I wasn't confident enough to make that happen. I managed to get one only slightly janky looking wing, then did the other eye with just as much apprehension. When all was said and done, I didn't look too bad. I'd definitely need more lessons from Alex, but I at least had the basics down.

After the makeup, I dug through my drawers for something feminine enough to quell my cravings. I found some black and purple striped leggings that I'd only ever worn to bed before, then went through my shirts. Nothing was good enough there, so I pulled a pair of scissors from my desk and took a plain black t-shirt and cut it into a crop top. I also cut some slits along the back and sleeves, then put the ensemble on. Looking in the full-length mirror on my closet door that I normally avoided, I sighed in relief. I still wished my hips were rounder, my frame less lanky, but it was a step in the right direction.

Finally, I climbed into bed, put some music on my phone, and settled in to do some homework. I needed to catch up, I couldn't let my grades slip as much as my relationship with my mother had. Otherwise, I'd never get into a college to get out of this place, and that was what I truly needed. The change, an environment that didn't hate me for who I was.

CHAPTER EIGHT

The next week flew by. Theo had insisted on doing the petition themself, but after a couple days they'd been feeling a lot better and needed something to keep them occupied while they were home alone anyway. We'd planned to launch our scheme next week – Theo still wouldn't be back in school, but Alex would deliver the petition with our essay and all the pictures to the principal. If she did nothing, Theo would be back in time for the walkout. Harriet and Alex had been busy gathering signatures, running around like wild during lunch to get everyone that they could while still keeping everything under wraps. We had well over 200 signatures, more than 10% of the school population. The principal would absolutely be in the wrong to not at least have a meeting with us.

Things were gearing up to explode on the day-to-day front, now that Kyle was roaming around unchecked without Theo there. He'd been on top of the world since knocking Theo out, taking it as a sign that he was so much stronger than them, and would always win. Alex and I had skipped our lockers all week just to avoid him, carrying every book we had for class all day long instead.

Today, I found another place to dread going: the bathrooms.

I wasn't sure which one to go into, knowing that I was a girl but still presenting so masculine. I'd been too afraid to wear makeup at school, but I'd been bold enough to wear my leggings and cropped shirt instead of my usual skinny jeans and baggy t-shirt. Every part of me wanted to use the girl's bathroom, but I knew I'd be met with pushback the minute I stepped foot inside. On the other hand, the boy's room undoubtedly meant ridicule and malice.

Taking in a deep breath and holding it, I opened the boy's bathroom door as quietly as I could. I didn't see anyone inside – it was the middle of a period, so most people were in class. I swiftly walked into a stall and dropped my heavy bag onto the floor before using the toilet. While I was in the stall, I heard the door open and a multitude of voices came in, one after the other. Then, a smell that made my nose turn up – cigarettes. Before flushing the toilet and making my presence known, I peered through the crack in the stall to see a group of guys congregating around the sinks with a pack of cigarettes sitting on the counter. Kyle wasn't there, but I recognized a couple of guys from his crew. *Great.*

I stood in the stall a few extra minutes to gather up the nerve to go out there – the group wasn't leaving any time soon. Then, I flushed the toilet and picked up my bag, putting it on my back before opening the door. All heads turned in my direction, at first in horror, as if whoever coming out would rat them out to a teacher. Once they recognized me, though, all bets were off.

I didn't look at any of them as I walked through the group to an open sink to wash my hands. They all stared at me in silence, the tension building in my chest as I reached for a paper towel. For a second, I thought I might get away without an altercation, but then one of the guys slapped his hand against the door as I went to open it, keeping me inside.

"What's the matter?" he taunted. "Your pint-sized friend not here to protect you?"

I glanced at him. He was one of the larger guys of the group – a player on the football team, broad shoulders, easily over six foot. His dark hair and eyes drew me in – he'd be attractive if he wasn't such an ass. He gave a sly smirk and leaned in close to me as I tried to yank the door from his grip and failed. I gave up pulling at the door, then sighed and turned to him, attempting to meet his eyes and not show the fear that was simmering inside me.

"What do you want?"

He took a slow drag of the cigarette, then blew the smoke in my face. Then, before I could react, he swiftly grabbed my arm and held the lit end of the cigarette to it. I didn't react beyond a slight wince – it was a pain I knew too well, scars dotted faintly up my arms from my mother doing the same thing.

"What, this just foreplay for you, freak?" He really ground the cigarette into my skin, ash falling to the floor.

"I just want to go back to class." My voice wavered slightly, my fear making a showing.

I didn't know what was going to happen, I was significantly outnumbered and out-muscled here. I should've never come in here, I should've just held it until I got home. Then, as if by an act of god, someone opened the door from the outside and it smacked the guy in the face, giving me the chance to escape. I took it, ducking around the person coming in and making a run for my classroom, my heavy bag only slowing me down slightly.

Stopping in front of the classroom door, I tried to catch my breath and regain my composure before stepping inside so I wouldn't draw everyone's attention. I looked down the hallway, no one was in sight, so I dropped to the ground as the panic overtook me.

I knew what a panic attack looked like from the outside from being there for Theo, and I'd felt something similar before, but this felt like a whole new level. My breaths were ragged, no matter how hard I tried to slow them down they just came quicker and quicker as I gasped and tried to take in air. My chest was so tight, it was like I was being squeezed inside someone's fist, lungs unable to expand. Shaking hands covered my face as tears forced their way out of my eyes. And god, the sounds that were escaping from my throat. Gasps and wheezing whimpers, loud – too loud. The door opened next to me, and my heart felt like it might explode in anticipation of who was walking out.

The door closed softly and a warm, familiar hand rested on my knee. "Jer, hey. It's okay, just breathe. What happened?" Alex cooed at me, similar to the way she approached Theo when they were in the same state.

It's amazing how little "just breathe" did to get me to *actually* breathe. Of course Alex meant only the best, but I knew I needed to breathe, it wasn't like I was doing this on purpose. Her presence was soothing, but not enough to calm my racing thoughts, my inability to control my body. It was like I was floating above myself, unable to control this meat puppet that wanted to flounder and flail.

When I failed to respond, Alex muttered, "shit," then dug through her bag briefly, pulling out a multicolored stress ball.

What the fuck was a ball gonna do?

She took one of my hands that were still shaking out of control, then pressed the ball into my palm. It had a texture of small beads inside it, and Alex closed my hand around it, forcing the tactile sensation to draw my attention. My breaths kept on running away from me – I was getting dizzy. This wasn't working.

Alex turned my hand over in front of me and pointed to a

stripe on the ball, "What color is this?"

What?

"I know it sounds silly, but humor me. What color is it?"

I tried my best to follow the instruction, "R...re-red."

"Good. How many colors are there?"

Squinting at the ball, I counted. There was red, pink, purple, orange, white...it was the lesbian flag. "Five."

"Squeeze it and count out five beads."

With all my strength, I squished the ball in my palm, feeling the beads disperse against the pressure. Then, I ran a finger over five of the beads, counting them mentally.

Alex placed a hand on my knee again, and I was brought back into my body. Everything was still dialed up to ten, but I was starting to feel a sense of control. I was able to meet her eyes.

"Now take a few breaths with me." She proceeded to count out a few breaths, and I was able to match her, my lungs finally expanding and bringing in some much-needed air. She sat down against the wall next to me, quiet and letting me take a few more breaths as I squished the ball between my hands.

After a few minutes, I was able to relax my shoulders and lean back against the wall. I felt exhausted, drained. Stealing a glance at Alex, I managed, "I've never seen you do that with Theo."

She gave a weak smile. "It doesn't work with Theo. They need pressure, and you just have to let the panic attack pass. I usually hold them through it. This," she plucked the ball from my hands, turning it over, "is what I do."

I'd never known Alex to have such a level of panic – she hid it well. She was always so strong for everyone else's sake, more than I think people realized.

"You get panic attacks?" I couldn't leave it alone, now that she'd opened that door. Alex spent so much time taking care of everyone else, it occurred to me that no one ever stopped to ask if she was okay.

She gave a half smile as she looked down at the ball, passing it back and forth between her hands. "They started after Theo's suicide attempt." Her eyes didn't meet mine. "But don't ever tell them that. They won't forgive themself."

She was right, Theo would be wracked with guilt knowing that. "Has it gotten better, now that Theo's gotten help?"

Shrugging, she put the ball back into her bag. "A lot's happened since then."

That was an understatement. Her life had been turned upside down since her and Theo had gotten together. In some ways, it was probably for the best, but she never let on how much of a toll it took on her.

"We should get back to class." Alex stood up, offering me a hand.

Taking her hand, my legs wobbled a bit as I rose from the floor. I was still dizzy, and Alex took my weight as I leaned against her. She steadied me, then placed a hand on each of my shoulders, looking me in the eyes.

"We just gotta push through it, you know?"

Part of me wondered how sustainable that was, but I didn't verbalize my apprehension as she led me back into the classroom.

———

I stepped over the threshold of my apartment, exhausted from the rest of the day, still drained from my panic attack. I didn't assess the situation with my mother, I didn't have the energy for it. I just walked in and went straight to my room, oblivious to everything else. Dropping my backpack at my door and flopping face down on my bed, I sucked in a deep breath and a groan escaped my throat. A soft knock came on my door that I'd forgotten to shut, and I didn't even move to see my mom standing in the doorway.

"Jer, how about I make us some dinner? Some sticky rice and teriyaki chicken? Are you hungry?"

She didn't sound drunk for the first time in weeks, her voice had a clarity that I rarely heard. Whatever was going on, I was too tired to question it.

"Okay," I said, muffled into my pillow.

Footsteps left my doorway and I heard the clattering of pans in the kitchen before the padding of feet returned.

"Would… would you like to cook with me? It could be like old times, you and me in the kitchen."

Okay, *something* was up. Was this her way of apologizing for my hair? Sobering up and offering me what used to be my favorite pastime before she'd completely lost herself in an alcoholic stupor?

We used to be a unit in the kitchen, I think that's part of why I enjoyed being Seth's sous-chef so much. Bringing me back to a time where I had my mom's undivided attention, her kind words, her sweet nature. The parts of her that were taken away from me by the alcohol.

"I miss you." Her voice was small, longing.

God damn it, I really did still love her.

Pushing myself up from the bed with my lengthy arms, I sat on the edge and rubbed at my eyes. I really looked at my mom for the first time since I'd gotten home, and I was blown away. She was completely put together – a distant picture that was once what I'd seen every day. It didn't seem real. She was wearing a nice, clean button-down flannel without a stain in sight, and a pair of crease-free jeans. Her eyes were bright, focused on me. Not a hair was out of place in her tight bun. This was a complete turnaround from the last few weeks. Hell, the last few *years*. I'd seen her like this maybe three times since I'd been a teenager.

"Mom? Are you okay?"

Her smile wavered a bit – she was putting on a show. How easy it would be to crack this facade. But I didn't want to, I wanted to pretend that I had this mother back, that this mother still existed somewhere inside her. That this was the rule, and not the exception.

"I'd be much better if you'd come cook with me."

I dragged myself out of bed and into the kitchen, actually noticing my surroundings this time. Everything was *clean*, put away in its place. The surfaces glistened as if they'd just been wiped down, I couldn't find a speck of dust on the floor. This had been an all-day preparation for my homecoming. She'd never apologized this hard before. Did she really feel that guilty? Was she trying to make up for years of abuse and neglect, or just this past week?

"Will you drain the rice? I'll get out the chicken."

I pulled a metal strainer from the cabinet and dumped the bowl of rice that had been sitting on the counter into it, before setting a pot of water on the stove and resting the strainer inside of it, placing a lid on top. My mom pulled chicken that had been marinating in teriyaki sauce in a bag from the fridge and placed it onto the cutting board and chopped it into strips. The chicken sizzled as it met a pan with a small amount of oil in it, and the smell of teriyaki rushed over me, making my stomach growl.

Stealing a glance at me, my mom smiled as I watched over the rice. Sticky rice was my favorite, and I'd been in charge of it whenever we made it since I was old enough to reach the stove. It was a waiting game though, so I briefly pulled out my phone to check the text I'd felt buzz in my pocket while I'd been in bed.

"Al told me you had a panic attack, how are you feeling?"

Theo, checking in.

"I like the shirt." My mom's voice called my attention up from my phone.

I glanced at her briefly. Every part of this felt like a trap. Not saying a word, I lifted the lid from the rice and flipped it over before replacing the lid. This whole thing was a ruse, an attempt to gain my favor. This wouldn't last, and I knew it. She stirred the chicken around, the whole time it sizzled in the pan. An awkward silence formed between us, brought on by my refusal to take this bait.

The rice and chicken being fully cooked, my mom turned off the stove and I grabbed two plates from the cupboard. We each filled a plate up, and I turned to take my plate into my room. My mom stopped, setting her plate on the kitchen table.

"Won't you eat with me, Jer?"

My footsteps froze, and I slowly turned around, setting my plate on the table across from hers and sat down, still not making eye contact. More awkward silence, but she was trying so hard that I started to feel a little bad about how cold I was being. I picked up a piece of chicken with the sticky rice and dropped it into my mouth, chewing a bit on the flavors of my childhood before finally meeting my mom's gaze.

"Will you call me Phee?"

My mom stopped chewing. Silence. She dropped her head into her hands and took a deep breath. "You really want me to say goodbye to my son?"

"I was never your son. I'm your daughter." My tone was flat, unfeeling. I had no emotional energy left for this. This arguing, this fighting to be who I was.

My mom lifted her head from her hands, looking me over with pleading eyes. "I want to make things better between us."

"This is how you do it."

"What you said the other night, about leaving for college and me never dealing with you again, did you really mean that? Are you really just waiting to be out of here?"

I guess we were really getting into it. I leaned back in my chair, looking up at my mom, no longer focused on the food on my plate.

"Can you blame me, mom? You're drunk all the time. If I'm not taking care of you, you're either embarrassing me or hurting me. You refuse to accept who I am. I can't be myself here, I'm just a caretaker who gets hit."

"No, I suppose not." She looked down at her plate. Neither of us were eating at this point, appetites sufficiently gone out the window. "I just don't want you to leave and never look back, I love you."

"You sure haven't been showing it."

"What if I get sober?"

And now we fell into the conversation we'd had dozens of times before. I wasn't having it. "You've tried that before, mom. You always go back to drinking. You've always chosen alcohol over me."

Tears brimmed in her eyes, and she scraped at a speck of dirt on the table with her nail. "What if it's different this time? I feel awful for what I've done."

"It's not going to be. It's never different."

"I poured out all the alcohol in the house."

"You'll get more. You always do."

A tear fell from my mother's cheek. I should've felt bad about shutting her down, but I didn't. I was telling the truth – she'd tried to get sober so many times I'd lost count. Alcoholics Anonymous, counseling, rehab, nothing ever worked. She'd fall away from her supports, call it 'just one drink', and then we'd be back in the same situation. I was tired of being given false hope that things would be different, and I wasn't going to accept the fake promise this time. It was always fake, whether or not she meant it to be.

Tears fell from my mother's face without restraint, and her voice wavered as she squeaked out, "You've given up on me, haven't you?"

Don't say it, that's an awful thing to say to your mother.

"Yes."

Shit.

CHAPTER NINE

I couldn't focus in school the next day. I felt awful. Why did I say it? Why hadn't I just held my tongue? But it was the truth, I'd given up and resigned to my life with my mother as it was some time ago. It wasn't news to me, but it certainly was to her. I didn't see her in the morning before I left for school, and our dinner had ended in an awkward silence, neither of us finishing our plates.

Opening the door to my apartment, I expected to find my mother drunk on the couch or something similar, turning to alcohol to soothe her wounds. I did find her on the couch, but in a much different state than I'd expected. She was wrapped up in a blanket, sweat beading her forehead. Her body shook with tremors, and she was incredibly pale with dark circles formed around her eyes. I dropped my bag at the door after shutting it and rushed over to the couch.

"Mom? What's wrong?"

Her teeth chattered as she failed to answer me, and I pressed a hand to her clammy forehead. She was burning up.

"You've got a fever. Should we go to the doctor?"

"N-no… it's just… I'm not drinking."

"You're having withdrawal."

"Yes."

"Can't alcohol withdrawal kill you? We should go to the emergency room."

She batted a hand and pulled the blanket tighter around herself. "No… no. I'll be fine. I'm going to do this for you. I can't hurt you anymore."

Her shaking was uncontrollable, and worry ate at me. I pulled my phone from my pocket and went into my room, dialing the number I knew by heart.

"Theo?"

"What's up?"

"Can you come to my house? It's my mom, she…"

"Did she hurt you again?"

"No, no. She stopped drinking. She's having withdrawal, and I'm worried. I thought you might… you might know what to do."

There was a silence on their end, and I worried that I might've offended them. While alcohol hadn't been their primary vice, they knew what it was to struggle with addiction. They'd come out the other side, so I hoped that they'd know what to do.

After a long pause, they answered, "I'll have Seth drive me over. I'll be there in five."

"Okay, thank you."

I walked back into the living room, just in time to pull my mother's hair back as she threw up into a small garbage can that had been placed at her side. I filled a glass of water and then returned to the living room, putting it in my mother's shaking hands. She brought it to her lips and took a sip, handing me back the glass and leaning back on the couch, exhausted. I changed the bag in the trash can and as I came back into the living room there was a knock on the door, Theo on the other side.

"Wow, you're right, she looks like shit." Theo walked over to place a hand on her forehead, which my mom pushed away.

"Who are you?"

"Mom, you've met Theo before." I sat down on the coffee table in front of my mom.

"No, I only remember that blonde boy." She shook and stared warily at Theo, who sat down next to me at the coffee table.

Theo leaned in towards me, "I don't think I've been inside your house since I transitioned, definitely not when she's been sober anyway."

My heart sank, I didn't want to out Theo like this, but there was no avoiding it. "Mom, do you remember the girl with the long hair that used to come by every once in a while? I think you threw a plate at them once."

My mom glanced between Theo and I, squinting while trying to conjure up the image in her memory. A flicker of realization came to her eyes, then she stared pointedly at Theo. "You're one of those transgenders? Are you the one putting ideas into my boy's head?"

"Mom!" My face flushed, but Theo's smirk put me at ease.

A slight chuckle escaped them, "It's okay, Phee. Alex's mom has said way worse."

The relief didn't last long as my mom grew more pale, which I didn't even think was possible. "I… I don't… feel…" my mom rambled a bit.

And then the shaking started — not the shivering and shaking hands, but violent, uncontrollable shaking that rendered my mother silent as her eyes rolled back in her head. Theo stood up from the table, acting quickly to guide my mother into lying on her side on the couch as she continued to shake and started spitting up saliva.

I was frozen in fear. As angry as I'd been at my mother, I wasn't ready to lose her completely. Not like this. "Theo, what's happening?" My voice cracked as panic rose up in my chest.

"She's having a seizure." Theo pulled out their phone, handing it to me with one hand while using the other to steady my mom on the couch and keep her from falling off. "Call Mom."

Quickly, I skimmed through Theo's contacts before landing on Monica's number, then paced back and forth as the phone rang.

She answered on the third ring, "Theo, what's wrong honey?"

I didn't even bother to correct her before the words spilled from my mouth, "My mom, she stopped drinking and she's been having withdrawal and now she's having a seizure I don't know what to do Theo told me to call you."

"Okay, okay, slow down, Jeremy. Is she still seizing? Is she in a safe position?"

"Theo has her lying on her side. She's spitting up a lot, oh god, is she gonna die? She can't die, Monica." Tears started forcing their way out of my eyes as my own hands began to shake.

"Okay. Can you bring her in, Jeremy? I can send an ambulance."

"I… I can drive her."

"Do that, I'll meet you in the emergency room."

Hanging up, I approached Theo as my mom's uncontrollable shaking started to slow. There was a glazed-over look in her eyes, and she still appeared out of it.

"We going to the hospital?" Theo asked, grabbing a napkin to wipe the spit from my mom's face.

"Yes. How are we gonna get her in the car?"

My mother was a small woman, but I knew for sure I didn't have the strength to carry her. Without hesitation, Theo scooped my mother into their arms, lifting her from the couch. They might've been small, but they were mighty.

"You get the doors."

I nodded, grabbing the car keys from the hook by the door and opening it for Theo to go through. The stairs seemed treacherous, but Theo handled them with ease. I opened the car door for the backseat, and Theo tucked my mother inside, fastening her seatbelt.

"No… I don't… I don't need to go…" my mom protested, apparently alert enough to speak, but still too weak to really fight us off.

"Mom, we're going." I shut the door as Theo and I got into the front.

My mom halfheartedly pulled at her seatbelt, no strength left inside her. She quickly gave up, resting her head on the seat and sighing. I turned the car on, taking in a deep breath. I didn't drive very often, the truth was that I hated it. Everything about it made me so anxious. But it needed to be done, and I was going to do this. I pulled out of the parking spot and onto the street, beginning the short drive to the hospital's emergency room.

I kept glancing at the back seat through the rearview mirror, watching my mom as she seemingly slipped in and out of consciousness. Before long, I pulled up to the emergency bay at the hospital, and Theo jumped out, rounding the car to open my mom's door. This time, she fought them.

"No, you're not taking me anywhere!"

Theo undid her seatbelt and went to lift her from the seat when she slapped them across the face. I jumped in front of them, grabbing my mom's wrist firmly.

"Mom! Don't hit them. They're just trying to help, we have to go."

She yanked her hand away from me, spitting in my face. "You… you just want me locked up! Nothing's going to help!

You don't even care!"

I wiped my face, exasperated. Monica appeared behind us with a wheelchair and Theo and I both looked at her helplessly. She held up a hand for both of us to take a step back, and so we did. She bent down to my mom's level in the car. My mom stared at her warily, shifting towards the other side of the car.

"Ma'am, Jeremy tells me that you had a seizure. He just wants to make sure you're okay, why don't we get you checked out?"

My mom looked between Monica and I before leaning forward and throwing up all over Monica's shoes. She seemed unphased by it, resting a hand on my mother's shoulder.

"At the very least, we can get you on some fluids and give you something for the nausea." Her tone was soft, there was no anger here, only concern.

Reluctantly, my mom took Monica's hand and got into the wheelchair, and we followed her inside. We got to skip the waiting room and Monica got my mom into a bed where a nurse helped take her vitals and hook her up to an IV. Then, the shaking started again, and my mom contorted back onto the mattress. Monica and the nurse quickly turned her onto her side, as another nurse ran over and medical commands were given from Monica's lips. The new nurse corralled Theo and I with her arms, escorting us away.

"Let's let them work, okay? There's no need for you to see this."

Before we knew it, we were in the waiting room, blinking against the fluorescent lights and looking at each other, dumbfounded. Theo put a hand on my shoulder.

"Phee, you okay?"

I didn't know. I was numb, unfeeling of what was happening around me. It felt like I should be worrying, and on some level I think that I was, but on the surface, nothing. Slowly, I looked up at

Theo, turning the car keys over in my hand.

"I'm… I'm gonna go park the car."

As if on autopilot, I stepped out of the automatic doors of the emergency room into the cool air of an autumn night. Taking in a deep breath, I walked around the car and shut the back door, careful to avoid the puddle of vomit that was still next to the car. Then, I got into the car, shutting the door behind me.

Keys turned in the ignition, and the car roared to life. It was a bit of an old car, so it always made loud protests when turning on, changing gears. Anything, really. At least it was reliable. I pressed my head back against the headrest and closed my eyes, tears suddenly taking over. The numb was starting to wear off, now that no one was around, my composure fell away. It was as if I was made up of a ton of tiny, fragmented pieces, held together dubiously, and someone had just taken a hammer to my very being. Sobs overtook my body, and I hunched forward, covering my face with my hands.

I couldn't do this anymore. It was all too much. I lost myself for what felt like an eternity, my whole body shaking uncontrollably and my sobs surely loud enough for everyone inside to hear. So loud, in fact, that I didn't hear the passenger's side door open, and had the fear of my life run through me as a hand rested on my shoulder.

Blurry through the tears, it was Theo.

"Hey, you're okay. It's gonna be okay."

"Why does she get to keep doing this to me? It's not fucking fair. It's not fair!"

"You're right, it's not. The nurse inside said we gotta move the car though, in case an ambulance needs to pull up."

I nodded, wiping the tears and snot from my face with the back of my hand. I managed to muster up the composure to focus enough to move the car into a nearby parking spot, then turned the keys back in the ignition, shutting the car off.

There was a small ticking sound the car always made right after you turned it off, but otherwise there was complete silence as I stared out the windshield into the bushes surrounding the hospital.

"Do you wanna go back to my house? We can do something, take your mind off things."

"I… I should stay here. What if she needs me?"

"Honestly, Phee, there's nothing we can do right now. Monica's taking care of her, but she's too in and out to know what's going on right now. We can come back in the morning."

I sniffled, wiping at my nose again.

Theo took my hand, not caring that it had become a makeshift tissue. I looked up at them, tears still brimming at my eyes.

"I've got some really good weed, I'll roll you a joint, okay? We've got snacks, too. Ice cream."

Theo pulled me into an embrace, and I let myself relax into their arms. Theo hugs were few and far between, a treasure to be savored. Only Alex got an unlimited number of them. They pulled away after a minute, brushing some pink hair away from my eyes.

"Does that sound okay?"

I nodded before turning the car back on.

CHAPTER TEN

I sniffled through the drive to Theo's house, blinking away the blur of tears the whole time. Thankfully, it was a pretty short drive – ten minutes, maybe. I parked on the street behind Seth's car, and Theo placed a hand gently on my shoulder before we both got out. My legs bounced underneath me and I glanced along the dark street while Theo unlocked the door.

We were met with the smell of a dinner recently cooked, cajun chicken wings, it smelled like. Seth was in the kitchen with a towel thrown over his shoulder as he walked away from the fridge, and Alex was at the sink washing dishes. Seth turned to see us coming from the door, a cool breeze disturbing the heat of the kitchen.

"Oh, shit, I just put the food away. I can get it back out for you two." Seth turned back to the fridge as Theo shook their head.

"I think we're gonna smoke first, don't worry about it, Seth."

Taking his hand from the handle on the fridge, Seth perked up a little. "I'm in."

Theo rolled their eyes. "Moocher."

Seth chuckled. "Act like I don't buy my own weed and share it with you."

Theo gave Seth a gentle shove of the shoulder before gesturing to me to follow them up the stairs. Their room was dim, but we all hated the overhead light in there. It was almost as bad as the fluorescent lights of the hospital. Instead, they switched on their desk light before pulling a box from the bottom of their dresser. I sat down on their bed as they brought the box to their desk, pulling out the grinder and some weed. And damn, did this weed smell. It was a wonder they'd been able to keep it hidden.

After grinding up some of the weed, Theo pulled a couple rolling papers from the box and made quick work of rolling two joints. They then pulled a lighter out of the box before returning it to its place in their dresser. They plopped down on the bed and opened their window, letting the cool autumn air rush in. Then, they handed me one of the joints.

"That one's just for you." They gave a weak smile, handing me the lighter.

I lit the joint just as the doorknob turned and Alex and Seth came in. Seth took the seat at the desk, while Alex sat down on the bed next to Theo. Handing the lighter back to Theo, I took a deep breath of the joint in before holding it and blowing it out the window. Theo lit theirs and took a hit before handing it to Alex, who had recently gotten better at not inhaling the entire thing and then coughing up a storm. She handed it to Seth, and he took a hit as well before handing the joint back to Theo, and the circle started all over again.

The three of them finished off the joint much faster than I could finish off mine, so I was left smoking while everyone else melted into their seats. Theo was right, this weed was *good*. My anxieties began to ease up a little and I leaned against the window, putting my head back and closing my eyes for a minute. I felt heavy, but not a terrible kind of heavy, just like my limbs were made of lead. I was an immovable object on this bed, ready to melt away into a puddle of nothingness.

"Do you want to save the rest for later?" Theo asked.

"Huh?" My eyes squinted, I was barely able to keep them open. Theo pointed at the joint.

"Oh, uh, yeah." I handed them the half-smoked joint, and they got up and deposited it and the lighter into the box.

Seth made his exit silently while Theo did that. I barely noticed in my haze. All I really wished for in that moment was for someone to hold me, tell me everything was going to be okay. I wondered if I'd ever have that person. It was a mother's job, but I couldn't remember the last time she'd done something like that for me. In absence of that, I'd have to wait for the right partner to come along, and I didn't know if I was really worth it.

Theo shut the window, the clatter of it against the pane bringing me back to reality. "You okay, Phee?"

"Ask me again in a year." I sighed, closing my eyes. I'd curl up and die right here and now if I could.

"Do you two want food? The munchies are already setting in," Alex asked, placing a hand on her growling stomach.

Theo snickered. "Sure, Al."

Alex giggled, kissing Theo briefly before sneaking out the door and down to the kitchen. She always got this giddy demeanor when we smoked, and there was no stopping her on the hunt for food.

I shivered, then tried to wrestle a blanket from underneath me, sighing in exasperation as I gave up and leaned back against the wall. Everything felt so impossible.

"Take your shoes off." Theo said as they got up from the bed and started digging around in their closet, producing the fuzziest looking blanket I'd ever seen.

"Ooh, yay." I gasped, kicking my shoes off onto the floor and then curling up with the blanket.

It was so soft, I just wanted to pet it with my hands, such a nice feeling. Undoubtedly enhanced by how high I was, I didn't care as I rolled into a cocoon with the blanket. Theo picked up their laptop and brought the desk chair in front of their bed.

"What do you want to watch?" They sat down with the laptop, clicking around to get to our favorite streaming site.

"Something sci-fi, or like, a cool ocean documentary."

Theo set to searching and we found a cool looking ocean-themed sci-fi, and just as they hit play Alex bounded in the room with a plate of dinner for each of us and a bag of cheese puffs for herself. My nose had been correct earlier – cajun chicken with Mexican street corn and twice-baked potatoes. A feast fit for royalty.

The fork felt heavy in my hand, and I struggled a bit, but the food was so worth it. I hadn't eaten since lunch, and it was now approaching nine PM. It took me so long to finish my plate that Theo was actually done before me. Alex offered us some of the cheese puffs, but we were both full. I think she was secretly hoping for that, as she took the bag back and continued to demolish its contents.

We were about halfway into the movie by now, and it was actually pretty interesting, but I was having trouble keeping my focus. I curled back up in the blanket before slowly slumping over on the mattress and slipping into the best sleep of my life.

———

I awoke late the next morning, Saturday. Neither Theo nor Alex were in sight. I checked my phone – nothing from my mom, although I'm not sure she'd text me anyway. I made my way down the stairs, wearing the same clothes from yesterday, and found

Monica in the kitchen.

"Hey, kiddo." Her tone was soft and sympathetic, as always.

I didn't even stop to exchange pleasantries. "How's my mom? Can I go see her?"

"She's resting, I just got off shift about an hour ago. She'll need her sleep to recover, but we got her the care she needed. She'll be okay. It's probably best to visit a little bit later. I'm not sure how lucid she'd be if you went now."

"Shouldn't I go still? Just so she knows that I'm there?"

"She knows you care about her, Jer. You shouldn't make this harder for yourself seeing her like that, you deserve better."

Jer. A shiver ran down my spine, this would be my last coming out for a while, hopefully.

"It's… it's actually, Phee now."

"What?" It wasn't an exasperated or angry 'what', at least.

"My name. I'm… I'm a girl."

"Oh, okay." She gave me a smile that eased my nerves. "Phee, I like it."

She set the coffee mug she'd been holding down on the kitchen island, then came and engulfed me in an embrace I'd been longing for. I wrapped my arms around her back and buried my face in her shoulder, tears threatening to make their appearance. I wished that my own mother would've done this for me. That she'd reacted to my coming out with love instead of anger. I rubbed at my eyes after we pulled away, and Monica let her hands linger on my shoulders.

"You'll be okay, hun. I know it's hard, you've got a lot going on. It's normal to feel overwhelmed. I can't imagine how much you've been dealing with."

"I wish my mom understood." My voice wavered.

"I'm sure this is all so much harder with her drinking. It can't be easy."

"I just… I just want her to love *me*. Not the idea she has of me. I want her to see me for who I am and not be mad about it."

"I'm sure deep down, she does. She's just got to work on showing it. She kept mistaking one of our younger nurses for you last night and told him how sorry she was, over and over."

That made the tears really come out. "I should've been there." I cried.

"No, no you shouldn't. It was messy, and touch-and-go for most of the night. That type of thing isn't fair for a child to witness of a parent. I'm glad Theo brought you home."

My legs were weak, and I was getting dizzy. I was so overwhelmed, and my breathing started to quicken as I shook.

"Hey, hey, come sit down." Monica guided me over to the couch where I collapsed into a sobbing mess for what number of time I'd lost count of this month.

Monica rubbed my back as I buried my face in my hands, and I heard other people enter the room before my ears started ringing so loud that I couldn't hear anything on the outside. More hands were added to my back, and I felt someone pull me into a hug – a tender compression that only came from Alex's arms. Eventually, things started to calm down, and the ringing in my ears died down.

"Hey, Phee?" Alex's voice.

I took a shaky breath in and then lifted my head.

"I've got a surprise for you. I was gonna show you when you woke up. Do you want to see?"

———

Alex held her hands in front of my eyes, which probably wasn't necessary with how blurry my vision was with tears. I sniffled as we entered the guest bedroom and stopped walking.

"Ready?" She asked.

"I guess." I wasn't really feeling it, but she'd been so excited that I couldn't refuse. All I really wanted to do at this point was crawl under a rock.

Alex removed her hands from my face and I tried to blink and rub away the blurriness. When my vision finally cleared up, all I could see was a bunch of boxes and packages sprawled across the bed.

"I know it's not really a *surprise* surprise, since you did pick them out and all, but your new clothes are here!"

"Ooh." I tried to sound excited, I really did, but my mood refused to be lifted.

"Do you want to open them now?"

The "not really" had to be tamped down, I didn't want to crush her excitement. Instead, nothing came out, and I just kind of stood there and blinked. I should've been excited, but I was so lost in my emotions that it was hard to find my way out. Alex's smile slowly faded, and Theo put a hand on my shoulder.

"Phee, what do you need right now?" Theo asked.

The only thing that had ever really helped when I felt like this was getting lost in my art. When I was looking for the perfect shot, I wasn't thinking about what was going on around me, wasn't worried about my mom, wasn't feeling sorry for myself or anxious. That's what I needed.

"Theo, will you help me with something?"

———

What do you like most about your body?

"Take a right here." Theo pointed as we drove away from the city.

What do you like least about your body?

"Where are we going?" I asked, glancing at our surroundings. We were getting further and further into the woods.

How do you see the beauty in other people's bodies?

"Right here," Theo announced, and I pulled off to the side of the dirt road we'd ended up on.

We both got out of the car, and I glanced around anxiously – this was the perfect place for a murderer to kill us and hide our bodies. We'd never be found.

"Why here?" I clutched my camera to my chest as Theo walked down the path a bit, finding an old, decrepit-looking tree that wound in every direction.

"I like the woods. You told me to pick some place significant."

"Yeah, I figured you'd take me to the skate park. Since when are you a tree hugger?"

They shook their head. "The woods are my real safe place. Back when I was with my bio father, I'd run to the woods behind the cabin when he was angry. I was quick and good at climbing, he'd never find me once I got ahead of him."

"Oh." *Shit.* Leave it to me to sound like an ass.

"Now I walk Dulce in the woods around that little park on the edge of town, but I've always loved these woods, they're just too far to walk."

I fiddled with my camera, bringing it to my face as Theo stepped up to the tree and placed their hand on it.

"Hold on." They held up their other hand, then pulled their hoodie over their head, revealing a black half-tank binder underneath.

Then, to my surprise, they unbuttoned their jeans and shed the layer down to a pair of black bicycle shorts that were tight against their frame. I lowered the camera. I had no idea Theo even owned a pair of shorts. I'd never seen them wear one in all the time I'd known them. Then, barefoot, they stepped onto the branches of the tree, hoisting themself up. I stared, watching the flex of their muscles and the curve of their back, down to their defined abs and thighs that could easily crush a man's skull.

I think they said something, but I didn't really hear it. All the emotions I thought I'd tamped down, gotten rid of, came flooding back to me. They were fucking *hot*, and every part of me wanted to run my hands along their muscles. Their perfect, heart-shaped ass, their capped shoulders that could bear the weight of another human, their elegant collarbones that stuck out as they climbed, it was all too much at once. I'd been so confused when I'd first developed feelings for them. I'd never been attracted to a girl in my life. I thought that maybe they'd be the one to "fix" me, make me straight. Then, when we figured out that they weren't a girl, everything started to make more sense, as my hopes of being "normal" slipped away. I knew they couldn't be mine. They were head over heels for Alex, and just didn't feel the same way about me. I'd accepted it. Or at least, I thought I had.

"Phee?" Their voice broke through my daze, and they blinked at me from their perch in the tree.

I closed my eyes tight and shook away the feelings. I couldn't have these feelings, no. They'd get in the way of our friendship, of the comfortable companionship we had. They hadn't made it weird when I told them how I felt, but I'd brushed it aside as quickly as I'd mentioned it. I couldn't lose this friendship for what it was. Opening my eyes again, my gaze fell to their legs.

The *scars*. I knew they were there, but I'd never seen them in person. Theo had talked about what their father did, however briefly, but it was so easy to forget. They were the reason I'd never seen them wear shorts, they kept them hidden from the world. The dark secret of their past, incarnate.

Theo glanced down at their legs, then rubbed a hand along one of them. "I know, they're ugly." Their tone was somber.

"No," I said, almost too quickly, "They're beautiful. They show where you've been, and how you've come out of it."

Theo flashed a slight smile as they adjusted their binder and shorts, getting the materials to lay flush against their skin. They were stunning, up there in that tree. I brought my camera to my face, and all bets were off. Taking all the pictures I could, I circled around the tree, getting different angles, and even taking some pictures when they weren't expecting it to get that candid feeling. I could've spent an eternity there with them, my perfect muse. We'd made it for the golden hour, elegant beams of sun peeking through the leaves of the trees, casting a pattern of shadows over Theo's skin. Losing all sense of time, we only stopped when the sun began to dip below the horizon.

They hopped down from the tree when I was mid-picture. "We should head back, it's getting late. I'm sure you want to see your mom."

I stared at them as they started putting their clothes back on, and I started feeling like a creep. If I knew they didn't feel that way about me, how could I look at them like that? Anger directed at myself rushed over me, and I squinted and looked away, blushing. Theo hopped, putting their last shoe back on and then approached me, gesturing towards the camera.

"Can I see?"

I tilted the camera so that Theo could see my favorite photo of the session. They were perched in the tree, back against the trunk, hands resting on a branch. Their gaze was off in the distance, as if something incredible were happening just out of frame. Golden eyes alight as the sun beamed into them, casting shadows of leaves in a pattern across their face. They were stunning, breathtaking.

Theo took the picture in before skimming through a few more, then smiling up at me. "These are really good. Do they say what you want them to?"

I took the camera as Theo handed it back to me, unable to make eye contact with a blush slowly forming across my face. "I think so. Are you able to write out the answers to those questions?"

"Yeah, I can have that for you soon. Are you going to do Alex, too?"

We started walking back towards the car, "Yeah, if she's okay with it. I might try to get Seth and Harriet, too. I don't know about Elliot. Our interactions are still a little… tense."

Theo put a hand on my shoulder as we sat down in the car. "It'll get better between you two. Breakups are tough."

"How would you know?" The words came out more bitter than intended, "You've never had one."

"Phee." Theo shot me a look that all but told me to watch my tone.

I rested my forehead against the steering wheel before muttering, "I'm sorry. I just… I'm really overwhelmed right now."

Theo put a hand on my back. "Then let's get back before dinner. Cooking with Seth always puts you in a good mood."

I nodded, turning the car on and driving out of the woods that seemed even more murderous in the dim light of dusk. Theo's association with them made sense, but I wasn't sure I'd ever see them the same way.

CHAPTER ELEVEN

Monica drove us to the hospital – I'd decided to see my mom alone, although now I was beginning to regret that decision. The anticipation of not knowing what state she'd be in overwhelmed me, and I picked at my nails while my legs bounced uncontrollably in the passenger's seat. We'd eaten dinner, but my stomach was still clenched into a knot, making me feel like it would all come up again. Monica glanced over at me while she drove, concern written across her face.

"You don't have to stay long if you don't want to. Seth's just a phone call away. Okay? I know this is hard, and you want to be there for her, but it's important to take care of yourself, too."

I nodded, unable to form an adequate response. We pulled into the hospital parking lot all too soon, and approached the front of the emergency room where Monica greeted a nurse and punched in before escorting me to my mom's room.

I wasn't prepared for what I saw. She was in four-point restraints, hair matted wildly to her forehead, IVs and oxygen hooked up. She was asleep, for the moment, but scratches ran up and down her arms, especially around her IV. Monica furrowed her brow when we walked in, addressing the nurse who was checking my mom's vitals.

"Why is she in restraints?" Her tone wasn't harsh, but she still didn't seem happy with the situation.

"She was hallucinating. She attacked a couple nurses and wouldn't stop scratching. Tried to rip her IV out a few times. They had to dose her, and she's been out ever since."

Monica nodded solemnly, glancing over at me. I kept wringing my hands together, my chest tight with anxiety.

"It's okay if you don't want to stay, hun. We can wait until tomorrow. I'm sure things will be better then."

I stared at my mother. She was pale, and it was almost as if all life had left her body. I knew she was just sleeping, judging by the rhythmic beep of her heart rate on the monitor, but it was as if all the fight inside her was gone.

"N-no… I'll stay for a little."

Monica placed a hand on my shoulder as she turned to leave the room. "Okay. I've got to go, but please let me know if you need anything. Seth can come get you when you're ready to go."

I nodded, then pulled the chair in the corner of the room up to my mom's bedside, and watched as the nurse finished recording her vitals and left us alone. I stared for a long time, not sure what to do, what to say. We'd been through this before, but never this bad. Touching my mom's hand, I shuddered at the cold. Her hands were like ice. I tried to warm them up between my own hands, but it proved futile. There was a spare blanket resting on the back of my chair, so I unfolded it and laid it across her. Her eyes fluttered open, then she blinked a few times, as if trying to assess her surroundings.

"Hi, mom," I said softly.

She turned her head to look at me, then realization came to her eyes. "Ooh, my baby." She lifted her hands as if to embrace me, but they caught on the restraints. Startled, she looked down at them and fought them a little before giving up and looking back up at me. "They took you away from me."

"No, mom. You were hallucinating. I left for a little while so you could get some rest, but now I'm back."

"No, no. You're… too little to be home alone. Who took care of you?"

"Mom, I'm seventeen."

She paused at that, squinting at me and then lifting her arms against the restraints again.

"You got so big! What happened? Please let me out, I want to hug you."

"I can't, mom. You hurt the nurses."

"Nooo…" She dragged out the word, the drugs definitely still affecting her.

I took my mom's hand, mustering up the best smile I could under the circumstances, "You've just gotta be chill, okay? I'm sure once they see you're calm, they'll let you out."

"Will you stay with me?" Her hand trembled in mine, still ice cold.

I lifted the blanket up to her chin and tucked her in. "Sure."

Sitting down in the chair, I scooted it a little closer to her, then clicked the tiny television in the corner of the room on, skimming the channels.

"Ooh, leave it here," My mom said as I passed a channel playing old cartoons. I flipped it back, setting the remote down as the misadventures of a cat desperately trying to catch a mouse played out on the screen. A smile lit up my mom's face. "I loved this one when I was little."

I grinned at her, this was nice. Who knew it would take a seizure-inducing detox for us to get along? Every interaction with her lately had been fighting, hurtful words and actions, on both sides. I almost felt like I could give her another chance to be the good mom I know that deep down she truly wanted to be.

Monica walked in, relief on her face to see that things were calm. "Why don't we get you out of those?" she asked, approaching my mom's bedside.

My mom's attention darted from the television to Monica, a scowl forming on her face. Monica paused, looking at me for a second before looking back at my mother, who began to writhe in her bed.

I put a hand back on my mom's arm. "It's okay, mom, she's just trying to help. You wanted these off, didn't you?"

She stopped, glassy eyes focused on me. "Ye-yes, I'd like that."

Monica gave her a sympathetic smile before slowly and carefully undoing the restraints holding my mom's arms and legs to the bed. My mom rubbed at her wrists afterwards, still watching Monica's every move with distrust. She was paranoid, that was for sure. Monica checked my mom's vitals, recorded them on her chart, then turned to leave the room.

"Let me know if you need anything, all right, Phee?"

I nodded, before glancing at my mother at the mention of my new name. She hadn't missed it.

"Phee." Her tone was longing, wistful. She turned to face me, reaching out her hand, "What a pretty name."

I froze in disbelief, "You really think so?"

"Pretty just like you." She put a hand on my cheek.

I was waiting for the ridicule, the slap, the denial. But it didn't come. There was no way this was happening, this had to be a joke. Everything began to overwhelm me, the paranoia of what this really meant making me antsy. This was the drugs talking, right? This couldn't be my mother.

My mom pulled her hand away, scanning my pained expression. "I've been thinking a lot. I shouldn't have treated you the way that I did. You have every right to hate me, it shows what a good person you are that you're still here."

Silent tears fell from my eyes, and I said softly, "You're my mom. I'm always gonna be here."

She reached over and wiped away the tears running down my cheeks, her own eyes brimming with water. "This… this is all for you. I'm going to do better for you, I promise. I have to. These past years haven't been fair to you."

I stood up, my lip quivering as I looked at my mom.

"Oh, baby, please don't leave."

Silently, I clicked down the railing on one side of the bed and climbed in, wrapping my arms around my mom as the tears came faster. This felt like a dream, this couldn't be real. She *apologized?* She's calling me a girl? When would the switch flip, when would she turn back into the mother who despised who I was? Was this all just the drugs she'd been given talking? There was no way this could last.

But I was going to take advantage of it while I could.

She wrapped her frigid hands around my back as I cried into her chest, clutching her tight. This was the mother that had been robbed from me all those years ago. The mother that had been turned by alcohol into an abusive monster whose moods I couldn't predict. The mother that wasn't completely overcome with fury and grief.

And it was amazing.

———

I'd stayed until my mom fell asleep, and everyone went into night mode in the hospital. We'd stayed cuddled up in the bed, watching cartoons like there wasn't a care to be had, like she wasn't in the hospital for a detox that had almost killed her. Like she hadn't spent years hurting me. Maybe now, things would start to heal.

For now, I was on my way back to Theo's house, staring out the window of Seth's car with the ugliest grin on my face, my crooked teeth showing and all.

"How was she?" Seth asked.

"She… she was *great*. Like, really great. Like she was before she ever started drinking, before everything went bad. I'm so afraid it was just the drugs they gave her, but she stayed like that the whole time, y'know? I would think it would've worn off if it was just the drugs."

My smile was contagious, Seth grinned back at me. "That's so good, Phee. I hope things stay that way."

"I hope so too."

Seth parked on the street in front of the house, and we both got out and Seth fiddled with his keys to let us in. Before we were even in the door, I was bombarded by Alex.

"*Now* can we go through your clothes? *Please?* I waited all day for you!"

"Al, leave her alone, she's probably tired." Theo waved one of their hands, their other hand wrapped around a mug of tea as they sat curled up on the couch.

"No, no," I laughed, "I'd like that."

"*Yes!*" Alex took me by the hand and led me into the guest bedroom where all the packages were laid out on the bed.

My eyes scanned the array of boxes and bags as Alex flipped the light on. It was overwhelming, to say the least. It must've shown on my face, because Alex looked at me and then picked up one of the bags and handed it to me.

"Start with this one!"

I sat down on the free corner of the bed, and Alex stood in front of me, hands clasped together in anticipation. Theo appeared in the doorway, cup of tea still in hand. A smile graced their face as they watched me tear into the plastic, revealing a beautiful, flowing off-white top with butterflies and flowers printed on it. There were ties around the neckline and draping sleeves.

Alex snatched it from my hands. "Oh my god, this is *so* cute. I didn't even see this one in the cart!"

I smiled at Alex's enthusiasm, then reached back into the bag, pulling out the black, rhinestone-studded leggings that I'd chosen to go with the shirt. Her eyes widened when she saw them, then she placed the shirt back into my hands.

"Put them on, put them on!"

"Al, if she tries them all on, this is going to take *forever.*"

"Just this one!" She clasped her hands together again. "Please?"

"Okay, okay." I laughed, then took the two articles to the bathroom and did a quick change.

When I came back into the room, Alex gasped in excitement before pulling me over to the mirror.

"You look so *cute!*"

I smiled, adjusting the top on my shoulders. I really wished that I had something going on with my chest to fill the shirt out, but I still really liked what I saw. It was me, free to express what had always been nagging at the back of my mind. Alex ran back to the bed and picked up a small package, placing it in my hands.

"Try this with it! It wasn't on your list, I ordered it special."

I glanced at her before taking the package, then pried the thin plastic apart to reveal a small velvet bag. Opening it, I pulled out a beautiful silver chain with a square charm on it. I flipped it over — it was a polaroid, with a small picture of the three of us together inside the frame. Running my fingers over it, I looked back at Alex.

"It's beautiful, Alex, I love it."

"Here, let me put it on."

I handed her the necklace, and she placed it around my neck, clipping the chain together in the back. It perfectly filled the empty space that the blouse left, drawing attention away from the ribs you could see below my collarbone.

"It's so perfect on you!" Alex placed a hand on my shoulder.

Theo came over from the doorway and picked the pendant up, squinting at it to see better. "Aw, that's sweet, Allie."

I turned to Alex, throwing my arms around her. "Thank you, for everything," Releasing her from my grip, I put a hand on Theo's shoulder. "You've both been so great."

"Of course, Phee," they both said in unison.

Then, Alex returned to the bed, picking up another package. "Let's keep going!"

———

The next day, I woke up in the guest bedroom, surrounded by the pile of clothes we'd folded and left on the free side of the bed. There'd barely been enough room for me to sleep. I yawned, emerging from the room in an oversized t-shirt and leggings I'd worn as pajamas. Seth was in the kitchen, but it looked like he'd just gotten started.

"Hey!" he called, "You're up in time to help today!" He gestured to a block of cheese that was placed on a cutting board next to a grater.

I grinned, washing my hands before setting to work on grating the cheese. Seth was carefully lining a muffin pan with bacon in each little compartment, and I cocked my head at him.

"What are we making?"

"Egg baskets. Little bacon baskets with an egg inside and

cheese on top."

My mouth watered, and I nodded as I continued grating the cheese. We made quick work of everything, Seth cracking eggs into the muffin pan after he'd laid out all the bacon. Then, it was my job to sprinkle the cheese on after he doused each one with seasoning. Into the oven it went, and Alex descended the stairs right on time to do her part and wash the few dishes we'd made.

"Where's Theo?" I asked, seeing no sign of them behind her.

"Out for a run with Dulce. They left me a text about forty-five minutes ago, they should be back soon."

They had a lot more self-discipline than me. I'd never be able to get out of bed and go out for a run so early. Then again, they actually *liked* running, so they had a bit more motivation than me.

Smells of bacon and eggs began to fill the kitchen as I made everyone's beverages, including Theo's tea. Just as Seth was pulling the hot tray from the oven, the door opened and Dulce went running up the stairs while Theo kicked their shoes off and hung up the leash.

"Aw, sweet," they said as they plucked the cup of tea from my hands and took a sip, sitting down next to Alex.

We ate together in a comfortable silence, everyone in a good mood this morning, until Theo's phone rang. They pulled it from their pocket and squinted at it before answering.

"Mom? Yeah, yeah, okay. Phee, she wants to talk to you."

My stomach dropped. This couldn't be good. Hesitantly, I took the phone from Theo.

"Hello?"

"Phee, your mom's up and trying to leave AMA. I'm sorry, kiddo, but I need you to come down here and try and talk her down."

"AMA?"

"Against Medical Advice."

"Shit," I muttered. Why did this perfect morning have to end so abruptly? "Okay, I'll be right there." I hung up the phone and handed it back to Theo before turning to Seth. "Can you give me a ride to the hospital?"

"Sure, everything okay?" He lowered his fork, the utensil clattering as he dropped it on his plate.

"My mom's trying to sign herself out. I gotta go talk her out of it."

"Shit, let me throw some clothes on." Seth ascended the stairs at a trot while I glanced down at my own attire and retreated to the guest bedroom.

Looking at the pile of clothes on the bed, anxiety bubbled up in my throat. What would happen if I actually wore some of this? I supposed that there was only one way to find out. I picked up the butterfly shirt and leggings I'd tried on yesterday. They were subtle enough, nothing over the top, this would be a good transition. I put them on and quickly laced up my black combat boots before emerging and finding Seth at the front door, wearing a t-shirt and jeans instead of the pajama bottoms he'd had on a few minutes ago. Nodding at him, I waved at Theo and Alex and stepped into the brisk morning air. The fabric of the shirt was thin enough that I thought about getting a jacket, but it was too late as we stepped into the car, Seth turning the key in the ignition.

"Do you want me to stay?" he asked as we pulled onto the street, "I mean, if you wanted to go alone you could've taken your car."

I glanced back at my mom's car, parked on the street in front of the house. "Honestly, I forgot it was here. But yeah, if you don't mind, could you wait for me? I don't know how she's gonna be."

Seth nodded solemnly, keeping his eyes focused on the road. We arrived at the hospital quickly, and Seth dropped me at the emergency room door before driving off to find a parking spot. When I walked inside, Monica was waiting there, ready to usher me into my mom's room. As I entered the room, I was met with a much different sight than I had been yesterday. She was out of bed, pulling at her IV line, threatening anyone that got near her.

"I want to go *home!* You can't keep me here! Bring me the papers!"

I walked up to my mom cautiously, trying to get her attention. I took a swift step backwards as she lunged at me, and Monica instinctively rushed to my side.

She put her hands on my shoulders. "Phee, I'm sorry, she wasn't like this when I left. I wouldn't have told you to come."

"No, it's okay." I turned back to my mom, "Mom? It's me, can we sit down for a minute?"

Her eyes focused a little as recognition flickered across her face. I walked over and sat on the edge of the bed, patting the space next to me.

"Come sit." I beckoned, holding an arm out towards her.

Slowly, she glanced around the room, at each person standing there, before sitting down next to me. She looked at me and squinted.

"Mom, you've gotta let them take care of you. They're only trying to help."

"Jeremy, what… What are you wearing?" She tugged at my sleeve, and I blushed.

"It's Phee mom, don't you remember? We talked about it yesterday."

She shook her head. "No, no. I'd remember that. Who's Phee?"

I sighed, smoothing out my leggings before looking back up at my mom. "I'm a girl. My name is Phee."

She squinted, looking me up and down. "Your hair… I did that. I remember, the makeup."

Solemnly, I looked down at my hands in my lap. I wasn't sure what she was going to do, her moods had been so unpredictable lately. Would she reject me again? How many times would we have to go through this?

I jumped as she wrapped her arms around me, pulling me into a hug. "I'm sorry, baby."

Tears stung at the corners of my eyes, and I sniffled, putting my hands around my mom's back. She squeezed me with what little strength she had left, and I felt her relax in my arms. A couple of the nurses filed out of the room, until it was just me, my mom, and Monica.

Finally, my mom pulled away and glanced at me with tears in her eyes. "I want to go home."

I held her hand. "We can't yet, mom. You're still sick. You've got to let them help you, we're just trying to take care of you. How much longer does she need to stay, Monica?" I turned towards her.

She swallowed before answering. "We'd like her to stay the night. She's doing better, but it would be best if she stayed just to be safe. After that, there's a number of facilities—"

"I'm *not* going to rehab," my mom barked, pulling her hand away from mine.

"Wouldn't it be best, to get you the help you need? I know you're trying really hard this time, but you can't do this on your own." My voice was unsteady, hoping she'd make the right choice.

"I'm not." Her tone softened, and she held my chin in one hand, "I have you."

I sighed, "Mom, I'm sorry, but your sobriety can't be my responsibility. I just can't do it. I've tried so many times before."

"This time will be different," she pleaded. "I promise. Rehab doesn't work, what I need is you. My son."

I glanced down at the floor before she corrected herself.

"My daughter."

I couldn't help but be enticed by the promise of a mother who loved me for who I was, who wanted what was best for me. Who didn't love alcohol more than she loved me.

Sucking in a deep breath, I relented. "Okay, mom. But you've gotta stay here tonight, okay?"

She smiled, placing her hands on my cheeks. "Okay, my baby. Will you stay with me?"

I nodded to Monica, who gave me a weak smile and nodded back before leaving the room. "I can stay for a little while, mom. But I've got homework, and school tomorrow."

"Oh, poo on responsibilities." She got under the covers and pulled me along with her.

I snickered a little, resting my head on her chest and pulling out my phone to text Seth. "All good, you can go home. I'll be here a little while."

CHAPTER TWELVE

Today was Theo's first day back at school after their concussion. It was time. We had the petition gathered, a couple hundred signatures adorning the list. Theo's request was there, and we had the pictures of every injury we'd endured since freshman year. Theo held it all in a very official looking manilla folder, and the three of us – Theo, Alex, and I – walked into the principal's office that morning instead of going to our lockers.

The secretary looked up from her computer questioningly as Theo approached the desk. "Can I help you?"

Theo ran their hand along the edge of the folder before answering, "We'd like to speak with the principal for a minute, if that's okay. We have a petition for her."

"Let me see if she's available." The secretary got up from her desk, shuffling quickly into the door behind her where the principal could be seen sitting at her desk, staring at her own computer.

The secretary said something, her voice muffled through the glass. She pointed at us through the windows, and the principal gave her a hesitant look, rolling her eyes before nodding. I already didn't like this. The secretary opened the door and waved us inside, closing the door behind us and retreating to her desk. We were left standing face-to-face with the principal, who wore a look of disdain.

"Good to see you back, Elizabeth. What was it this time, a suspension?"

"I had a concussion. And it's Theo." They bristled against the deadname, I could see them trying to contain the flare of anger inside them.

The principal waved a hand in the air. "Right, right. I suppose whatever petition you have isn't about getting a suspension scrubbed from your record, then."

"No, it's bigger than that." Theo stepped up to the principal's desk and laid the folder down in front of her, ignoring the dig at their character.

A sneer on her face, she opened the folder and flipped through the pages quickly, barely glancing at what was there. "This is about Kyle Ritter? From what I understand, you start the fights just as much as he does, if not more."

Theo twitched a little, balling their hands into fists and releasing them a couple times before speaking. "I haven't instigated a fight with him beyond just trying to get to my locker. He always puts his hands on someone first. And it's not just me that he attacks, the pictures there prove that."

"All these pictures prove is that injuries happened, not who they came from. If he denies accountability, it's your word against his."

"My word and over two hundred other people, including teachers *and* the nurse, if you'd look at the signature pages." Theo was trying really hard to keep the snark out of their voice, their frustration level visibly rising.

"Now, don't get short with me." The principal looked down her nose at the papers before pushing her glasses up and leaning back in her chair and crossing her arms. "What do you expect me to do with this information?"

"Expel him, suspend him, break up his group, *anything*. Give him consequences for what he's done. Make the school a safe place for queer kids."

"I'll have a talk with him, but I'm really not sure how much I can do. None of this happened recently enough, I can't just punish him for something that happened in another school year."

Theo placed their hands on the edge of the desk, leaning in slightly – a look that would've made me shrink back in my seat if it had been directed at me. "We have a video of him giving me the concussion I was just out for. If you don't do anything, we're going to release it, let the news get ahold of it."

The principal leaned in towards Theo, matching their energy, "I don't appreciate threats, dear."

"It's not a threat." They stood up straight again, taking a step back towards us. "It's a failsafe."

———

I walked into Clare's classroom, trying to shake off the severity of the conversation we'd just had with the principal. Her eyes lit up when she saw me, and she stood up from the desk where she'd been drawing and wiped the charcoal from her hands with a rag.

"What've you got for me, kiddo?"

"I've got to edit them still, but I did Theo's pictures this weekend. I'm going to try and do Alex's later today." I held out my camera for her to look at, and she took it eagerly.

The buttons clicked as she flipped through the pictures, a smile growing on her face, "These are beautiful. You really captured them. I think this one's your best shot." She turned so that I could see the camera as well, and on screen was my favorite picture that

I'd picked out the day I'd taken them.

I smiled. "That one's my favorite, too."

She patted me on the back, placing the camera in my hands. "Good work, kiddo. Also, love the outfit."

I glanced down at what I was wearing, remembering for the first time that I'd chosen some of my new clothes to wear. They weren't over-the-top feminine, my combat boots, a pair of galaxy patterned leggings, and a cropped hoodie. I blushed a little, pulling at the strings of my hoodie.

"Thanks." I managed, sitting down at the computer in the corner of the room and pulling up some editing software before plugging my camera in and pulling up the pictures. Unable to focus, I glanced between Clare and the computer a few times, before relenting. The classroom was empty, just her and I. Surely it was safe? "Clare?" I asked.

Without raising her head from her work, she answered, "Yeah?"

"Would… Would you call me Phee, when there aren't other people around?"

She stopped smudging with her hands to push her glasses up and make eye contact with me. As she blinked at me for a few seconds, I started to squirm, suddenly regretting the request. I knew I wasn't ready to come out at school yet, what had possessed me to do this?

Clare stepped away from her work, and sat on a chair next to me, before saying in a hushed tone, "Of course. Would you like different pronouns?"

Relief washed over me, and my posture immediately relaxed. "She/her, if you don't mind."

She smiled at me with a knowing glance. "I always had a feeling you weren't a boy. I'd give you a hug, but…" She showed me her hands, which were black with charcoal.

I let out a small laugh, then got up and hugged her. My hoodie was black, anyway.

"So we're keeping this under wraps?" she asked after I pulled away.

"For now. I'm not ready to deal with all the backlash I know I'll get here. Plus, we just turned in that petition to the principal, so there's enough going on with that to keep me busy for a while."

"Oh, the petition! How'd you all make out?" Clare had been one of the first teacher signatures on the list.

"We got a couple hundred. The principal didn't seem too impressed, though. She gave Theo a lot of attitude about the whole thing and it didn't seem like she was planning on doing much about things."

Clare shook her head. "The woman isn't known for her tact. I guess we'll just have to wait and see."

"If she doesn't do anything, we're releasing the video of Theo getting punched unconscious. And we're going to stage a walkout, but that's under wraps too."

Clare nodded. "I'll be at your side for all of it. This school needs to be a safer place. What you and the other LGBTQ+ students go through isn't fair. I'm sure there's a lot more staying closeted because they don't feel safe here."

I nodded back solemnly, "I just hope our plan works."

———

After school, I followed Alex into Theo's room.

She flipped on the obnoxious overhead light and turned to me. "What did you want to talk about?" she asked, flopping down onto the bed.

"My senior project, uh—"

"Oh! Those pictures you took with Theo?

"Yeah. I was wondering if you'd do it with me, too? I have these questions, if you could write some answers, and then we can go anywhere you want, someplace you like, and take some pictures."

She pressed a finger to her chin, squinting her eyes as she looked at me, "You know I love getting my picture taken, as long as I'm ready for it."

I echoed the laugh she let out – she was notorious for trying to get pictures while Theo shoved the camera away. I'd been surprised when Theo agreed to help me with my project.

"Let me change and put some makeup on, then we can go to Best Boba."

I nodded, retreating from the room to get my camera out of the backpack I'd left in the guest bedroom. I sat on the edge of the bed, taking in a deep breath – my mother was going to be released from the hospital later today, and I'd go home with her. As worried as I'd been about her, these past few days at Theo's had been really nice, a sense of security had been provided to me when I went to bed at night, a feeling I didn't have in my own home. Hopefully now things would be better at home, my mom being sober, but I still took her words with a grain of salt.

She'd proclaimed that she would change before. She'd even stopped drinking before, on several occasions. Rehab, Alcoholics Anonymous, the works. Every time, she'd slip into a depression and start drinking again. She was never the same mother that I'd had before she picked up the bottle in the first place either, even when she was sober. The way she'd treated me the last few days surely wouldn't last. I was ready for her to take back all the understanding she'd shown me about my transition, go back to being disappointed in me for liking boys, for not being one myself.

I was broken from my thoughts when Alex came bounding in the room. She looked beautiful – she had on a green satin dress, one that we both knew drove Theo nuts. She was wearing a golden chain around her neck and her makeup was smokey and perfect, glittery highlights in the corners of her eyes and all. Her feet were adorned in a pair of goddess sandals.

"Isn't that a little much for Best Boba?"

"They've got that pretty arch in the window, I figured we could take pictures there. You know, with all the potted plants and everything, the bench right in front of it."

"Ooh, you're right. That'll be nice."

She smiled at me and pulled me by the hand from the room as I held the camera in my other hand. We scurried through the living room quickly, but not fast enough to get past Theo, who was in the kitchen making a cup of tea.

"Holy shit," they breathed. "Al, you're gorgeous."

"I know, I know, you love this dress. Don't kiss me, you'll ruin my makeup." Alex smiled, loving the attention and playing with Theo at the same time.

"Oh, c'mon. What if I don't kiss your face?"

Before Alex could object, Theo pulled her in close and kissed her on the neck. She shivered a little, but the grin on her face said it was a good chill. Running her hands through Theo's hair, she kissed them on the forehead, leaving behind a small smudge of red lipstick. Giggling, she wiped the smudge away, then turned for the door, leaving Theo longing for more as they watched her go.

"We'll be back in a bit!"

I followed Alex as she picked up her keys from one of the hooks by the door, and before I knew it we were out into the crisp autumn air. We shut the door behind us and started walking towards Best Boba, about ten blocks away.

"What were the questions you had?" Alex asked as we plodded

along the sidewalk.

"Oh! Um, the first one's 'What do you like most about your body?'"

"Hm," Alex squinted, like she was thinking hard. "I guess... I like my lips? Maybe my legs."

"Why do you feel good about it?"

"Theo always tells me how pretty my lips are, I guess it kinda rubbed off on me. My legs... are strong. They get me places. That's kind of a double-edged sword though, a lot of the time I feel like my thighs are too big."

I nodded, not judging, but acknowledging her feelings. I knew how it felt to have a love-hate relationship with your body. Moving on, I asked, "What do you like least about your body?"

"That one's easy. My stomach and my shoulders."

"What has made you feel that way?"

"My stomach sticks out way too much, I wish it were flat like Theo's. My shoulders are too broad, they make me feel manly."

"That's what you don't like about them, but what made you feel those things?"

Alex exhaled slowly, a look on her face like she was thinking hard. "I guess... my mom always used to tell me I eat too much, that I'll get fat. She's always the first to comment on my weight, and I carry a lot of the extra weight in my stomach. My shoulders didn't used to bother me that much, I mean, I never felt great about them, but I really started noticing them when I found out I'm intersex. Now every little thing that feels too manly about me sticks out so much more."

Alex was the least "manly" looking person I'd ever met. I had no idea these things bothered her, but then again, I'd never asked.

"When you look in the mirror, what do you see?" I went off script, my own curiosity getting the better of me.

Alex looked down at the ground. "All the things wrong with me. All the places I'm too fat, all the bone structures that are too masculine. Sometimes I just have to try and turn that part of my brain off while I get ready for the day, otherwise I'll spiral and be stuck in a rut. I don't really like mirrors. I only use them when I have to."

"Alex, you pull things off so well and look so flawless most of the time. You really feel that way?"

She rubbed a hand against her upper arm, still staring at the ground. "Theo thinks I might have body dysmorphia. I don't really talk about it much, it's always been more of an internal struggle."

"I know the feeling." I sighed.

"It's funny, isn't it? You want my curves, I want your leanness. I wish we could just trade." She laughed a little, a hollow sound.

We'd gotten a little more somber than I'd intended, so I decided to try and press forward. "Last one – how do you see the beauty in other people's bodies?"

"There's so much beauty in diversity, the different things that make up a person. Take Theo – they're tiny, but pure muscle, their strength shows just as much on the outside as on the inside. Or you, you've got this ethereal vibe to you that shows even more now that you're wearing makeup and clothes that you like. When just thinking about a person makes you happy, every inch of them is beautiful to you. It's easy to find the beauty in other people, their defining features that you'll never forget. That lens just falls short when I think about myself."

"Hopefully you'll see it in these pictures." I gave her a faint smile as we entered the door to Best Boba.

We were in luck, the bench in front of the archway lined with plants was open, so we gravitated to it immediately. Alex sat down on it, crossing one leg over the other and smoothing out her dress.

I had her do a few different poses, ones where she was interacting with the plants, or looking off into the distance instead of directly at the camera. Once we were done, I offered to buy us both a tea, returning to the bench with two strawberry bobas. I sipped at mine while I clicked through the pictures.

They were just as stunning as Theo's. Granted, I wasn't attracted to Alex so it didn't hold that same wonder for me, but there was no denying that she was beautiful. Her smile, most of all, was gorgeous. Holding the camera so that Alex could see too, I picked out one picture where I'd gotten her to laugh. It was so pure, so spontaneous, the sparkle in her eyes captivated the viewer.

"Ugh," she grimaced, "I've got horse teeth."

I turned to her, squinting. "Have you *seen* my teeth?" I bared them, showing off the crooked mess that I often hid with a lips-only smile. "Yours are practically perfect. And your smile, it's so beautiful."

She cocked her head, reaching for the camera to get a closer look. "I guess, Theo always says how much they love the way my lips curve at the edges, and the way my nose wrinkles when I laugh."

"What do *you* like about it?"

"My eyes. They're so green and the dress really brings them out."

I nodded, flipping to the next picture with the camera still in Alex's hands.

"Oh, wow," she breathed.

This picture was one of the ones where she was ignoring the camera – her arm was outstretched, reaching towards the leaves of some ivy. Her lips parted slightly in wonder and her eyes sparkled, her gaze fixed on the plant. It was like she was the only person in the room.

"That one's really nice, too." I smiled, looking at her.

"How do you do that? Capture people with such raw emotion?

My pictures always look so staged."

"I try to put the person at ease, like the camera isn't even there. That's part of why I wanted you and Theo to pick your own locations, someplace where you're comfortable."

"Which one do you think you'll use?"

"Both, I think. There's no hard and fast rule of how many I have to use per person."

"Who else are you gonna get? I know it's not just going to be me and Theo."

"Seth, Harriet, Rachel if she'll let me, and maybe Elliot."

"Things still awkward between you two?"

I sighed, looking down at the camera in my lap. "Yeah. He just doesn't understand my situation, everything with my mom. He took it pretty personally, I just don't like bringing it up."

"I know you don't want to, but I feel like things could be solved there pretty easily if you just communicate."

"Yeah, but then he'll want to get back together. I can't play with him like that."

"You don't want to?"

"No, things kinda fell apart between us for a bunch of different reasons. I don't think we're a good fit, also he doesn't like girls. I feel like if we get back together he'll be thinking of me as a boy pretending to be a girl the whole time, not as the girl that I am."

"You think Elliot's transphobic? I never got that vibe from him."

"No, not exactly. I think it'll be more subconscious, he'll be wishing for a version of me that doesn't exist."

"Ah, I get it."

I sipped down the last of my boba, then got up and threw both our cups in the trash. "We should get back, I've got to go to the hospital for my mom's discharge soon."

Alex got up and we left the shop, the bell on the door ringing behind us as we went.

"How're you doing with everything with your mom, anyway? You haven't talked about it much," Alex asked as we started the trek back to the house.

"Okay, I think. She's been really nice, kinda like how she was before she started drinking at all. I'm just afraid to believe it, this has happened before. She's okay for a few days and then things turn sour real fast. I don't want to get my hopes up this time only for everything to crash and burn."

"It's gotta be tough. My relationship with my mom was pretty hostile, but I feel like it would've been more devastating if it was a rollercoaster like yours with your mom. At least with how my mom was, it was easy to cut her out of my life, there wasn't anything good for me in that relationship."

"Don't you ever wish she would love you for who you are, though? Just because she's your mom?"

"Of course, but I had to let that go. Once I did, things felt a lot better. I don't need her love to be whole."

"See, every time I get to that point, my mom flips a switch and starts being nice to me again and I realize how badly I craved it. I can't let it go the way it's constantly dangled in front of me like a carrot on a stick."

We walked in silence for a few minutes, until we were at the front door, where Alex put a hand on my shoulder. "I hope it lasts this time. But if it doesn't, just try to remember you don't need her to be whole. We've always got your back."

I gave her a slight smile and a nod as she turned the doorknob and we walked inside. Theo practically tackled Alex as we closed the door behind us, as if they'd just been waiting for us to get back the whole time like an expectant dog waiting by the door for its person. Suddenly, Alex's pet name of "Puppy" for them clicked in my head.

They kissed her on the neck again and she let out an excited giggle as they took her by the hand and were gone in a flash up the stairs. We all knew what would happen next.

Seth looked at me and shook his head. "I'd better get my headphones."

I let out an understanding chuckle, then picked up the keys to my mom's car and got my backpack out of the guest room. I turned to Seth, who had opted to put the television on blast over getting up from the couch.

"I'm gonna go to the hospital, my mom should be discharged soon."

Seth turned down the volume a little — a mistake, we could already hear Alex's moans. He shook his head and turned it back up and instead yelled over the reality show he had playing.

"Shit, that's today? Do you want me to come with?"

I shook my head. "Nah, I'll be fine. Thanks, though."

Once out the door and sitting in my mom's car, I turned it on and sat for a minute, taking in a deep breath. Anxiety rose up within me over seeing my mom again, and I shook my head to try and ward it off. I had a bad feeling, like everything was going to fall apart once we got home. How long would the reprieve last this time? When would the angry, disapproving mother be back? Shutting my eyes hard, I rubbed at them with my hands and tried to take in a deep breath, then started the short drive to the hospital.

When I arrived there, my mom was sitting up in her bed, looking slightly disheveled and completely zoned into the television, rocking slightly. A tightness formed in the pit of my stomach.

"Mom?" I asked hesitantly, entering the room.

She turned her head, dark circles under her eyes, but greeted me with a smile, "My baby! I was afraid you wouldn't come back."

"Of course I came back, mom."

"They said I could go home once you got here. I'm not supposed to drive, they gave me some medicine."

"Okay." I started gathering up my mom's clothes so that she could change out of the hospital gown, when Monica walked in the room.

"Oh good, Phee, you're here. I've got a couple things to go over with both of you before she's discharged."

I sat on the edge of the bed while Monica pulled up the rolling table and laid out some paperwork. "This is her discharge packet, it's just got a visit summary and some aftercare details. Stay away from alcohol mostly. We've also set her up with a psychiatrist and a therapist—"

"I don't need that," my mom jumped in, furrowing her eyebrows.

"Mom, maybe it'll help? Why not give it a try?"

My mom had always been resistant to the idea of psychiatric care. She didn't want to admit that she needed it, but I felt like that was the reason every treatment had failed. I was reminded of Theo's insistence that they didn't need it, and how bad things really got before they finally accepted help. Needing help means you're vulnerable, and to any kind of survivor being vulnerable was a big no.

"It's just a bunch of bullshit." She looked at me. "They're not going to help, they never do."

"Because you never let them. Maybe this is the piece that's missing, maybe this is what will make you being sober stick this time."

My mom sighed and rolled her eyes, looking down at the ground.

"Please, for me?" I asked, putting a hand on her shoulder.

She looked at me, tears welling in her eyes. "Fine, I suppose."

Monica nodded slightly and placed a pill bottle on the table next to the discharge papers. "The psychiatrist already started her on these antidepressants. She shouldn't drive until you know how they affect her, just to be safe. These ones can make you a little drowsy."

I picked up the bottle, looking it over and then holding it in my lap.

"She's already had her dose for today, but going forward she should take it before bedtime. It's important to stay consistent." Monica made a point of looking at both me and my mom, and I nodded while my mom looked away. "The appointment days and times are in the paperwork for you. Do you have any questions?"

"Can I leave now?" my mom asked, sounding a little irritated.

Monica gave a patient smile, then handed my mom a clipboard and a pen, "Just as soon as you sign this."

My mom took it eagerly and scribbled a signature down before hopping up from the bed. I handed her the change of clothes I'd gathered up and she took them into the bathroom.

Monica placed a hand on my shoulder to quietly reassure me. "If you need anything, anything at all, just call me, okay? Do your best to get her to those appointments, I think it'll be really beneficial for her."

"Thanks, Monica, for everything."

She smiled before exiting the room, leaving me there holding the pill bottle and discharge papers as my mom emerged from the bathroom, still looking like a mess, but a more familiar mess in her own clothes.

"Ready to go, Mom?"

CHAPTER THIRTEEN

As we walked in the door, we were greeted by the mess we'd left in our haste to get my mom to the hospital in the first place. I hadn't been back here since. Setting my backpack by the door, I guided my mom to her bedroom.

"Why don't you take a shower, mom? I'll clean up the house and make us some food."

My mom sat down on her bed and looked up at me. "Will you eat with me when it's done?"

"Sure, mom."

I rummaged through her drawers and pulled out a fresh change of clothes and put them in her bathroom along with a clean towel. She followed me inside and wrapped her arms around me. She smelled like sweat and antiseptic, but I didn't complain. I'd never complain about a hug.

Shutting the door behind me, I got to work cleaning up the living room and kitchen. The rest of the house wasn't too bad, since I'd cleaned everything a couple days before we had to take my mom into the hospital. I took out the trash after I'd gotten everything picked up, then washed my hands and peeked in the freezer to see what was still good as far as food went. I pulled out some hamburger and stuck it in the microwave to defrost before rummaging through the pantry and finding a box of hamburger helper. It was a go-to comfort food of my mom's, perfect for the occasion.

Setting a skillet on the stove, I turned it on and put a little oil in the pan before dropping in the thawed hamburger. The sizzle brought me back to Theo's kitchen, cooking with Seth. He'd never be caught dead using hamburger helper, though. After the meat was browned, I dumped in the contents of the box, some water, and stirred.

A silent hand on my shoulder made me jump before I realized it was my mom, and I relaxed a little when I saw her smile. She looked much better now that she'd cleaned up and was in a fresh change of clothes. Gesturing to the back of her hand, she looked at me.

"I couldn't get this off, no matter how hard I scrubbed."

There were bits of adhesive on her now reddened hand, and I took it into my own hands before looking up at her face.

"I can get it off for you," I said, leaving her in the kitchen and running to the bathroom to dig up the rubbing alcohol – a trick I'd seen Alex use getting the same adhesive off of Theo in the hospital.

Bringing it into the kitchen, I put some on a cotton pad and rubbed at the back of my mom's hand lightly, and the adhesive began to break down and wipe off with ease. Afterwards, I rinsed both her and my hands with water to get rid of the rubbing alcohol before returning to the simmering pan.

"Thank you… Ooh, that smells so good." My mom leaned over the stove to take in the scent.

"It's almost ready." I stirred the pan, holding up the wooden spoon with a noodle on it for her to taste.

She eagerly accepted the offering, and grinned afterwards. "It's perfect."

I pulled the pan from the burner and turned the stove off. Getting out two plates and forks, I handed her one of each, letting her take a helping first. Once she sat down, I got my own and sat down across from her.

"This used to be your favorite, you know. We always had it with…" She smiled at me and jumped up from the table, digging through the fridge before coming out victorious with milk and chocolate syrup I didn't even know we still had.

I laughed slightly as she grabbed two glasses and spoons from the cabinet, pouring milk and then dumping a generous amount of syrup into each glass. She gave them each a stir and put one in front of me after putting the ingredients away. Sitting down, she gave me a proud look of accomplishment as I took a sip.

"*Now* it's perfect." She reached over and tousled my brightly colored hair like I was her little kid again. Like everything was right in the world and she hadn't just come home from the hospital for an alcohol detox.

I decided to let it be perfect and smiled back at her as we both dug into our food. My mind wouldn't let the moment rest, though. Thoughts racing about all the ways this could turn sour, how eventually she would fall apart and go back to alcohol, just like she had every other time.

"What's wrong, my baby?"

I hadn't realized my racing thoughts had decided to show through on my face. Quickly, I unfurrowed my brow and tried to blink away the emotions, but it was too late, I'd been caught. I sighed, deciding to breach the subject that was really gnawing at me.

"I'm just worried about you, mom."

"I'm fine! I'm much better, really."

"When you said you'd go to therapy, were you just saying that so we could leave sooner?"

She stopped eating and looked down at her plate, pushing the food around as if I wouldn't notice. "I really don't think I need it."

"Mom, I think you do. Someday, however close or far off it might be, you're going to get sad again. You don't know how to handle it and always end up drinking to make the pain go away."

Staring down at her lap, she avoided eye contact. "You're all grown up, aren't you? I feel like I missed it."

"That's because you did. Alcohol took it from you, from us. It took my childhood, and it took your parenthood. We can't get that back. All we can do is try to protect the future. If we can do that, you'll still see me graduate, get into college. I want to be able to go and know that you'll be safe, you'll have somewhere to turn if things get difficult."

"And you think therapy will help make that happen?"

"Yes. One of my friends, you might not remember, the one that came over when you were detoxing and carried you to the car, things got really bad for them until they agreed to go to therapy and put in the work to get better. Before that they were using drugs, alcohol like you. It was just an escape, and I know that's what it is for you, too."

"How bad did it get?"

I broke eye contact, staring at my own plate before answering. "They tried to kill themself, mom."

A moment of silence filled the room, the kind of silence that felt harsh, like it might explode at any minute. Neither of us looked at each other, and I glanced at my mom before shattering the air around us.

"But they're so much better now. They had a really hard life before their mom adopted them, and it was too much to deal with alone. You shouldn't have to deal with things alone, either. I don't want you to get to the same point they did."

A tear ran down my mom's otherwise stone-cold face, and I studied her to try and guess what she was thinking. She ran her fingers along the side of the rickety kitchen table, and it wobbled slightly against the pressure.

I leaned over and placed a hand on my mom's. "I know you said you'd do it for me, but you need to do it for yourself, too."

She clasped her hands around mine. "What will I do when you're gone? You said before, you'll leave here and never come back. I don't want that."

"I was just angry. At the world, at the way you treated me. If you're really trying to get better, I'll come back. I promise. You just have to let me be who I am, and not hurt me. Especially when you're sober. It feels so much worse when you're sober."

"I know I haven't treated you fairly. I let my problems become yours, I took things out on you that weren't your fault. Just this whole 'girl' thing and you liking boys is hard for me."

"You hurt me before that. And it's not easy for me either. You don't have any idea what it's like in school, and I'm not even out as trans there. No one at school knows I'm a girl. The bullies are rampant. They gave Theo a concussion just a few weeks ago."

My mom looked down at the table and started tracing circles with her finger. "I grew up in a very conservative family. My parents were disappointed that they had me instead of a son. My whole childhood I was taught that my worth was attached to my future husband, that my job was to take care of a man. Things got better when I met your father. He was so kind and helped me unlearn all the ways my parents put me down. When he died, I just… it was like I'd lost everything, even the air in my lungs. My soulmate was gone, and everything I'd learned along with him."

"I know losing dad was hard for you. I wish… I wish I knew more about him. You never talk about him."

Tears welled up in her eyes and she put her hands over her face. "He'd be so disappointed in what I've done to you. He loved you so much."

"Would he still love me now?" My voice was small, begging for the answer I wanted, but terrified to get one that I didn't.

"Absolutely. He'd be so much better with all this stuff than I am. He never would've done what I did, he'd be so angry if I did it while he was here. He would've protected you."

I felt so robbed. My father's death had taken both parents away from me, set my childhood on fire and let it burn.

My mom brushed tears away from her face. "I'm… I'm going to try and be the person he would've wanted. I owe you that much."

"So you'll do the therapy?"

"Okay, my baby."

————

At Theo's house, in the guest bedroom, I started packing the vast array of clothes Alex had gotten me into a bag. With my mom's acceptance seeming more sound, I'd decided to take most of them home. Alex was helping me, looking each piece over as she folded them and put them into the duffel bag.

"If this stuff would fit me, you'd already be missing half of it."

I chuckled, carefully placing a small bag of jewelry on top of a pile, and hung up a couple sets of clothes in the closet. I'd decided to keep a couple changes here as a backup, since I was over so often.

"I mean, it's your closet, and you bought the stuff, you've got more claim to it than I do."

"Let's just give each other closet-raiding rights, deal? Just, the green dress is off limits."

I laughed loudly. "I don't think it'll have the same effect on Theo if I'm wearing it."

"Still. Just in case."

I shook my head with a smile as we finished packing up the clothes. Then, Alex picked up my camera and started flipping through yesterday's pictures. "Are you going to do like, a self-portrait at all? Or only interview other people?"

I sat down on the edge of the bed as Alex handed me the camera. "I was going to be in it, but I'm kinda anxious about it. I've just been putting it off."

"Why not get it over with?"

I rubbed my arm with my free hand and glanced between Alex and the camera. "I guess it's the questions that are really the hard part."

"So let's do the pictures! C'mon, I'll help. What's your perfect place?"

"I've been thinking about the skate park."

"Oh, we could get some cool action shots! My camera work is nowhere near as good as yours, though."

I smiled, handing her the camera. "Just take a whole bunch. That's what I do when I'm unsure of something, if you take a ton of them one is bound to be good."

"Ah, the old shoot and pray." We both chuckled, then Alex gestured to the duffel bag. "Are we gonna have to unpack everything to get the right outfit?"

"Nah." I waved my hand, getting up and going to the closet. "I've got it right here."

Out of the closet, I pulled a hanger that had a galaxy-print cropped hoodie and a pair of black skinny jeans. I'd gone through all my clothes and selected this one for my pictures. It had the punk vibe I wanted, especially with the spiked choker and bracelet I'd ordered. The jeans were adorned with a bunch of chains and zippers, the sound making it clear whenever I entered a room.

"Do you want to do makeup?" Alex asked, an eager look on her face like she was waiting for me to ask for her help.

I did just that. "Yeah, will you help me? I want something that matches the hoodie, but kinda edgy, if you get what I mean?"

Alex grinned, picking up the makeup bag she'd given me and sitting cross-legged on the bed. "Well, come over here! Let's do it."

Sitting down on the bed in front of her, I let Alex get to work. She pulled out some concealer and applied it under my eyes, covering up the dark circles of stress and lack of sleep. Then, she moved on to foundation and contouring, putting product in all the right places to feminize my face.

"What's so hard about the questions for you? Which part?" she asked while patting my face with a beauty blender.

"I have so much negative, and it's really hard to come up with positives. My hair used to be one of the positives, and that got taken away from me."

"You can't find one thing you like about yourself?" Alex furrowed her brow a little as she kept working.

"I mean, I guess I like my hands. They're pretty and elegant, but I feel like none of the rest of me matches. I wish I had your curves, or at least a *little* substance. I'm gangly and awkward."

"That's not how I would describe you."

"How would you describe me?"

Alex smiled while she pulled out some eyeshadow. "Elegant is definitely a good word to use. You're willowy, almost ethereal, like

I said before. You've got this otherworldly vibe, especially now that you've come into yourself more."

I blushed a little. "You really think so? I feel like I've got all the elegance of a baby giraffe."

"Have you *seen* a baby giraffe? They're adorable. And they grow up to be just as elegant as you are. You're just growing right now, you have to look at yourself as a work-in-progress, not the final product. You've just started to express what you like, I bet you felt awkward before because you were forcing yourself to be something you weren't."

I took a deep breath. "I guess you're right."

"You know how awkward Theo felt? How they still feel? I have to hound them to take off their binder at night so they don't hurt themself, they hate not having it on. Thing is, I don't see their chest as feminine, I just think it's handsome like all the rest of them, but that's not how they see it. To them, it doesn't match, so it feels wrong."

"That's dysphoria, Alex, a lot of trans people have it."

"Do you?"

"A little bit, I think. My hair being short definitely makes me uncomfortable, I feel naked. And then all the angles I have in my face, my body. Angles feel masculine to me."

Alex leaned back for a second. "You know how many girls would kill for your cheekbones?"

I waved my hand. "They can have them. I want a round face, like yours."

She gave me a sympathetic smile before lowering her hands and taking a look at her work. "What do you think, full glam for the photoshoot or no?"

"I mean, I might as well go all-out, it's basically going to be the only way I'm coming out at school."

Alex jumped up from the bed. "Okay, hang on a sec, I've gotta get some stuff."

In a flash, she was gone from the room, but she returned just as quickly, carrying a bag full of products. I didn't understand how we could possibly need more than what she'd gotten me, when I saw her pull out false lashes and rhinestones.

"Which ones do you want?" She held out various boxes with a pair of lashes in each box, ranging in style.

I picked up a couple, inspecting them before going with a pair that almost looked feathery. Alex smiled and opened the box, applying a bit of glue to the lash. She leaned into me, and I did my best to hold still, an anxiety rising within me that happened whenever she worked around my eyes. I had no reason to be anxious, she'd never poked me or gotten anything in my eyes before, but it was still so foreign to me. She had the advantage of doing this for years.

She leaned back with a smile once the lashes were applied, then started picking some rhinestones off a sheet and applying them to my face with lash glue as well. I had no idea what direction she was going with this, but I trusted her to do something good for the final look. After she finished with everything, she grabbed a small stand-up mirror from the dresser and handed it to me.

I gasped, it was so much better than I'd ever expected. My skin looked flawless, almost airbrushed. My lips had a distinct pout that I'd never been able to replicate on my own. It was the eyes that were the showstopper, though. She'd matched the colors to the hoodie, creating a galaxyesque gradient on my lids. The eyeliner was perfectly angled up in a sharp line. The best part was her final touch of the rhinestones, which adorned my eyes, looking like stars against the galaxy backdrop. I grinned, putting the mirror down and hugging Alex.

She giggled slightly, embracing the hug. "I'm glad you like it." I picked the mirror back up to get another look, when Alex brushed some stray pink hair from my face. "Your hair's starting to come in a little more."

I lifted the mirror to look at my hair, still a pink and purple pixie cut, but a slightly longer one than the day my mom had cut it. I could see the dark roots starting to come in. I sighed, "It'll take forever to get back to where it was."

Alex offered a sympathetic smile. "You know, when we first met, I never would've imagined we'd end up friends this close. It just didn't seem like we fit together that well."

Putting the mirror back down, I glanced at her. "It was because I was jealous. All the attention Theo gave you, how in love with you they were. I wanted it for myself. I've had a crush on Theo since the day we met, but you already had their heart."

"I thought you only liked boys? Theo presented as a girl when you met them."

"I know, that didn't make sense to me either. I thought that maybe that meant they would be the one to 'fix' me, like I just needed the right girl to come along."

Alex shook her head. "You don't need fixing."

"It sure feels like I do sometimes."

"I get it, my mom didn't know I was pan until she caught me kissing Theo. I guess she still doesn't know, just thinks I'm gay."

"How did you figure out you were pan, anyway? It's not like your environment was any more accepting than mine, why not just go with guys if you had an attraction to them?"

She smiled slightly, looking away from me. "The heart wants what it wants. Sure, I was attracted to guys, but I felt the same way towards girls. I was curious, so I dated a couple. It felt just as right as when I dated guys. Then, there was Theo."

"Does Theo feel the same?"

Her eyes met mine. "No. They're so much better. I've never been as in love with someone as I am with Theo."

I sighed. "You two are right together. There's so much love. If I can't be with them, I'm glad it's you instead."

"That's awfully grown up of you. It's okay to be sad about it, I know what it's like when someone doesn't love you back. They do love you, just in a platonic way."

"I know, I've gotten myself to be okay with that. They're my best friend. The three of us have been through so much together, I hope we never lose each other."

Alex put an arm around my shoulders. "We won't. That's impossible. You should get changed so we can get the photoshoot done before it gets dark."

I leaned into her slightly before standing up and picking up the hanger with the outfit on it. I took it to the bathroom and changed, looking at the mirror to take myself in. I wished to everything that my hair was longer, but when I looked, I could see myself more than I usually could. Between the outfit and my makeup, I looked like a girl with a pixie cut, not the boy pretending to be a girl that I felt like most of the time. The hoodie was loose enough that it could've been hiding a small chest, instead of my flat-as-a-board situation I had going on. The way the jeans sat on my hips made them look a bit wider than normal, giving the illusion of an hourglass figure. I smiled a little, then emerged from the bathroom victorious, rather than the defeat I usually felt when I looked in the mirror.

Alex clapped when I came back in the guest bedroom. "Oh, you look *amazing!*"

My grin widened as I picked up my skateboard from the corner of the room. "Let's do this."

Entering the skate park, there was about an hour of daylight left. The sun was golden, shining down and casting long shadows on everything it hit. This kind of lighting was notoriously difficult to capture in photos, but when it was done correctly, it was beautiful. I took the camera from Alex's hands and adjusted the settings, trying to give her the best chance of getting good photos. I snapped a couple test photos, then handed her back the camera.

"Okay, it's got the right settings, so only mess with the zoom when you take pictures. It's right here." I turned the dial around the lens, showing her how to zoom in and out.

"Got it. Now go on! I'm so excited."

Leading us to a less crowded area of the park, I struck a couple poses with my skateboard, then tried to show off a couple tricks to get a more natural photo. I alternated between posing and just doing my thing to try and get a good range.

We were just about to call it a day when a guy walked up to me, apprehension clear on his face. My heart jumped into my throat. I recognized him from school. He wasn't one of Kyle's groupies, but I didn't know what to expect from him. I'd only ever seen him in passing.

"Hi, um…" He held his skateboard in his hands, looking down and fidgeting with a peeling sticker on the back of it. "I, uh, I've never seen you here before. I'm Chris."

"Hi Chris." I didn't know what else to say.

I glanced between him and Alex and noticed him glancing back at a small group of guys who looked like they were urging him on. Was this a prank? A dare? How sour was this going to turn?

Finally, he lowered his skateboard to his side in one hand and looked at me with his fawn-like brown eyes and asked, "You're really pretty. Can I… maybe… get your number?"

What? What??

I looked over at Alex who had the biggest shit-eating grin on her face, proving she'd only encourage this encounter. I still felt like there were ulterior motives here, but the guy looked genuinely anxious, and anyone trying to pull a prank wouldn't be this afraid.

"Sure, uh, give me your phone."

He dropped his skateboard while fumbling around in his pocket, trying to pull out his phone. When he finally got it, his skateboard was rolling away on the incline and he chased after it before returning to hand me his phone.

"Sorry," he muttered.

I smiled. He was awkwardly cute. I typed in my number and made it a contact before handing his phone back to him. He looked at it, then tried to hide the smile that grew across his face. He was trying really hard to play it cool.

"Thanks, uh," he looked back down at his phone again, "Phee? That's a pretty name."

I chuckled. "Thanks."

All the nerve he'd mustered up left him as he scurried back to his friends, and I looked at Alex to try and confirm whether that had actually just happened. She ran up to me with a giggle, tapping my shoulder playfully.

"I told you that you looked good."

I rolled my eyes, shoving her back slightly. "How do you know that wasn't a prank, they're not trying to lure me somewhere and beat the shit out of me?"

"Did you *see* how nervous he was? That was real. Plus, he's pretty cute. Did you give him your real number?"

"Against my better judgment."

Her grin widened. "We could do a double date if you still think it's something bad. That way you're not alone. You've gotta do it!"

"He looked pretty straight."

"And? You're a girl!"

"I don't know, Alex. I don't trust it."

"C'mon, we'll be right there! You know Theo won't let shit fly if he's a weirdo."

"Okay, fine."

"Yes!" She bounced up on the balls of her feet, holding my camera tight so as to not drop it.

I gestured towards the camera. "Let me see what we've got."

Alex handed it to me eagerly, and I started flipping through the pictures. Her camera work wasn't as bad as she'd made it out to be. Sure, there were things I would've done differently, but overall her work was pretty good. There were definitely some pictures in there that would work. Stopping on one in particular, I held the camera closer to my face to get a better look.

"Did I mess something up?" Alex asked.

"No, this one's just… really good."

It was one of the more natural looking photos, with me riding my skateboard, seemingly not a care in the world. My stance was wide to keep my balance, and there was a focus that only came to my face when I was skating or taking pictures. A determination to complete a task to the best of my ability. The rhinestones around my eyes caught the light perfectly and left me wishing I had a close-up portrait of the shot, until I flipped to the next photo, which was just that. Alex had good instincts.

The same look of determination was on my face, my brow

furrowed slightly to create an intensity that only showed when I was doing something I really loved. My eye makeup was striking, and my hair perfectly framed my face despite its length. I smiled as I looked up at Alex, who was waiting with apprehension. The colors needed a bit of brightening and touching up, but it was nothing I couldn't do with editing software.

"You did good. I can definitely use some of these."

"Oh, good! I was worried."

"All those selfies paid off." I gave her a smirk.

She rolled her eyes. "Shut up."

I laughed, the kind of laugh that I hadn't had in a while. It felt good. For once, things felt good.

"C'mon, let's get out of here. I hate this place after dark." Alex's eyes darted around, like she was waiting for something awful to happen, so I obliged and we started walking towards the exit.

CHAPTER FOURTEEN

Two weeks had gone by, and we'd heard nothing from the principal. Kyle hadn't received any kind of punishment, at least nothing that we could tell. He hadn't missed any school. We knew that from him faithfully showing up at our lockers to harass us every day. I'd be lying if I said that Theo hadn't thrown any punches in that time, but all of them could be chalked up to self-defense. Alex had gotten a little more feisty too, we were all sick of this and under no circumstances were we going to let Theo get another concussion.

We decided that it was time, we were going to release the video. Sitting at a computer in the library during lunch, Theo and I watched as Alex logged into her socials. We'd decided to have Alex post the video on her account, since she had the most followers. We plugged my phone in to upload the video to the computer and as soon as it was finished, Alex posted it and deleted the video off the computer.

"Everyone that knows us, knows that this is going on. Teachers and the principal know it's going on. No one is helping, no one that can make a difference cares. This happens every day."

And then we waited. We all attempted to work on a little homework, but truth be told we had our eyes glued to the screen more often than not. Theo and I instantly retweeted the video to our accounts for more visibility. Theo's repost added, "This gave me a concussion, I was out for 2 weeks." Mine added, "Why won't anyone in power stand up for us?"

By the end of lunch period, we'd gotten absolutely no work done, and the post had gathered a few likes and reposts from friends. Harriet, Elliot, Seth, Rachel, a few other queer kids that we'd gotten to know over the course of making and passing around the petition. Anxious, we all exchanged glances before we split up and made our way to our classes.

My next class was my time for my senior project, so I made my way to Clare's classroom, heart heavy and brain unfocused. There was no one else in the room, as usual, so I approached Clare's desk, and she looked up at me questioningly.

"What's up, kiddo?"

"We posted the video."

"What video?" She cocked her head slightly, squinting as she looked up.

"The video of Kyle giving Theo that concussion. We gave the principal the petition over two weeks ago, and nothing's been done. No meetings, no consequences, nothing. We just need this shit to stop."

I pulled up the video on my phone and handed it to Clare, which she took and watched. Her eyes widened in horror and she placed her hand over her mouth as it played. When it was done, she laid my phone down on her desk and looked up at me.

"This is horrible."

"This is every day. I gave the principal pictures that I've taken to document every injury we've had, and she rolled her eyes like it was nothing."

"Did you show her this video?"

"No, but we told her we had it and that we'd release it if she didn't do anything."

Clare shook her head as I picked up my phone and slid it into my pocket. "I wish there was something more I could do. You know this classroom is always a safe space, right?"

I gave her a weak smile. "I know. It's one of the things that make this place bearable. We protect each other in the halls. Theo just didn't fight back that time because we were taking the video. Normally, they're pretty quick on their feet."

"They shouldn't have to be. If you think it'll help, I'll bring this up and have a talk with the principal."

I shook my head, "She'll see it soon enough."

As if to prove me right, my phone vibrated in my pocket. I pulled it out to see almost 100 likes on the post, and one particular repost – Kyle.

"The gays get what they deserve. This girl is such a pussy, and my form was great."

My blood started to boil. He was *proud* of what he'd done. My hands shook and my cheeks felt hot. Suddenly, all the lights in the room were too bright, all the noises too loud, yet somehow so completely muffled that I barely made out what Clare said.

"Phee? Hey, what's wrong?"

My hands shaking so badly that I almost dropped my phone, I turned it around and showed her.

"What the fuck." Her brows furrowed.

I'd never heard this woman swear. I didn't know she was capable of it. My knees started to feel weak and I landed – luckily – on a stool behind me. I dropped my phone, and it clattered against the linoleum floor. Air escaped me and I choked to catch my breath. Clare got up from her desk and put her hands on my shoulders, causing my blurry vision to zone in onto her face. Tears fell from my cheeks, and Clare was saying something I had to focus hard to hear.

"Breathe, Phee. You've gotta breathe. Take a deep breath."

I tried to follow her instructions and took in a shaky breath, trying to fill my lungs. Every part of me tingled, like the electric feeling you get right after your foot falls asleep. I covered my face with my hands and curled in on myself, all the while Clare's voice told me to breathe. Focusing hard, after what felt like hours, I caught the air enough that my lungs didn't hurt, and I wiped my face of the tears that had streaked down to my jaw. Clare let go of me and leaned back on her desk in front of me.

"You all right, kiddo? Do you want me to take you to the nurse?"

I shook my head, words failing to come out of my mouth as we sat there in silence. It was still taking an incredible amount of focus to keep air in my lungs, so Clare just sat with me quietly until I came around.

"S-sorry," I muttered.

"You've got nothing to be sorry for. Has that ever happened to you before?"

I nodded, sniffling and accepting the tissue that she handed to me.

"I'm no doctor, but that really looked like a panic attack. Has anyone ever helped you with that?"

"Theo's pulled me out of them a few times, so has Alex, they both get them too."

"I mean, have you seen a professional for them? It might be helpful. The school has a counselor—"

"I don't... I don't want to see a counselor." The words felt familiar. Mom. I sounded just like my mom. Immediately, I doubled back. "Maybe I should."

Clare gave me a sympathetic smile, then stood up straight, reaching her hand out towards me. "I'll take you. She's pretty cool, I think you'll like her."

"N-now?"

"Yes, now."

Clare had a gentle force that couldn't be argued with. I got up from the stool, knees still weak, and wobbled after her like a baby deer as she led me out of the classroom. We walked to the front offices, going in one set of doors before Clare knocked on one of the doors inside. It was decorated with some signs – a "safe space" sticker with a progress pride flag in particular caught my eye. All the decorations surrounded a nameplate: Quinn Alexander, L.I.C.S.W.

Inside, there was some shuffling of papers, then footsteps, then the doorknob turned and the door opened to reveal a woman a bit taller than me, with long black hair pulled back into a fishtail braid and a pair of cat-eye glasses that framed dark-brown, almost black, eyes. She wore a kind smile that immediately put me at ease.

"Hi, Clare. And who's this?"

"Phee," I said, still a bit anxious despite the kind demeanor that this woman had. Residual anxiety from the panic attack, maybe.

"Hi, Phee. Why don't you two come in?"

The office was small, but it was thoroughly decorated with artwork from students, and a few pieces that I could tell were Clare's from the style. There was a desk with two chairs in front of it, where Clare and I sat down as Quinn settled into her small and uncomfortable-looking office chair.

"What can I do for you, Phee? I assume Clare brought you here?"

"I, uh…" The sentences wouldn't form in my head. There was

a ringing in my ears and my eyes darted to the floor as I wrung my hands together.

Clare to the rescue. "She just had a panic attack in my classroom, for valid reason, but she told me she's had them before, so I thought it might be worth paying you a visit."

"I see." She looked down her nose before pushing her glasses up by the frame, "Phee, you look very anxious right now. Is that correct?"

I nodded, still avoiding eye contact.

"Is there anything you do that usually helps? Is there anything you know of that we can do for you?"

"If… If I'm at home I wrap up really tight in a blanket, but I can't exactly do that here."

"Have you ever tried grounding techniques?" Quinn asked.

"Are those, like, counting and naming things? One of my friends did it with me once."

"There's a few different exercises, I can teach you one if you're open to it."

"Okay."

Clare, standing up from her seat, put a hand on my shoulder. "I'm going to head back to my classroom, I've got a class starting in a few minutes. Take as much time as you need here, Phee." She then exited the room, closing the door behind her, and I was left alone with Quinn.

She gave me a patient smile. "Okay, one of the easiest ones is 5, 4, 3, 2, 1. First, name 5 things you can see."

My eyes darted around the room, before settling on a few objects, "A plant, some pictures, your glasses, a computer." I glanced down at my still-shaking hands. "My hands."

"Good. Now 4 things you can touch."

Without thinking, I felt the softness of my oversized hoodie, then the coldness of the metal chair I was sitting in. Everything around me started to slow down as I focused on specific sensations through the entire exercise, until we got to the last one, 1 thing you can taste. I suddenly became aware of my teeth gnawing at my cheek. Who knows how long I'd been doing that.

"Blood," I muttered.

Quinn squinted. "Blood from what?"

"I bit my cheek."

"Oh, okay. As long as it's nothing serious."

I shook my head, taking a deep breath that filled my lungs to the brim, expanding my chest until I couldn't take any more. Then, I let it out slowly through my mouth. The room felt more real. Everything around me had slowed down, and the tightness in my chest relaxed as I settled more comfortably into the chair.

"How do you feel now? That was a good deep breath. I see you've already got some self-regulation skills, even if you don't realize you're using them."

"I feel a little better."

"Good, good. Clare said there was a good reason for your panic attack, do you mind if I ask what it was?"

"It's… It's kind of a long story."

"I've got nowhere to be." She leaned back in her chair, placing her hands on the desk in front of her.

I looked around the room again, trying to avoid the topic. My eyes were drawn to her hands, where I found a ring – married. Squinting, I looked around the desk. There was no sign of a man in any of her pictures. I found a picture of her laughing with another woman, the woman's arm around her shoulders and leaning in. It could've been a friend, but there was something in the woman's eyes that told me otherwise.

"Are you a lesbian?" slipped out of my mouth before I could stop it, and my face flushed red as I realized how blunt and personal of a question that was.

Thankfully, I didn't have to wait long for her reaction, because she started *laughing*. It was a carefree, unbridled laugh. She picked up the photograph I'd been looking at before chuckling out, "Would you believe she's my sister?"

I glanced between her and the picture, squinting a little harder to try and find a family resemblance. "I, uh…"

"The principal does." She wrinkled her nose. "She keeps asking me to bring my husband to faculty functions."

"The principal's an asshole."

"I'm not disagreeing with you, but what makes you feel that way?"

"It's… There's this whole thing. It's part of why I had my panic attack."

"Well, go on."

"Kyle Ritter… He comes after us almost every day."

"Who's us?"

"My friends and I… Theo Venia, Alex Kenzington…"

"Oh, I know all about Theo. We've never sat down and had a conversation, since they've got their own therapist, but I know they've needed a bit of extra support over the years. I know they get in trouble for fights a lot."

"That's the thing, they never start the fights. It's all Kyle, Theo just defends us and tries to keep everyone safe from him and his goons."

"And the principal won't do anything?"

"No. A couple weeks ago, we brought her a petition that we got hundreds of signatures on, and photo evidence of all the injuries Kyle's caused. We just want school to be safe, and it's not as long as he's here. She rolled her eyes at us, barely listened, and hasn't done anything since. We have a video of Kyle giving Theo a concussion, and just released it today. And then Kyle, he…" My chest began to get tight again, and I pulled my phone from my pocket, opening up the post and placing it on Quinn's desk.

She picked up the phone, squinting hard with disdain for a moment, seeing Kyle's retweet. She tapped the screen, presumably to play the video. Her hand covered her mouth, and she put the phone down quickly, shaking her head and closing her eyes tightly for a minute before opening them and looking directly into mine.

"I'm so sorry this is happening to you. I can see why you're carrying so much stress. Is home at least a good respite?"

My gaze fell to the floor before I blurted out, "My mom's an alcoholic."

Something about this woman made me lose all tact and nuance to my words, it was like my brain just wanted to get as much information out there as possible, regardless of how it sounded or what repercussions it might bring.

"Is dad in the picture? Or another parent in general, I don't want to assume."

"My dad died when I was really young. It's what started my mom's drinking."

"Do you remember him at all?"

"It's… kind of fuzzy. But I remember how my mom used to be, around him. She was so in love, she was practically a different person."

"How is she now?"

I bit my lip, scanning Quinn's face, suddenly wary of what I might say. "Please don't call CPS."

"Right now, do you feel like you're in imminent danger when you're at home?"

Right now… Right now was okay. "No."

"Then I don't see any reason to call CPS. Everything you say here stays between us. I've seen some kids through many difficult situations. I'm not going to react badly, no matter what you say."

"For now, she stopped drinking. Just stopped a couple weeks ago, and things have been better. She's gotten sober before though, and always goes back to drinking."

"What's she like when she's drunk?"

"She's… She's either great, or awful. No in-between. She'll coo over me and be so happy that I'm there, or she'll be so angry, she just…" I glanced up at Quinn again, my leg bouncing as I leaned forward in the chair.

"Does she ever get physical with you?"

Reluctantly, I dropped my gaze from her face to the floor and muttered, "Yes."

"What kind of things has she done?"

"It… She… Everything got worse when I came out as gay. Then even more when I told her I was a girl. Before, the anger wasn't usually directed at me, I was just her outlet. Once she knew I was queer… I was a disappointment, something she was ashamed of."

Quinn's eyebrow quirked a little, and I could see the gears turning in her head. "Phee, how old are you?"

"Seventeen. I'll be eighteen in a couple months."

"Do you have a place to go when things aren't safe?"

I nodded. "Theo's house is always safe. We're like our own little family there."

"And your mom hasn't put hands on you since she got sober?"

"You said you wouldn't call CPS."

She gave me a weak smile. "Kiddo, if it were a matter of your safety, I'd have no choice, I'm a mandated reporter. Have you dealt with CPS before?"

I shook my head. "I've always hid the marks, for the longest time no one knew, until I told Theo. Well, I didn't really tell them. They figured it out. But Theo went through DCF since they were really little. They don't really talk about it, but I know some horrible things happened to them while they were in the system."

"Well, thankfully things seem to be okay for you at home right now, so I have no reason to call. But foster care would look very different for you as a seventeen-year-old than as a young child. And then you'd be free to make your own choices once you turned eighteen. I'm just trying to assess the situation. Have you ever met with a counselor before?"

"No."

"So you've just kept all this inside?"

Suddenly, I became very overwhelmed. My cheeks got hot and I could feel tears trying to force their way out. My voice wavered as I spoke, "I, uh... I talk to Theo sometimes..."

"How long have you known Theo?"

"Three years."

"You said your father died when you were young, and that's when your mother's drinking started. Did you talk to anyone before Theo?"

"No."

"That's an awful lot to keep inside."

I failed to keep the tears from falling, and I sniffled and wiped at my eyes before Quinn handed me a tissue.

"What about Theo made you feel safe enough to talk to them?"

"They... They understand. People have hurt them, too, they know what it's like."

Quinn nodded, keeping a neutral face while leaning back in her chair. "Theo sounds like a good friend."

"They are. They don't deserve the bad reputation they've got here. The anger they have, it's just. If people looked at the reasons why they did things, they'd see they're really not a bad person."

"Do you believe that your mother's anger is justified? And if so, we should just let it go, she shouldn't be held accountable?"

"I never said people shouldn't be held accountable when they hurt other people. But yes, to an extent, my mother's anger comes from grief and mourning, and I understand that. She drinks to numb those feelings. But hurting me because of it, that's the part that's not okay."

Quinn nodded. "That's good, that you recognize her actions aren't your fault. That's where a lot of kids get hung up."

"At least, it wasn't until I came out."

"Tell me about coming out, how did that go?"

"I did it one of the few times she was sober, it was a morning before school, and she was hung over, but sober. I'd just made us breakfast… pancakes. I remember because she threw the plate at the wall and syrup went everywhere. And then she hit me, hard, across the face. Said that no son of hers would 'be one of those freaks'. I grabbed my backpack and ran out, then stayed at Theo's for a couple days. When I came back, she was drunk and it was like nothing ever happened, except her anger was so much more pointed. Like I was the conduit for everything that had gone wrong in her life. We didn't talk about it for months, until eventually it seemed like she came around to the idea a little. She still wasn't happy about it but… less angry."

"You're not wrong for it, but if her reaction was so negative to you being gay, why did you come out to her as trans? Surely it didn't feel safe."

"I didn't mean to. She found some makeup that I'd been messing with and it just… came out. As soon as I said it I was terrified."

"How did she react?"

"She dragged me into the kitchen by the arm and cut all my hair off. It used to be really long, down to the middle of my back." I sniffled, mentally reliving the moment I heard the crunch of the scissors in my hair. The anguish, the fear, the regret. I ran my hands through my hair and wiped a tear away from my face.

"I see that's still fresh, how long ago was this?"

"A little over a month."

"Does she ever show remorse for what she's done to you, try to make it right?"

"She apologizes when she's in a better mood. It doesn't feel genuine most of the time, but I think this past time she got sober was her way of trying to make it up to me. She's been… so nice, I still don't trust it, like it's leading up to something awful. She said she was doing it for me, to be a better mom."

"Do you believe that?"

"I think she believes that, but like I said, I don't trust it. She's always ended up hitting a wall, picking up alcohol again. This time, I've been trying to get her involved with meetings and therapists, the hospital psychiatrist put her on an antidepressant, so I'm hoping against everything that this time will be different, but she's been through rehab before, and went right back to drinking once she lost the routine of the placement."

Quinn squinted a little. "Where were you while she was in rehab?"

"Alone, mostly. I can take care of myself."

She nodded, leaning forward and putting her elbows on her desk. "It sounds like you've had to take care of not only yourself, but your mom, for a very long time."

"Yeah…"

"That's not fair to expect of someone your age. You should be out with friends, looking into colleges, worrying about your grades. Not taking care of a parent."

I shrugged, looking out the window briefly before staring down at my lap where my hands twisted together.

"Phee, would you be willing to come back and talk with me some more? It seems like there's a lot to unpack here, more than we can talk about in just one session. I want to give you the support you need. Your anxiety could have many causes, between your home life and school. I think anyone in your situation would be overwhelmed."

"Okay." I sighed. It felt good to talk to someone, but I was still apprehensive about the idea of seeing a therapist regularly, probably rooted in my mom's resistance to the idea.

"Good, let's set up a time a couple times a week. You're a senior, right? That means you should have a free period somewhere in your schedule."

I nodded, pulling out my phone to look at my calendar.

CHAPTER FIFTEEN

I arrived at home a couple hours later than usual. Since the visit with Quinn had taken up my entire senior project time period, I'd stayed late in Clare's classroom editing the photos I had of Alex. I wasn't ready to move on to mine just yet. That, of course, meant that I missed the bus, and had to walk home, which took up another chunk of time.

Turning my key in the apartment door, I was met with the most unexpected sight. Instead of the barely livable mess that it had been for years, a minimum state of cleanliness that I struggled to keep up with following my whirlwind of a mother, the apartment was *spotless*. Shelves were organized and dusted, tables I hadn't seen the surface of in years were cleared off, the floors had a shine to them, and the whole place smelled wonderful. Not like air freshener even, but the smell of baked goods.

"Mom?" I beckoned quietly, a little wary of what I'd discover. Was she okay? Replaced with a clone that decided its purpose in life was to clean?

I heard quick footsteps, and my mom popped her head out of the kitchen and grinned when she saw me, "My baby! I was getting worried, it's so late."

"Yeah, sorry, I had to finish up some stuff at school. The house looks… amazing. Are you feeling okay?"

"You always try so hard to keep it clean, I thought I'd finally do my part. I feel great! I woke up with so much energy, more than I've had in years. I needed to put it to use somewhere. Come, come! I made fresh rolls and there's a pie in the oven for dessert! I couldn't decide what to make for dinner." Her speech was quick and breathless, like she had to get everything out all at once.

"Slow down a little, okay mom? I'll help with dinner."

I dropped my backpack off in my room, then entered the kitchen which smelled more heavenly than it had in years. Usually, there was a distinct smell of spoiled food in there, science experiments in the back of the fridge that needed to be thrown away. When I walked in, I noticed that it was just as spotless as the living room. All the dishes organized and put away in the cupboards, counters a clean, shining white, stovetop spotless and free from grease. I opened the pantry door to find all the food organized, all the stale items gone from the shelves.

"Wow…" I muttered. The stale food had been doing a pretty good job of making it look like we were better stocked than we actually were, the shelves looking a bit empty.

"We should go grocery shopping together when you get back from school tomorrow! It's the beginning of the month, so I just got food stamps in. Everything looks so empty now that all the bad food is gone."

"Okay," I agreed, then pulled out a bag of rice and some furikake seasoning, then chicken and soy sauce from the fridge, along with some cucumber and carrots. "Poke bowls, mom?"

"That sounds wonderful." She pulled a bowl out of the cabinet and took the bag of rice from me to wash it.

I opened the drawer where I usually kept the cutting board, and instead found all the silverware organized neatly in stacks. While I was there, I pulled a knife out before closing it.

After a glance around the kitchen with no success I asked, "Where are the cutting boards?"

"I moved some things around, we'll have to get used to it." She smiled and pulled open the drawer she'd been standing in front of, handing me the two cutting boards – one for meat, one for vegetables.

Taking them from her, I nodded and set to work cutting up the chicken before checking the cabinet where we usually kept the pots and pans. Luckily, that was still the case. I pulled a skillet from the cabinet as well as the rice cooker. I put the rice cooker on the counter next to my mom, then set the pan on the stove and turned on the heat before pouring in a little oil and dropping in the chicken. Once the chicken had a good sear on it, I dumped a liberal amount of soy sauce into the pan and stirred it up and put a lid on it, reducing the heat. Then I set to work cutting up the vegetables. By the time I was finished, the chicken was almost ready and my mom had put the rice in the cooker, so all that was left to do was wait.

Cracking the oven door open slightly, my mom checked on the pie and smiled, shooing me away from in front of the stove. She grabbed a couple potholders and pulled the pie from the oven, setting it on one of the back burners of the stove to cool. Then, she sat at the table while we waited. I joined her, pulling my phone out of my pocket to check my messages.

"Didn't see you on the bus, you good?" That was Theo.

"Yeah, just had to work late on my senior project. Can we talk a little later?"

I looked up from my phone for a second, my leg bouncing

underneath the table when I almost immediately heard another ping. My attention was drawn down to see the "Sure." from Theo, then glanced over at my mom. Setting my phone face down on the table, I started wringing my hands together in my lap, my nervous tell I'd never get rid of.

My mom caught it, apparently much more perceptive when she wasn't drunk. "What's the matter?"

I didn't want to dance around the issue, maybe if my mom saw that I was trying she'd be more open to it herself, "I saw the school counselor today."

"Did something happen?"

"I had a panic attack. She wants me to start seeing her regularly."

"Have you ever had a panic attack before?"

"Yes."

"Oh. I… I missed it. I'm sorry."

"I know." Sounded a bit more passive aggressive than I intended.

"Are you going to do it?"

"I think so. After everything that's happened… I think I need it, too."

My mom's eyes became glassy as she stared into space, and I didn't know what to say. I knew those words were going to hurt, but they were the truth, and I was done lying to protect her feelings. She hurt me, whether or not she was sober didn't matter. She'd hurt me enough, and I'd kept it to myself for so long. She needed to see the reality of what she'd done.

After a deep inhale, my mom spoke. "I have my first session with the therapist tomorrow while you're at school."

"Are you gonna go?"

She looked at me, tears begging to free themselves from her eyes. "Yes. I have to be better, for you. It's not fair, what I've done to us."

"Me." I was being selfish now, but the words spilled from my mouth without my brain's consent. "What you've done to me."

There was an uncomfortable silence between us, until the ding of the rice cooker saved us. My mom wiped the tears from her eyes and got up, dishing the rice into two bowls. I got up as well, giving the chicken one last stir and turning the heat off completely. Taking the bowl of rice from my mom, I mixed in the furikake and then took some vegetables and chicken, adding another dash of soy sauce. I pulled a pair of chopsticks from the silverware drawer and sat down at the table, not really making eye contact as my mom sat down across from me. She stirred up her bowl with her chopsticks far longer than was necessary as I brought the first bite to my mouth and my foot bounced against the floor. Nervous energy all around.

"Can… Can you ever forgive me?" My mom sniffled, poking at her food.

I stopped chewing. My eyes met hers, and I stabbed my chopsticks into my bowl and leaned back, my back hitting the chair hard. Still, I stayed silent. I didn't want to lie and say yes, but I couldn't break her heart with a no.

"I don't… I don't deserve it." Tears fell from her eyes, and she dropped her chopsticks on the table to free up her hands and cover her face.

I placed a napkin in front of her, still unsure of what to say. Sighing, I propped my elbows up on the table. "Mom, you just… You have to do better. I still don't know that you're not going to go right back to drinking, it hasn't been long enough. You've lasted longer before, saying you'll never drink again for my sake. It was a lie every time. I'm just not ready to believe you yet."

"I have to earn it, I *will.* I will earn it this time, I promise."

"You just have to show me. I can't live on hope any longer."

She slowly lowered her hands, picking up the napkin and dabbing it at her eyes. "I don't remember if I'd said it before, but I'm sorry. I'm sorry for everything. I know you'll never forget what I've done, and there's no excuse for it, but I really am."

The most sincere she'd ever sounded. She wasn't saying it just to gain my sympathy, she really meant it. I sighed deeply and untwisted my hands, picking my chopsticks back up.

"I won't say it's okay, mom, but thank you for apologizing."

When we walked through the doors to the school the next morning, all chatter hushed around us. The video had gotten around. Stares followed us in the hallways, especially Theo. We could hear whispers talking about the incident, kids turning to each other and glancing between us and their friends.

We expected to be met with Kyle, a cocky bastard proud of his harassment of us, but instead we heard the clack of high heels colliding with the linoleum flooring. The principal approached us, seemingly having a heated conversation on her phone when she walked up to us.

She covered the phone with her hand and snarled, "My office. Now."

The three of us looked at each other before apprehensively following. On the way to her office, we passed Kyle, who the principal also rallied to follow us. Theo's gaze narrowed and they put themself between Alex and Kyle to block any hits that might come our way. With the principal's track record, she'd ignore anything that happened behind her back. As we approached her office, the secretary looked up at us and gave a sympathetic look before turning back to her computer, seemingly hiding from the principal. She marched into her office and pointed at the chairs where Kyle and Theo sat, Alex and I taking a spot against the wall near Theo.

"Yes, yes. I'll see to it that everything's taken care of. Just bury it." The principal hung up the phone and glared at Theo before addressing them. "Take it down."

She was *livid*, hands shaking and her face the brightest red I'd seen. Theo's snarky side was always ready to make an appearance, especially in a situation like this.

"I don't know what you're talking about." They leaned back in the chair, a casual smirk on their face.

"Wipe that grin off your face. Take that video down. You're using it to slander me."

Theo waved a hand in the air. "If you'd done something when we first came to you, it never would've gone up in the first place. Tell me why he's here." They nodded their head towards Kyle, who had his perfect angel face on.

Playing the fool was his strong suit, "What happened? Why did you want to see me?" His tone sickly sweet and infuriating.

Theo rolled their eyes and scoffed as the principal turned to address him. "Don't you play innocent here, you can be seen clearly assaulting someone in the video and to make matters worse, you posted bragging about it! This whole thing is a nightmare on the school's image, on my image."

She didn't care about us. She just cared that she looked bad. It was a wonder how she got this position in the first place when she cared so little about the students.

"I should give suspensions all around."

Alex's prior face of stone broke, as did mine. While Theo was no stranger to the school's disciplinary actions, Alex and I had never gotten so much as a single detention. A panic rose up in my chest before Theo jumped on it.

"You can't suspend us for this. We didn't do anything wrong. The only one who should be getting disciplinary action is him." Theo growled and shot Kyle a sideways glance.

"I'm the principal, I'll damn well do what I please."

"And suspending the students that brought a rampantly queerphobic hate crime to light will look great on your part."

The principal froze at that.

"The only thing that will save your ass here is doing what you should've done in the first place." They knew they had the upper hand, and they weren't about to let things go. Not anymore.

Looking down at her phone that hadn't stopped pinging with notifications the entire time we'd been in the office, the principal pinched the bridge of her nose and shut her eyes, letting out a breath filled with frustration. "Fine. Kyle, you're suspended for a week. Go home."

Theo and Kyle exclaimed at the same time.

"What?! I didn't post that video, why am I in trouble?" That was Kyle.

"That's *it?!*" That was Theo.

The principal turned to Kyle, ignoring Theo. "Again, you are seen clearly assaulting her—"

"Them." Alex spoke for the first time.

Rolling her eyes, the principal continued, "on the video. You can't get out of this for free, the press would have a field day with it. You're lucky you don't get more. Take your week and be happy with it."

"He *should* get more!" Theo dug their nails into the arm of the chair.

Finally turning back to them, the principal didn't hide her

contempt. "It's his first offense. I'd be playing favorites if I gave him more."

"How the fuck is this his first offense?!"

"Watch your mouth."

Theo rolled their eyes. "You said it yourself, it's *assault*. He's eighteen. I could press charges!"

"So press charges. It's none of my concern."

Theo's whole body was shaking, and I could hear the noise of them grinding their teeth from where I was standing a few feet away. They were going to blow up if we didn't step out. This was too much.

Alex saw it too. She walked up and placed a hand on Theo's shoulder gently and leaned over close to their ear. "T, let's go."

Theo glanced up at Alex but remained firmly seated. "This is a load of crap. You have to do more than this. Why won't you just *help* us? Do your fucking job!" Tears welled in the corners of their eyes, their composure cracking.

Alex leaned over and whispered to Theo, something unheard by the rest of us in the room. Whatever it was, it was enough to convince them to get up and start walking towards the door with Alex at their side. I followed them, and Kyle filtered out after us. Once we were out of eyesight and earshot of the principal's office, Kyle jogged to catch up with us. He shoved Theo, who was already on edge.

"You'll never get rid of me, pussy. I'm invincible."

Theo wheeled around on him, inches from his face. "Kyle, I will *fuck you up*." The tips of their ears flushed red, and their entire body shook with rage.

"Do it. You won't." He laughed in their face.

Alex moved fast, but Theo moved faster. Before Alex could put herself between the two, Theo punched Kyle squarely in the face.

A cracking sound echoed in the hallway, and blood gushed from Kyle's nose. He wailed in pain, turning and running back towards the principal's office. I watched helplessly as everything happened, and Alex put her hands on Theo's shoulders.

"We're going to the nurse. You need your meds."

Tears began to fall from Theo's eyes as they wiped the blood on their hand onto their already scuffed-up jeans, and let Alex guide them down the hallway towards the nurse's office. I followed, continuously glancing behind us in the direction Kyle had run. Was he going to do what I thought he was about to do?

The nurse jumped up as soon as she saw us in her doorway. She ushered Theo to sit on the couch in her office, looking them over as the tears continued to silently fall. Their eyes were glassy, unfocused. They weren't here.

"Are you hurt?" the nurse asked them, finding the remnants of blood on their hand.

No answer.

Alex glanced between Theo and the nurse before sitting down next to Theo. "The blood's not theirs."

The nurse gave Alex a solemn look before walking away and returning with some alcohol wipes and cleaning Theo's hand. Alex tried to get Theo's attention, but they were long gone – a flashback, *somewhere*. Their whole body shook as the tears streamed down their face, but otherwise they were immovable stone, rigid and cold.

Alex glanced back at the nurse. "We gotta get them to take their meds."

The nurse nodded, placing Theo's hand back in their lap. She went up to the glass cabinet where all the student medications were held and retrieved Theo's, putting a pill in a small paper cup and filling another with water. She returned, extending her hands towards Theo.

"Hey, kiddo, you've got to take this." Her tone was gentle, knowing enough not to be harsh with them.

Not a single movement in her direction.

Alex placed a hand under Theo's chin, turning their head towards her and cooing to them softly, "T, you've gotta take your meds, it'll help. You know it will."

Still silent, Theo slowly extended a shaky hand towards the cup with their medication. Alex placed her hand around it to steady them as they brought the cup to their mouth. She then took the cup of water before Theo could, not wanting it to spill everywhere. Theo took a sip as the cup touched their lips.

Before Alex could even put the cup down, the principal came marching into the office with Kyle and his bleeding nose in tow. He had a bunch of bloody tissues pressed against his face with his hands, tears mixing with blood onto them. The nurse rushed over to him to assess the damage, while the principal didn't even address her, but instead angrily stomped until she was standing over Theo.

"You think this is okay? Isn't this what you're 'trying to prevent' with all these stupid petitions and videos? Two weeks, Venia."

Rage built up inside me. How was the principal going to give Theo two weeks on nothing but word of mouth when Kyle only got one with video proof?

I couldn't stop myself. "What do you mean, two weeks? Kyle only got one."

"This isn't her first offense. The way I see it, Elizabeth, is you're the only menace to this school. You're the one who should have charges brought up on."

Theo was still lost in their world that wasn't this one, and had no response to the principal. Alex tried to soothe them, bring them back to this place, but maybe their world was better right now.

The principal grew angrier the longer they didn't respond, squatted down, and got in their face.

Alex put a hand out between them before pleading. "Don't."

Shoving Alex's hand out of the way, she raised her voice significantly. "Do you hear me, Elizabeth?"

And then they were gone. Up off the couch, running out the door. They hadn't said a word. I'd seen them run like this before, after dealing with my mom. They'd pulled me out of the apartment, but the slam of the door, my mother's shouts, and breaking glass sent them running. I never knew where they went, but they were always faster than me.

"Shit," Alex said breathlessly before getting up and running after them.

"Back to class, Kenzington!" the principal shouted after Alex.

Anger and fear overcame me. I'd never been one to talk back to authority, but this was too much. This wasn't fair, any way you looked at it. No, Theo shouldn't have punched Kyle, but after everything he'd done, who could blame them? He called Theo a pussy, but here he was running and tattling to the principal.

Without intending to, I pushed myself away from the wall that I'd been pressed up against next to the couch and threw my arms out in the air in a genuine "What the fuck?" motion before speaking. "You can't yell at them like that! Don't you know they have PTSD?"

The principal rolled her eyes. "I don't care. There's no excuse for her behavior."

Baffled by how hard-headed this woman was, I shook my head and ran out of the office, following Alex, who was already out of sight.

I heard a call from the nurse's station. "To class with you, too!"

Shaking my head, I sprinted down the hallway. No way was I going to class right now. I barreled through the glass doors and almost straight into Alex who was panting and had her phone pressed to her ear. She turned around and looked at me, tears in her eyes.

"I have no idea which way they went. They won't answer their phone."

"Shit. The skate park, maybe? Or home?"

"I don't know, they were so out of it, I don't want them doing anything dangerous." Her breaths quickened, and I put a hand on her shoulder.

"Hey, we'll find them. Why don't you check home and I'll go to the skate park? Maybe we'll find them sooner if we split up, cover more ground."

"Okay, okay." Alex tried to reel herself back, pressing the call button on her phone again and putting it on speaker so that she could jog back home but still hear if they picked up.

I ran in the opposite direction, towards the skate park. I took a shortcut behind the school, when I glanced over at the woods that lined the property. That's when I remembered our photoshoot – what Theo had told me about running into the woods, it being their safe place. My gut told me I was right, and I turned and ran headfirst into the woods.

How was I going to find them in here, if they even came in here? Some of these trees were huge, an infinite number of hiding places laid out before me. I tried to scan the environment as best as I could while I was running and trying not to trip over roots and sticks. There was no path back here, only solid trees and bushes. Was this really a good idea? It was just a passing thought, something to consider. Surely they'd run somewhere more familiar, like the skate park. They could be hiding in the tunnels, or like Alex said, something dangerous. Would they turn to drugs when they were like this? My brain started to spiral.

Then, I heard it. Theo's ringtone for Alex. My thoughts began to fall away as I skidded to a stop on my heels and listened to the sound echo through the woods. It was difficult to tell what direction it was coming from, so I played a game of hot-and-cold walking in directions and seeing where the tone was at its loudest. I came to a place where the noise sounded like it was right on top of me – I checked behind trees, in bushes, even in a pretty small fallen log. Nothing. I squinted, looking around the landscape, and then thought about the notion that it might be literally on *top* of me. Looking up, I peered through the leaves, and on a branch pretty high up I saw Theo's skater shoes, firmly planted.

Looking around the tree, I found the lowest branch and began climbing. I definitely wasn't built for this, and it took everything I had to hoist myself up onto each subsequent limb. Upper body strength? We don't know her. After what felt like forever, I climbed up onto the branch next to Theo, limbs shaking from the exertion.

Theo didn't acknowledge me. Tears still fell from their face, and their breath was shallow and quick. They had no idea what was happening around them. I leaned over and pulled their phone from their pocket, answering Alex's call.

"Hey, I got them. It's gonna be a minute, but I'll bring them home."

An audible gasp of relief came from Alex's side of the phone between her shaky breaths from running.

"You tell Monica what happened, okay? Everything. Including what we've been doing with the petition and video. We're gonna need as many adults on our side as we can get."

"I will," Alex breathed.

"And Alex?"

"Yeah?"

"What did you tell them, to get them to leave the office?"

"I told them we still have the walk-out. We're gonna end this shit."

CHAPTER SIXTEEN

I hung up the phone, tucking it into my pocket and sat there quietly for a minute, trying to catch my breath. Theo's breath was shaky too, and I couldn't tell if it was from the running or from the panic. After I got my bearings a little bit more, I turned on the branch so that I was facing Theo and placed a hand over theirs. I noticed their nails were digging so deep into the tree bark that their knuckles were white. Gently, I pried their hand away from the branch and held it in one palm while rubbing the back of it with my other.

They seemed unchanged. I'd never seen them this far gone. I was pretty sure Alex had, but they still hid some things from me. Sighing, I stared out at the sky over my shoulder, trying to remember anything that could help them. The day I'd had my panic attack with Alex, she told me grounding things don't usually work for Theo, you just had to wait it out. They'd taken their medication, so that would kick in soon and hopefully help bring them back.

Carefully, I scooted closer to Theo on the branch and put a hand around them on their shoulder, pulling them into me. This would work better for Alex, but I decided to give it a try. I ran my hands through Theo's hair, hoping that the sensation would remind them that everything was okay. Alex always did this, but I didn't know if it was more for her or for Theo.

It felt so intimate, like I shouldn't be doing this. My crush on them had never left, no matter how much I shoved it down. A friend would do this too, wouldn't they? I shook my head, trying to fight away the guilt I felt for my emotions. Was this how Theo felt with Alex, before they told her they were in love with her? It was an awful feeling, like I was betraying them by showing any affection.

Nails digging into my arm that was across their shoulder, I gasped slightly and brought myself back to the present. Theo was clinging to me, and instead of silent tears, audible sobs shook their body. I pulled them tighter to my chest, rubbing their arm as they grabbed at mine.

"Shh, hey, you're okay," I whispered, resting my chin on the top of their head and closing my eyes. I despised how much pain they were in. I hated Kyle, the principal, for setting them off like this. They'd been through enough, why did these horrible people have to add to it? Why was this world so full of horrible people? We're all constantly just hurting each other, making mistakes, but these acts felt so intentional, so cruel.

Theo started coughing through their sobs, gasping, struggling to catch their breath. I squeezed them tightly before holding them at arm's length by their shoulders. Their face was flushed red, a mess of tears. They still clung to my hands. There was a difference in their gaze, though. Something more present, more aware of this world.

"Theo?" I lowered my head a little, squinting at them and getting a little closer.

They looked at me. It was a quick glance, and the sobs didn't stop, but they looked at me.

I took full advantage of their awareness. "Okay, hey, you've got to slow down. Breathe."

They shook their head, closing their eyes and hunching over more.

Trying to keep them here, I moved my hands to their face and wiped away some of their tears, which were quickly replaced, but the gesture was enough to get them focused on me again.

"Do it with me, okay?" I took in a deep breath, filling my chest with air and raising my shoulders.

Theo didn't get quite as far, but they tried. They inhaled, their sobs breaking it up, but they kept trying. Eventually, they mirrored my stance with a chest full of air. I let mine out slowly through my mouth, and they tried to do the same, choppy and clumsy just the same.

"Good, again." I moved my hands to their arms, grasping them firmly but gently, giving them a pressure that I hoped was helping. Then, I inhaled as I had before, and Theo followed, a little more solid this time. We kept breathing like that until Theo's sobs slowly stopped, and all at once their posture deflated, slouching in on themself.

"I'm so tired," they whispered, closing their eyes.

"I know," I said, pulling them into me in a hug.

They grasped my arms that were around them, but not in a clinging desperation as they had before. We sat there for a few minutes, the silence growing between us. The sounds of the forest crept in – trees creaking in the light breeze, birds chirping, bushes rustling. I closed my eyes, wishing that we were here under different circumstances. Wishing we could enjoy the quiet together without this heaviness looming over our heads.

Eventually, I broke the silence. "Can we get down now? If your meds kick in too much, I'm afraid you'll fall."

"Okay." Their voice was hoarse, but they followed the answer by pulling away from me and beginning the descent to the ground.

I followed them, but much less surefooted. They caught me a

couple times as my feet slipped from beneath me, and my arms
gave out from a lack of strength. It was a wonder that I'd gotten
up here on my own. The relief I felt when our feet were planted
firmly on the earth was second to none. I fell back against the
trunk of the tree and took in a few solid breaths, while Theo sat
down on the small log I'd noticed earlier. They wiped at their eyes
with their sleeves and sniffled. I joined them shortly after.

"What… What happened, T? I've never seen you like that before."

"I wish you hadn't."

"What was it? A flashback? Something more?"

"Rage, flashback, dissociation, panic attack. In that order," they
muttered, kicking at the dirt beneath their feet.

"Shit," I looked around us before my gaze fell back on Theo.
"The dissociation, that was you not talking? You were just gone."

Theo nodded, wiping at their reddened nose with their sleeve again.

"That shit was scary. I mean, none of it was good, but I've seen
the rest of it before."

Theo patted at their pockets, and a brief look of panic crossed
their face. "Shit, where's my phone? Alex is probably freaking out."

"Oh," I pulled their phone from my pocket and handed it to
them. "I already told her I was with you, but I'm sure she'd feel
better hearing your voice."

Theo scrolled briefly and then tapped the screen, lifting the
phone to their ear. I'm sure it didn't even ring once before I heard
Alex faintly on the other end. I couldn't make out what she was
saying, but it must've been a string of anxieties with how fast the
speech sounded.

"It's me," Theo said softly. "No, I'm okay. Phee's here. I'll be
home soon." Their voice cracked in the middle, still hoarse from
crying. "I love you too." They hung up the phone and stood up

from the log, extending a hand towards me. "We should go."

I took their hand, nodding.

———

The walk back to the house was silent, but I watched Theo become more and more weighed down by their medication. They tripped over their own feet a couple times, and I caught them, as they had with me in the tree. I was reminded of the first night we spent together – they were a drunken mess after playing poker with their dealer. So much had changed since then. We were different people now, but all the same as well.

Shaky hands brought the key to the door of their house, and they made a few attempts to get it into the keyhole before growling and giving the keyring to me. I unlocked it with ease, and before the door was even fully open Alex had Theo in an embrace in the doorframe. All the tension that was in Theo's body fell away as they melted into her arms, burying their face in her chest. Alex held them close, kissing the top of their head and squeezing her arms around them.

"I was so scared, T. You can't run off like that."

Theo's voice wavered like they were crying again, and the sound was muffled from their face being pressed against Alex's chest, but I could make out, "I'm sorry. I didn't mean to."

Alex slid her arms up to Theo's shoulders, applying pressure to try and lift them from her chest. Reluctantly, they loosened their grip on her back and their face was visible again – tearstained and wet. Alex ran her hand through Theo's hair and pulled their forehead to her lips, kissing them again.

"C'mon, baby, come lay down." Alex guided Theo towards the couch where they collapsed, sniffling and weary. Covering them with a blanket, Alex retrieved a box of tissues from the coffee table and Theo took one, blowing their nose before Alex sat down on the couch and they rested their head in her lap. Alex turned to me. "Will you make some tea, Phee?"

"On it," I said, retreating to the kitchen and washing my hands of the sticky tree sap that had stained them from climbing.

Pulling chamomile tea from the cupboard, I laid out three cups – one with water, one with milk, and one with milk and honey. I heated them all up in the microwave while unwrapping the tea bags. Glancing back towards the living room, I watched Alex as she stroked Theo's hair, then the confusion on her face as she pulled a twig from it.

"Where were they?" She squinted at me, tossing the twig to the side.

"The woods behind the school. I had an inkling from something they told me once, so I ran in there, and once I was there, I heard your ringtone."

She nodded, looking back down at Theo, who I assumed was already asleep from the state of them.

The microwave beeped, and I pulled the three hot mugs from it and put the tea bags inside. Accompanying them with spoons, I carried the mugs into the living room, setting Theo's on the table and handing the one with milk and honey to Alex. Theo was out cold, face still a mess, some dirt even showing on their forehead. I set my mug down on the table and put warm water on a washcloth in the bathroom before coming back to the living room and kneeling down in front of Alex. I gently wiped the dirt and tear stains from Theo's face. They didn't wake up, so I moved onto their hands that were sticky with the same sap that had been on mine.

Sitting back down and picking up my mug, I looked back at Alex and asked, "Where's Monica?"

Before Alex could answer, I heard Monica's voice descending the stairs, the angriest tone I'd ever heard out of her as she spoke into her phone. "I don't care what they did, you shouted in the face of my child, who you are very much aware of having PTSD. There's better ways to handle that. And hearing all that has been going on, I can't believe the approach you've taken to all of this." She was silent for a moment, but I could feel her seething in the very air around us. Then, she spoke again, her voice even harsher, "THEY have plans in place for things like that. If you had followed up with the nurse, who was taking care of THEM, you would've been told that. And when the plans were first made, they were sent to your desk, it's not my fault if you ignored them."

I turned around to see her cheeks and the tips of her ears flushed red while she rolled her eyes and cut the principal off. "The school board will be hearing from me. I'd be fearful for your job." With that, she promptly hung up the phone, taking a deep breath and exhaling before entering the living room. She turned to me, placing a hand on my shoulder briefly. "Thank you for finding them." Shemoved Theo's tea, sat on the coffee table in front of Alex and brushed a stray spike of hair from Theo's face. "They weren't hurt at all?"

Alex shook her head before I answered. "Not physically. They got triggered really bad though, I've never seen them like that before. I found them in the woods."

With that, Monica snapped her head in my direction, "The woods?"

I nodded.

Monica's face fell, and she got up and sat in the chair opposite of me in the living room. "They used to do that, when they first came to stay with me. Once they started feeling safer here, I thought they'd stopped. I stopped finding dirt marks and tree sap on their clothes. They'd still do it sometimes, after an argument, consequences of something they'd done, but I don't think they've done it in a long time. They must've been in a really bad way."

Solemn looks all around. Eventually, Alex broke the silence, "That was the principal?"

Monica leaned back in the chair, rubbing her face with her hands. "Yeah, what a useless and hateful woman. I wish you'd come to me sooner."

"Have you watched the video?" I asked.

Monica glanced in Alex's direction with her brows furrowed. "What video?"

Alex shot me a glare, and my face flushed red. "Sorry, I thought you told her."

Monica's gaze didn't waver from Alex, forcing an explanation out of her, "I didn't want to stress you out more, I already dropped so much on you."

Monica shook her head. "Let me see."

I pulled up the video on my phone, then handed it to Monica. She took it, squinting at the screen at first. Her expression morphed into horror, then anger. Tears brimmed at the corners of her eyes.

"That's how they got their concussion?"

Alex and I nodded as Monica scrolled a little bit on my phone, then handed it back to me. "You should look at this."

I took the phone, looking at what Monica had left on the screen. A local news organization had shared the video, its numbers had skyrocketed. I had a ton of notifications, and there were hundreds of replies to the video.

"Shit," I muttered.

"We're in it now," Monica said, "What do you three have planned?"

I got home late that night, we'd been brainstorming our next steps with the school. Monica would be talking to the school board, bringing up the video if they hadn't already seen it. Alex and I would go back to school – enjoy the week without Kyle – and continue to rally people for the walkout. Monica would fight Theo's suspension, but she wasn't sure how much she could do since Theo *did* punch Kyle in the face, and they had a record, although they'd gone a pretty long time without an incident. We were going to get in touch with local news outlets, a couple had even messaged Alex and I already. That would put more pressure on the principal and school board to do something about what was happening.

Everything was planned out, but it still felt like so much. Theo was still in a pretty bad state, once they'd woken up they were still on edge and just not themself in general. They'd taken another dose of their medication and gone to bed early after taking a shower to get the rest of the forest debris off of them that I hadn't cleaned off with the washcloth. Alex and I were worried about them, but Monica promised she'd take a couple days off work to take care of them while we were at school.

I turned the doorknob to my apartment and was met with nothing but darkness. Blindly, I felt around for the light switch and was scared nearly to death by the figure that appeared on the couch. I gasped and jumped back before I realized it was my mom, then took a deep breath and shut the door behind me.

"Mom, why are you sitting in the dark?"

She didn't answer me, and my eyes darted around to assess the situation. She was sitting cross-legged on the couch, holding a bottle of her favorite liquor, tears staining her cheeks. My heart dropped. I knew this wouldn't last.

Dropping my backpack by the door, I slowly walked over and

sat down next to her. I sighed, leaning forwards and putting my head in my hands.

Finally, she broke the silence, "I… I didn't drink."

Raising my head, I looked at her, then the bottle. It was still sealed. Gently, I pried the bottle out of her hands and set it on the ground next to me. "Why did you buy it, then?"

"I… I wanted to. Therapy was really hard. I don't think it's going to help me. It made me worse."

"Therapy's not supposed to be easy, mom. It brings up a lot of hard stuff. But you have to work through it so you can feel better for longer, not fall apart at the first thing that challenges you."

"I don't know if I can do it."

"You can, you have to."

Fresh tears joined the dried ones on her face, and she sniffled and rubbed at her nose.

"If I can do it, if Theo can do it, so can you. I know it's difficult, but you'll be better for it." I placed a hand on my mom's shoulder.

She placed her hand over mine. "I didn't even realize it had gotten dark. Why are you home so late?"

"We had kind of a bad day. There's a lot going on at school."

She shook her head. "There's too much pressure on you kids. Life shouldn't be so hard."

I leaned back on the couch, and she leaned into my shoulder. "I know."

Putting an arm around my mom as she sniffled again, I held her hand. "What did you talk about in therapy that hurt so much?"

A long pause. I didn't think she was going to answer me, when finally her voice broke and she managed, "I miss him so much."

I sighed. "I know you do, mom. I'm sorry. I don't really remember him."

"It's so unfair to you, you basically lost both of your parents with his death. It's a wonder you turned out so good. I'm so sorry."

"Will you tell me about him? You never talk about him."

She sat up, placing both her hands on my cheeks. "You're so much like him, sometimes it hurts. He was so good, he would be so disappointed with what I've become. He loved so fiercely, he never would've let me hurt you the way I have. I think sometimes it's because you remind me of him so much. It's like he's here, but not really, and that's what hurts so bad. The illusion of him, just out of my reach."

"He was like me?"

"Yes. You've got his spirit, his looks. His kind heart. I should've loved you for it, but instead I let it fuel my pain, got angry at you for not being him."

"I know it was hard, but it sounds like therapy was pretty productive." I tried not to show how much the words hurt. It was something she had to work through, something she was newly realizing. But why did she hate when there was the option to love?

"I do, you know."

"Do what?"

"Love you for it."

She wrapped me in her arms, and my face got hot and teary.

"You really think he would've loved me still?"

"Why wouldn't he?"

"Because I'm trans."

"Oh, I think he would've loved you even more because of it. He was always fiercely himself, he refused to change himself to make other people happy. What you're doing is the same thing. I'm sorry I made it so hard for you, made you think you weren't worthy of love because of it. You are. You deserve so much love.

So much more than I've given you. I hate myself for all I've failed to give you."

"You shouldn't hate yourself, mom. You're trying so hard to fix it now. I know it's tough going, but don't think I don't see it. I do. I know we can't forget everything that's happened, but we can move past it. We survive. It's what I've been doing my whole life. I know I've been kind of angry and blunt with you recently, but it doesn't mean I don't still love you. You're my mom."

"Thank you for saying that. You're such an old spirit, too mature for your years."

"I've had to be. I wouldn't have made it otherwise."

She rubbed my arms and kissed me on the top of my head, sniffling. "You know, I think he would've been so happy. He always wanted a girl."

CHAPTER SEVENTEEN

When I got off the bus in the morning, school was an absolute zoo. There were reporters and cameras everywhere, questions being shouted as I saw the principal shield her face as she forced her way into the building. I never thought it would get this big, but apparently after I'd gone home Alex had done some work in contacting news outlets. As I stood there, taking in the situation, reporters caught sight of me and flooded around me.

"Jeremy, word is that you recorded the video, what do you have to say about it?"

Cameras flashed in my face, and I squinted against the onslaught of media. I hadn't prepared for this. I should've seen it coming.

"I, Uh—"

"Do you know Theo Venia and Kyle Ritter? Alex Kenzington, who posted the video?"

"Yes, I—"

"We found that Kyle was suspended, but so was Theo, who didn't even fight back in the video, can you confirm this?"

"I'm—"

"Was this a hate crime?"

My anxiety was at a peak, my hands shook and my breathing started to quicken. I was so overwhelmed and glanced around for an exit. I was surrounded.

Then, Alex came to my rescue, pushing her way inside the circle of reporters.

"This was absolutely a hate crime," she started, her confident tone commanding silence around the circle as she stood in front of me, placing a hand on my shoulder. "Kyle has harassed and bullied every student that he has identified as part of the LGBTQ+ community. Up until now, he's received no consequences for his actions, and it's progressed far past casual schoolyard bullying. He's broken bones, caused concussions, drawn blood and so much more. He runs rampant around the school, a group of followers in tow, attacking our community at will. We've brought a petition to the principal, as well as pictures of injuries he's caused, and we were ignored, no consequences were given to him, and so we decided to release the video to force action on the principal's part."

The reporters scribbled furiously on notepads, while various cameras recorded us and flashed as Alex stood tall. She had such confidence, like she was born for this.

One of the reporters leaned in. "Why was Theo suspended?"

"Theo wasn't just suspended, they were verbally accosted by the principal herself just shortly after she pulled us into her office over the video. She demanded that we take it down and was clearly reluctant to give Kyle any consequences. She gave Theo twice as much time on their suspension as she gave Kyle, and only seemed to care about the school's image rather than the violence going on underneath her nose. She threatened to suspend Jeremy and I as well."

"She wanted to suspend you for posting the video?"

"Yes. The only reason she didn't was that Theo brought up

the fact that she'd look even worse if she were to suspend us for bringing this out into the open. After the meeting, Kyle verbally attacked Theo and they defended themself, which led to their suspension. The principal yelled in Theo's face and told them that they were the only menace in the situation, despite being aware that they have PTSD and can be triggered by something like that."

I glanced at Alex at the mention of Theo's mental health, unsure of if they'd want something like that shared. But I trusted Alex not to release something that Theo wasn't comfortable with, and put it to rest in my mind by assuming that they must've talked about it.

"How long have hate crimes like this been going on?"

"Years. We've been punished so many times for defending ourselves, while Kyle gets nothing."

"Why have you decided to bring it out in the open now?"

"We're tired of this. We want it to end. We deserve to feel safe in our own school."

The reporters seemed satisfied and began to disperse, some standing in front of camera men and reporting live, while others scurried off after other students. One apprehensively approached Alex – she was very young, but immediately I picked up on a progress pride flag sticker on the back of the notebook she'd been scribbling in.

"You said there were pictures of your injuries, would I be able to get access to them? And possibly the petition you turned into the principal as well? I'm not some big news outlet, but I work for a pretty influential queer activist group, and we'd like to help. You're absolutely right, you deserve to feel safe in your own school."

Alex nodded, taking the notepad from the reporter and writing down her email. "Message me, and I'll send you everything."

The reporter dipped her head at Alex. "Thank you. You," she

looked around Alex and nodded at me as I practically hid behind her, "Jeremy, and Theo are incredibly strong for what you're doing."

Smiling as the reporter left, Alex turned around and put her hands on my shoulders. "You okay?"

I took a deep breath, the ringing in my ears beginning to die down, "I… I think so. How… How did you do that? You shut them all up so fast, and you were so confident, and…"

She shrugged. "We've gotta get them on our side. I don't know about you, but I like it when my voice is heard."

"You made it look so easy."

Smiling, she put an arm around my shoulders and started to walk us towards the school. "We've all got our strengths. We'd be nothing without your camera work."

The inside of the school was buzzing with talk about us and the reporters. Security guards ushered us in, bouncing the media at the door. So many people were happy to greet us with high-fives and smiles, and Kyle's group was nowhere to be seen. Alex seemed almost giddy until the principal and a security guard met us with scowls on their faces.

"What, you gonna threaten to suspend us again?" Alex didn't hold back, perhaps a little high on her power trip at the moment. "Everyone's watching, do what you want." She smirked, reminding me of Theo's sass towards the principal yesterday. They had this in common, it just took a little more to bring it out of Alex.

The principal's face contorted, as if she'd just bit down on a lemon. Her fury was at a peak, face red, hands shaking, pointed glares in our direction. Then, through clenched teeth, she uttered, "My office. Now."

She marched in the direction of her office, the security guard herding us after her. We were both instantly uncomfortable with this large man ushering us through the hallways and looked at each other knowingly. It was a good thing Theo wasn't here, this surely would've set them off. Cops, guards, large men in general.

He stopped at the door of the principal's office, holding it open and gesturing for us to go inside. One last wary look at him, and we sat in the chairs in front of the principal's desk. Alex leaned back, crossing her arms with a distinct pout as if this was a waste of her time. I, on the other hand, nervously wrung my hands together and glanced around the room, unable to focus on any one thing. The principal leaned forward on her elbows placed on the desk, hands against her forehead, staring down at the mousepad and taking in a deep breath. In this moment, her stoic facade was showing some cracks. She gathered herself, then lifted her head from her hands, fury alight in her eyes.

"This slander has to stop. News outlets. You went to *news outlets!?*"

The hair stood up on the back of my neck and I avoided eye contact, trying to shrink myself into my seat, disappear. Alex, on the other hand, sat up straight, shoulders back, a commanding presence that I'd never really noticed before today.

"We're doing what it takes to keep ourselves safe, since you won't. It isn't slander if it's true."

The principal slammed a hand down on her desk and leaned back in her chair so hard I could hear her shoulders collide with the padded plastic. The chair squeaked, complaining about the sudden impact.

"I should suspend you both," she growled.

The sentence stabbed me in the chest, and my throat began to close as my hands grabbed more frantically at each other. Alex, on the other hand, showed none of the fear she'd had yesterday. Clearly, she felt she had a leg up in the situation. Her posture remained proud and tall as she struck the principal with her words.

"So suspend us. Like Theo said yesterday, I'm sure that'll look good on your part. We're not going to stop. Here's an idea: do your fucking job."

"I *AM* doing my job!" the principal shouted. "Do you have any idea what it takes to corral literal *thousands* of you ingrates? Petitions this, suspensions that, I get more shit from your group than anyone else in the school. Do you understand how *difficult* you make my job?"

"I'm sorry, but if you actually cared it wouldn't be so hard to keep track of us. You'd recognize an issue as big as this and do something about it, not let it get out of hand like this. None of this would've happened if you'd actually bothered to protect us."

"A juvenile delinquent like Elizabeth doesn't need protection. She's the real problem here, I don't understand how you two don't see that."

"Theo!" Alex and I shouted in unison. I glanced at Alex, who had leaned forward in her seat as her face reddened. Neither of us liked the attack on Theo's character, but Alex was quicker to defend them as she went on. "They're not a delinquent, they're the only one protecting us in the first place. You punish the self-defense, not the attacks. You're not looking at the whole picture here."

"I know what kind of kid Elizabeth is, I've seen them before in my decade of being a principal. No direction, no motivation, useless to society. A scourge to the community. She's just been the most vocal about it, defiant to all authority. I'm sure her first step once she graduates will land her in prison. *If* she graduates at all."

As the principal talked, Alex's legs twitched with each insult that was hurled in Theo's direction. I'd never seen Alex this angry – her teeth clenched and everything. She wasn't as prone to blow up as

Theo, but I really wasn't sure what would happen at this point.

"You two, you've got a future ahead of you if you just stop hanging around with the likes of her. I don't understand why you're wasting your time, you could be applying yourselves to your schooling, getting into good colleges with your grades. Instead you're stirring up a ruckus you never had to be involved in."

Alex was biting her lip, she was trying hard not to say something that would make this turn into an even worse conversation, so it was my turn to speak. Inhaling deeply, I straightened myself in the chair and made eye contact with the principal for the first time.

"You really think this has nothing to do with us?"

"Of course not, you're just trying to make this bigger than it is."

"You know how Theo and I met? Kyle had shoved me to the ground and his entire group was kicking me as I curled in a ball trying to protect myself. Theo pulled them off of me, stood up to Kyle and got him to tuck tail and run. They didn't even know me, but they saw that I needed help and protected me. You think that's delinquent behavior?"

"Looking for a fight is delinquent behavior, yes."

Alex let out a huff and got up from her chair swiftly, placing her hands on the edge of the principal's desk. "Okay, do you actually have anything concerning us, or were you just trying to scare us into stopping? Because I've had enough of this bullshit."

The principal recoiled at Alex's sudden movement, but then leaned in, trying to take command of the situation. "Whatever you're planning, it needs to end. I'll be watching, and I won't tolerate any more of this."

Alex *laughed*. Literally laughed in her face. My jaw almost hit the floor. What little respect she had for this woman was completely gone, and she followed it with, "You know, you tell us not to make threats, when you're the one throwing them out there. You won't know what's happening until it's already happened."

With that, she turned on her heels and walked out, leaving me blinking anxiously at the principal's stunned expression before scrambling out of my chair and running out to catch up to her.

"Fuck, Alex, are you trying to make up for Theo not being here? You definitely just pissed her off more."

"I'm not afraid of her, I'm done with this shit. The way she treats and talks about Theo, she doesn't deserve the respect I was holding out for her. She's a petty, insecure woman that shouldn't have that job. I'm done trying to be civil."

"Should we really be pissing her off, though? What if she steps on everything, suspends us? We can't run a walk-out if we're out of school. I don't know about you, but I don't want a suspension on my record."

"She can't, and even if she does, we'll fight the suspensions because they'll be unfounded. If we're out, Harriet can run the walk-out, the principal has no idea she's involved. Jer, this is water tight. We're doing this."

I sighed, my chest so tight I could barely breathe. Wringing my hands together, I tried as hard as I could to take deep breaths, staring at the floor as we walked and tears starting to brim in the corners of my eyes.

Alex stopped me, getting in front of me and placing her hands on my shoulders, "Hey, it's okay. We're going to be okay."

"It's just... all so much. It's too much." My voice cracked and I rubbed at my eyes where tears began to escape.

"Phee," she whispered, so no one but me would hear the name, "We've got each other's backs. We always have."

Reluctantly, I nodded, and she pulled me into a hug, squeezing me tight. I sighed, letting the pressure soothe me as I wrapped my hands around her back and sniffled.

Eventually, we pulled away, Alex still holding my shoulders as she repeated, "We're going to be okay."

Taking in the array of stickers just as I had the first time, I knocked on Quinn's door. I ran my fingers along the progress pride flag, then jumped back a little as Quinn opened the door.

"Come in, come in," she said softly, turning back to her uncomfortable-looking desk chair. I closed the door lightly behind me, then sat in the chair across from her, dropping my backpack to the side and wringing my hands together as I sat down. I bit my lip and stared down at the floor.

"Phee, you okay?

"I… I…" I broke. Sobs started to take over my body, and I covered my face with my hands and felt the wet of tears. I didn't know how to stop it, and frankly I was too exhausted to try. I brought my knees up to my chest in the chair and wrapped my arms around them, rocking slightly. I buried my face in my knees to try and muffle the sound.

I heard Quinn get up from her desk and walk towards some of the shelves, then felt a weight on top of my knees. Picking my head up, I was met face to face with a dog plush that was way heavier than it looked.

Quinn sat back down, giving me a faint smile I barely made out through the blurriness of my tears. "Let it out, kiddo, we can talk about it when you're ready."

I picked up the plush, pulling it into my chest, the weight grounding me a little. Slowly, the sobs began to stop, and I started to catch my breath. Reaching out for a tissue, I wiped my face dry and blew my nose, trying to take a few deep breaths. My eyes stung and were still a bit blurry, but I'd managed to compose myself for the most part.

Quinn took a deep breath, then rested her hand on her desk while propping her chin up with the other. "His name's Digby."

I looked down at the dog I was clutching to my chest and felt the soft, furry fabric with my hands while sniffling a bit. "That's a good dog name."

She smiled. "So tell me what's been going on."

"A lot. Everything. Too much."

"Let's start with the most recent."

"The principal's been threatening us with suspensions because of the video. She pulled us into her office again this morning. Alex stood up to her, but the principal's just… so awful."

"Again?"

"Yeah… she pulled us in yesterday too with the same threats, except Theo and Kyle were there too. She suspended Kyle for a week and then when we were leaving Kyle provoked Theo and they punched him, the principal gave them two weeks. When we were in the nurse's office she yelled at Theo and they got triggered really bad… they ran off, we had to run after them. I found them hiding in the woods."

Quinn's eyebrows furrowed. "She yelled at them?"

I nodded. "Right in their face. They already weren't okay, we were in there getting their meds."

Quinn shook her head. "And how do you feel in all of this? Them running off must've been scary."

"It was. We were afraid they'd hurt themself or someone else. And then, when I found them they were just… gone. I couldn't get their attention, they were just staring into space, somewhere else. I didn't know how to help."

"Had that happened before?"

"Not that I've ever seen, they were just *gone*. I felt so helpless. Eventually, they came out of it and had a panic attack while I held them. That sucked too, but at least I knew what to do, how to help them. They've been through so much I know they haven't told me... It hurts knowing how much they must hurt."

"I'm sure, as a friend, you want to try and fix it."

I nodded slightly. "I know that I can't fix everything, but... I still feel like I should."

"It's hard to let that go, not have that healing power. We never want our friends to hurt like that."

"Everything's so fucked... Alex hasn't had it easy either. I don't understand why people have to hurt others like this. Parents... principals... all the people that should be protecting us. Why does it always get taken out on us?"

Quinn gave a knowing nod, taking in a deep breath. "People fail each other, it's human nature. Some of it is inexcusable, but we're all constantly just making mistakes, some bigger than others."

"Some of it seems so purposeful, though."

"Something being on purpose doesn't mean it's not a mistake. That doesn't mean people shouldn't be held accountable, by any means."

I sniffled, running my hands along Digby's fabric. "Is it a mistake, what we're doing?"

Quinn leaned back in her chair, the squeak of the plastic making me cringe. "Absolutely not. You're standing up for what's right, trying to ensure safety for more than just yourselves. It's a difficult journey, but hopefully one that's worth it. I'll be doing everything I can to help you."

A silence grew between us, too many things pinging back and

forth in my head for me to figure out what to talk about next. I was so overwhelmed, the room felt like it was closing in on me, and I blinked hard to try and shake off the feeling.

"Aside from all you've been dealing with here, how is everything at home? With your mom?"

Something to focus on. "I went home last night and she had a bottle of wine in her lap, sitting in the dark in the living room."

"She drank?"

I shook my head. "It was still sealed. She told me that therapy was really hard and it wouldn't help her."

"It's tough work, someone who hasn't done it before might find it daunting, especially after a first session. Is she going to keep going?"

"I don't know. We talked a little and she seemed a little better. I dumped out the wine after she went to bed."

"Good. It's best not to keep it in the house."

"I thought about drinking it."

With those words, the air in the room went cold. Quinn blinked at me for a couple of seconds, and for a minute, I regretted what I'd said.

"Have you ever had substance abuse issues?"

"I get high with Theo sometimes, but it's just weed, and I don't do it all the time. I've never really drank."

"When you get high, are you trying to escape from things?"

"Sometimes. Sometimes I just want everything to stop, slow down for a minute. Dull all of the big feelings that I'm having, make it so everything isn't screaming at me all at once."

Quinn nodded silently. I wasn't sure what to make of her expression. Anxiety started to overtake me, my face got hot and tingly, while I felt a stabbing in my chest.

"Am I in trouble?"

"No, Phee. You're a teenager, teenagers experiment. As long as it's not taking over your life and affecting you on a daily basis, it's fine. As long as you're just talking weed – heavier things can lead to a lot of trouble, especially down the road. I wouldn't recommend it."

I shook my head. "I'll never touch it, not after seeing what it did to Theo."

Quinn nodded knowingly. Theo's suicide attempt hadn't been made known around the school, but a lot of people assumed drugs were involved in their absence sophomore year. I'm sure Quinn had been made aware, being the social worker at school, even if Theo didn't see her regularly.

"What do you think would've happened if you drank the wine?"

"I… I don't know. I've never gotten drunk before, I've always been too afraid to drink because of the way my mom is. That shit's hereditary, isn't it?"

"It can be. It's probably wise to be careful about it. What made you think about drinking it, if you've never wanted to before?"

"Sometimes, when my mom's really drunk, she's so *happy*. It can turn on a dime, but that happiness is something I've always envied. I want to know what it feels like, being so carefree, like nothing matters in the world, like nothing bad has ever happened. I want to turn my fucking brain off for a couple hours."

"I know there's a lot going on, and it's very overwhelming, it's understandable that you feel that way. I don't blame you for thinking about it."

"It doesn't mean I'm weak?"

"Well, you didn't drink it, now did you?"

"No…" Digby's ears were really soft. I hadn't noticed that I'd been rubbing them between my thumbs and index fingers.

"That's absolutely not the behavior of someone who's weak."

I sighed, dropping my shoulders and tossing my head back until it hit the top of the chair and I was staring up at the ceiling. Everything spun a little for a second as I tried to focus on the tiles above me, until I gave up and closed my eyes.

"What else has been overwhelming you?"

"I have to edit the pictures for the self-portrait part of my senior project. And do the written part. I don't want to."

"You're just putting off the work, or something's stopping you?"

"I… I don't want to look at myself that hard. Dysphoria has been a pretty big issue, especially since my mom cut my hair." I lifted a hand to run it through the strands that now touched the tips of my ears.

"Did you dress masculine in your pictures?"

"No. Alex even did my makeup. Some boy came up to me and asked for my number."

"How did that feel?"

"Weird. Good, I guess? I still don't believe it wasn't a prank."

"Did he seem genuine?"

"Yeah, he seemed really nervous. I don't think he clocked me. Alex said we could do a double date if I wanted to see him. I'm still not sure."

"A double date would take the danger out of the situation. If he's not for real, you can just have a nice night out with your friends and tell him to fuck off."

I snickered a little, picking my head up and feeling the rush of blood run from it.

With that, the bell rang for the next period, startling me into putting my feet on the floor and dropping Digby in my lap.

"What's your next period? We can continue if you'd like, I can write you a note."

"I can't, it's with Clare and my senior project that I don't want to look at, but I have to."

Quinn nodded with a patient smile. "Feel free to come back if you find it too difficult."

I set Digby down on Clare's desk before hoisting my heavy backpack on and walking out the door, blinking at the rush of students making their way through the halls. Waiting for a gap I could slip into, I held my breath as I was carried to Clare's room by the sea of traffic. Stepping out of the hall, I let the breath go and inhaled the scents of an art room that I'd always taken for granted. The earthy smells of clay and charcoal, the sweetness of pencil wood. It wasn't as intoxicating as the chemical smells of the dark room, but it felt like home nonetheless. I dropped my bag next to the stool in front of the computer I used for editing my pictures, wordlessly sitting down.

"Hi, Phee."

I jumped at the name, here, in this setting, before I remembered that I'd already told Clare, and the room was empty.

"Hi, sorry, I've kinda been in my own world."

Clare approached the desk, pulling a stool up next to me. "It's been a while since we've done a check-in, why don't you show me what you've got so far?"

Happy to put off working on my pictures longer, I plugged in the thumb drive that held all my pictures. Opening the file of completed pictures, I started with Theo's. My heart skipped a beat as I pulled up my favorite picture, their golden eyes alight in the sun.

Clare smiled, saying something about the framing and composition of the piece, while I was lost staring at it. She must've stopped talking at some point, and I jumped as I felt a tap on my shoulder.

"Phee, you with me?"

"Yeah, sorry. Should I change anything?"

"Not at all, it's a captivating photo. Do you have the written piece of it?"

"Yeah, I…" I squinted, before clamoring through my bag to pull out a manilla folder with some lined paper inside. "I haven't actually looked at it yet, they gave it to me last week."

"Well, let's have a look, then!"

I set the folder on the desk, flipping past the notes I'd scrawled down from my conversation with Alex to get to Theo's handwritten paragraphs. I leaned forward as Clare leaned in as well and we silently took in the words.

"My body is something I haven't always loved. I've taken out my anger, my frustration, my pain on it. I haven't always treated it right. Neither have other people. I've come to love a few things about myself in recent years, though. My strength – the weight it can bear without breaking. Once I started transitioning, I began to like specific aspects – the visual appeal of my muscles, the sharp line of my jaw, the freckles that Alex says she loves so much. There's a few things I still struggle to appreciate, though. My size – I'm always underestimated. My chest – it burdens me and makes me dysphoric. And my scars – although a good friend once told me they were beautiful, that they told the story of where I've been and how I came out on the other side. I think it might be the reminder of the people that hurt me that I really don't like."

"It's so much easier to see the beauty in other people's bodies than my own. Distinguishing features become visual cues that make you happy because they mean you're with a person you like. The body language your friends use when they're happy, it's beautiful in its own right. Every part of someone you love is beautiful, because it's them. You hate when your friends talk badly about parts of themselves, because you don't see it. No parts of your friends are ugly to you. Everyone is beautiful in their own unique way, whether they see it or not."

"Wow." Clare exhaled the word before looking to me for my own reaction.

I took a deep breath. Theo's writing always caught me off guard, blew me away. They were always so raw, so honest in a way you don't expect.

"They really have a talent for it," Clare said. "Is it what you were looking for?"

"It's perfect."

Clare smiled. "What else do you have?"

I showed her Alex's pictures and the parts of the conversation we'd had written down. Then moved on to Seth. He'd chosen the kitchen as his location, of course. His picture made me smile – he looked so happy, a kitchen towel thrown over his shoulder as he held a pan in mid-flip. Stir-fry, one of his classics. His paragraph was a little more to-the-point, it might even look thoughtless to someone who didn't know how analytical his mind was. He was always direct, didn't stop to calculate every part of a situation, just gave the most accurate and short answer he could. That's how we ended up with:

"I like my hands, they make things. Beautiful and delicious things."

"I don't like how lanky I am, people view it as weak."

"Other people are beautiful for who they are, and that's just embodied in how they look to us. If they're beautiful inside, they're beautiful outside too."

I clicked through to Rachel's photo, then Harriet's, then Elliot's. Elliot looked so stiff in every picture, regardless of how candid I tried to make it. I just couldn't put him at ease, a tension still straining our relationship. How I wished I could make him understand why I ended it, and that I still loved him, just not in the way he wanted me to. A pang of guilt hit me as I studied his face – there was a sadness behind the stiffness of his face, one that he was trying to hide from me. One that I'd caused.

I was pulled out of it when Clare patted me on the back. "You've got some really good stuff so far. Do you know how you're going to display it?"

"I was thinking of mats for the photos, and then the typed answers next to them in their own mats. White for the photos, black for the answers."

"Hm." Clare tapped her index finger to her lips. "Maybe go with gray for the answers instead? Black might stand out too much, take focus away from the photos."

I nodded. "Like a light gray? Actually, maybe even gray for all of them, to look more uniform. I just didn't want the white frames with the mostly white pages of text."

"Now you've got it." Clare smiled and turned back towards her desk. "Continue."

I sighed as she walked away, then pulled up my photos, closing my eyes after I selected the set to open. After another deep breath, I opened my eyes and they frantically scanned the computer screen.

This wasn't me, surely. This person was beautiful, held grace and confidence as she skated across the screen. I got to the picture I'd pointed out when Alex took them, and the portrait that was right after it. Why couldn't I be this person? Me, all the time. This person didn't care what people thought of her, she knew she was beautiful, and no one could tell her otherwise.

And she certainly wasn't a boy.

My skin started to crawl a little and I squirmed against the fabric of my clothing, suddenly painfully aware of every inch of myself. I was wearing a baggy black hoodie and skinny jeans. Not my most boyish outfit by far, but one that still wasn't me. One that was used to hide, remain ambiguous and unseen. It let people wonder, but didn't scream 'girl' or 'boy' at any point. To me, though, 'boy' might as well have been plastered on my forehead. I scratched at my arms, everything feeling awful, just *wrong*. This wasn't the reaction I'd expected to have to these pictures. I thought I'd just be upset by how I looked, but no, I was getting dysphoric by comparing myself to, well, myself.

That's when I realized I couldn't hide anymore. Hiding was killing me. Tomorrow, I'd do it. I'd come in full femme and just deal with the backlash, be brave like I wished I'd been in the first place. Brave like Theo was, not giving a damn what anyone else thought. This would be the time to do it, anyway, with Kyle gone.

For now, I had to separate myself from this. I shook my head, focusing on the colors and framing of the photo rather than the actual subject. Taking on an analytical perspective with an editing eye helped, but the itching in my skin didn't stop. When the bell rang, I closed the file so fast I wasn't even completely sure if it had saved correctly, but that was a problem for future me. I'd had enough for today.

CHAPTER EIGHTEEN

The mirror hated me. I'd tried on six different outfits, and none of them were right. I was running out of time, the bus would be here in twenty minutes, and I still had to do my makeup. I dug through my drawers until I landed on a floral blous\e with a cream background. I put it on with a pair of black leggings and stared for a minute, finally at least a little satisfied. I rummaged around and added some bangles to the look, then headed to my bathroom with my makeup bag.

Alex made it look so easy. This shit was *hard.* I wiped off the eyeliner at least six times, my skin starting to get red and irritated. Eventually, I got a pair of wings to look good enough and tried to remember all the steps that Alex hurriedly performed on my face. Blinking in this mirror that hated me just as much as the last one, I had to call it quits without being completely satisfied as the final alarm rang on my phone. I grabbed my backpack from my room and rushed towards the door, when words from my mom stopped me.

"You're going to school like *that?*"

My blood ran cold, hand freezing on the doorknob. Slowly, I turned my head to look at her quizzically.

"It's just… don't you get bullied enough already? Do you really want to add to it? This is all fine and good when you're here, or with your friends, but school?"

"I can't hide anymore, mom. I'm so tired of it."

She looked me up and down, then got up from the couch and approached me. I took a step back against the wall, waiting for the impact, a slap to the face. Flinching, I closed my eyes. If I didn't see it coming, maybe it wouldn't hurt so much.

The slap didn't come. Instead, I felt arms engulf me in a tight hug. Opening my eyes, tears threatened to ruin my makeup as my face got hot. This wasn't what I'd expected, I didn't know what to do. After an awkward amount of time, I returned the hug, leaning into my mom's shoulder and trying desperately not to cry. As she pulled away, I sniffled, vision blurry as I tried to wipe away tears before they ruined my face.

"Okay, my baby. Just please be careful."

I nodded, turning towards the door and rushing out of the apartment before she could see me fall apart. I wasn't used to this, the affection and acceptance. I'd lived my seventeen years not knowing if I'd receive violence or screaming, and feeling uncomfortable the few times she did show kindness when she was happy drunk. This was sober, intentional affection. I couldn't remember the last time I'd had that in reaction to daring to be myself. I felt so silly, crying over a hug. Taking a deep breath, I composed myself and descended the stairs and was out the door just in time for the bus to pull up. I rushed onto the bus, keeping my head down and taking a seat towards the back, hoping no one noticed me. No one seemed to care, so I released the breath I was holding and pulled out my phone, realizing I hadn't given Alex a heads up. I texted her, letting her know that I was going to be out today, no matter the consequences. She sent me back a heart emoji right as the bus pulled up to school.

As soon as I got off the bus, I was caught in an embrace – a warm hug that Alex was notorious for. I laughed a little, hugging her back. When we let go, she leaned in towards me, looking at my face before taking a step back and admiring my outfit.

"You did so good! How many times did you fuck that eyeliner up? Your eyes are so red."

I didn't particularly feel like telling her that the redness was probably from a hug my mom gave me and not what she assumed, so I chose to just answer her question. "I lost count."

She giggled a little. "You'll get better at it, it just takes some practice." She wrapped an arm around my shoulders, and we started walking towards the school.

The slew of reporters were nowhere to be seen, so I guessed we were just yesterday's news. Something more exciting must've happened somewhere else in the city, a new shiny thing for the news to focus on. We walked in the doors and were mostly ignored by the students already there. I got a couple of sideways glances, but nothing more. Then, I caught sight of someone.

"Alex, hey," I nudged her arm and pointed in the direction of Theo walking through the hall behind Monica who held a manilla folder just like the one we'd deposited on the principal's desk over a month ago.

Alex's eyes lit up and she started to rush towards them, but they held up a hand to stop. They gave us both a weak smile and stayed by Monica's side. They were on a mission, not to be interrupted. Eyes forward, headed directly towards the principal's office.

"I wonder what's in that folder," I whispered to Alex.

"Probably a lot, it looked kinda thick. Theo was up late putting something together last night. They didn't explain, just said that it would help us, that this was our last attempt before we do the walk-out."

"I wonder if Monica's still trying to get their suspension lifted?"

"That's probably part of it. Maybe with Monica here the principal will actually listen. I know she thinks we're all just incompetent brats, but maybe an adult bringing up the issues will get her to actually take them seriously?"

"Ugh, I hope so." I stole a glance as we walked by the principal's office, Theo sitting in a chair with their legs bouncing and arms crossed, a sneer on their face. Monica was standing up, leaning against the principal's desk and physically flipping through the pages in the folder, forcing her to look at them. I wondered if she'd ever actually seen the contents before, if she ever opened the folder we gave her in the first place.

The rest of the day was pretty uneventful. I hadn't seen Theo or Monica again after I went to class, so I had no idea how long they were in the office with the principal. I'd edited more photos in Clare's classroom, and told Quinn about coming out at school. I'd gotten a few more sideways glances and looks of disdain, but nothing I couldn't handle.

That is, up until now. Right now, I was standing in front of the bathrooms, legs crossed, trying to figure out which one to go into. I'd avoided them all day, but I couldn't wait any longer. Eventually, I took a deep breath, and as silently as possible snuck into the girl's room. I kept my head down, rushing into a stall and hoping no one noticed me. The relief I felt almost made up for how uncomfortable this experience was, but then any good feeling left me as I heard a group of girls enter the bathroom. I waited in the stall, hoping they would leave and I wouldn't have to walk by them, but the bell rang, and they remained.

Reluctantly, I pushed the stall door open, eyes on the floor, and approached the sinks to wash my hands. All conversation stopped, and the girls stared at me, a couple with their mouths hanging open. I still didn't look, grabbing a paper towel from the dispenser when an impact knocked me against the wall.

"What the *fuck* are you doing in here, pervert?" The girl was about my size, not terribly menacing, but with a group of friends to back her up this situation still didn't feel safe.

"I just had to pee." My voice was small, trying not to sound confrontational.

"And you thought you'd peep at some girls while you did it, freak?"

I shook my head and tried to push past her to leave, when the whole group cornered me. One of the girls stayed back, texting on her phone, but the rest surrounded me.

"Please, I just want to leave." I pulled at the strap on my backpack nervously, unsure of what would happen next.

The girls took turns shoving me into the wall every time I tried to make my escape, until the ping of a text received on a phone stopped them all in their tracks. They nodded at each other, then took a step away from me, letting me leave.

This didn't feel right, something was going on. I rushed past them, hoping I could make my escape into my next class, when I ran straight into what felt like a brick wall as soon as I got into the hallway. I took a step back, my heart dropping into my stomach as I looked up from the ground to see a group of boys, cocky grins on their faces. Turning to run in a different direction, one of the boys stepped in front of me. They surrounded me, and my breathing started to quicken as I felt my heartbeat in my throat.

They didn't need Kyle to rally them, he'd already shown them that people didn't care if they hurt me, people like me. The principal only suspended Kyle because we'd forced her hand, and she'd given Theo twice as long. I so desperately wanted out of this situation, but there was no exit in sight. My face got hot and tears started welling up in my eyes.

"What'chu crying for, pussy?" One boy stepped forward, putting his hand on my shoulder and pushing me back against the wall. "You're not a girl, you don't belong in the girl's room."

I struggled against his grasp but was unable to free myself. I wasn't strong enough. Why wasn't I a fighter, like Theo? Even Alex had thrown a punch or two. I felt weak, helpless. The boy grabbed me by the back of my shirt, a ripping sound heard as he forced me into the boy's room. He threw me against the mirror, drawing blood from my lip and cracking the glass. I fell to the ground in front of the sink, dazed. Then, I was dragged up by a few of the boys, and they held me bent over the sink.

One of the boys leaned over, inches from my ear and hissed, "You really think you're a girl, I'll make you feel like one."

Another boy pulled my leggings down as I struggled to get free. Then, I heard the zip of a pair of jeans as hands pressed into my back.

No, no, no.

Panic engulfed me. I fought harder, leaning forward onto the counter and throwing my legs out behind me in as hard of a kick as I could manage. There was a yelp, and the hands on my back disappeared. One of the boys holding me down let go, and I took the opportunity to rip myself away from the other one. I pulled my leggings up and ran, and ran, and ran.

I ran until I couldn't run anymore, out the doors of the school, across the street, halfway downtown. Not knowing *where* I was running, I collapsed when my legs refused to take me any farther. Pulling myself under the awning of a store, the sobs overtook me. Shaking, I pulled out my phone and called Theo.

They answered after the second ring. "Hey Phee, what's up?"

I couldn't speak, the sobs took over my whole body. My shaking hands almost dropped the phone as I cried harder, barely hearing Theo's "What's wrong?" and "Where are you?" The phone slipped from my hands eventually, and I buried my face in my knees, covering myself with my hands. I couldn't breathe, everything was so loud yet unperceivable at the same time, just a blur of noise around me. For what felt like an eternity, I was gone from this world.

A gentle touch on one of my arms, and a scream from my lips as my head shot up. I couldn't see through the blur of tears, so I recoiled from the touch until a voice broke through the ringing in my ears.

"Phee, it's me, it's okay."

Theo.

Practically tackling them, I threw my arms around them. I wanted to crawl inside of them, safe from this world and all of its monsters. My sobs didn't stop, and Theo put their arms around me, rubbing my back slightly and squeezing me tightly. After a minute, they started to nudge me upward.

"Come on, hey, let's go home."

My feet refused to carry me. Theo lifted me from the ground, taking most of my weight as I leaned against them. I heard a car door open, then Monica's voice vaguely in the background. "Is she hurt? I see blood."

I fell into the car and Theo slid in next to me, trying to get me to sit up so they could look me over. "Her lip's bleeding, but she looks okay otherwise."

I buried my face in their chest as they rested their arms around me after closing the car door. I wished they'd been there, it never would've gone so far. They never would've let that happen. They were so much stronger than me. Why couldn't I be strong?

We pulled up to Theo's house in what felt like the blink of an eye, and I was able to pull myself from the car as Theo ushered me inside. All at once, I broke away from their grasp and ran into the bathroom, turning on the shower as hot as it would go, kicking my shoes off and climbing into the tub as the water burned at my skin. I tried to breathe, let the water soothe me, but it was just searing the images that were flashing through my head into me.

Theo's voice broke me free again.

"Phee, hey. You've still got your clothes on and everything." They pulled back the shower curtain and hissed as the water hit their hand. They turned the water to a more bearable temperature, then sat down next to the tub. "I do shit like this when I have my nightmares. Please, tell me what happened." Their voice was low, soothing as they rested a hand in the middle of my back.

Hands. On my back.

I jumped away from them, even though I knew who it was this time. I wanted to scream, punch things, lose my shit. Instead, a guttural growl escaped my throat as I pounded the heels of my hands against my head. Everything felt so awful, so wrong. I was lost, and I didn't know how to come back.

Suddenly, Theo's voice was in front of me. They'd climbed into the tub with me, and had their hands wrapped around my wrists to keep me from hitting myself. Pressing their forehead to mine, they whispered, "Phee, did they touch you?"

I nodded, and immediately felt heat rush through Theo's hands. They were silent, but I felt their grip begin to shake. Their anger overtook the room, and they clamored out of the bathtub, squelching steps of their damp socks against the tile as they left. I heard yelling, some words my ears wouldn't let me understand, some almost definitely in Spanish.

My heart rate finally started to slow down as Monica entered the room, Theo behind her. Monica turned off the water and knelt down next to the tub. Once the water was gone, the cold air started to creep in and my shaking turned to shivering. Theo grabbed a towel from the cabinet and wrapped it around me while Monica spoke softly.

"Honey, I need to know how far it went."

I tried as hard as I could to get the words out, "Th-they were gonna… they held me down, they pulled my pants down, and I heard a zipper and then…"

Tears started to rush from my eyes again, mixing with the water already on my face.

"And then what?" Monica's voice was smooth, even. Too calm for the situation. Eerily so.

"And then I kicked them, as hard as I could and one of them let go, and I ran. I ran forever."

"Okay." Monica's tone didn't shift, but something in the air did. "Theo, why don't you get her dried off and warmed up? I'm going to make some calls."

With that, she left the room, and Theo started to pull me from the bathtub. I stood up slowly, leaning into them as I stepped out of the bathtub.

"I… I never should've come out."

"No," Theo held me by the shoulders, looking me in the face as I avoided eye contact. "No, don't do that. This isn't your fault, you hear me? Don't ever think it's your fault."

"I couldn't fight them off at first. I wish I was strong, like you."

"You are strong, you still fought them off. Being strong didn't save me, either. It's not up to you to stop people from hurting you, it's up to other people to not hurt you in the first place."

Theo led me into the guest bedroom and pulled out a comfy looking hoodie and a pair of joggers, handed me another towel, and turned to leave the room. "Come on out when you're ready, I'm gonna change too and then we can watch something. I'll make you hot cocoa."

After the door shut, I started to peel away the layers of soaked clothing. Tossing the clothes into the laundry basket, I wrapped myself in the towel and stood in front of the mirror. My face was already beginning to bruise. My lip had stopped bleeding, but was slightly swollen and I could see bruises on my arms from where the boys held me down. I made the mistake of looking myself in the eyes and felt nothing but hatred, disgust.

I didn't think I could ever love myself.

Shaking my head, I stepped away from the mirror, dried myself off, and put the new clothes on before venturing into the living room and collapsing on the couch. Before I knew it, Theo handed me a mug brimming with marshmallows on top and I took it eagerly as they sat down next to me.

We could both hear Monica ranting on the phone upstairs. The words were muffled through the walls, but her tone was that of someone who no longer had any patience for the school's incompetence. This was going to end, one way or another.

————————

I didn't go back to school the rest of the week. I didn't want to step foot into that place. Monica had been making calls non-stop, and I spent that first night at Theo's, sleeping fitfully in the guest bedroom.

I didn't tell my mom what happened. I didn't know how she

would react. Not wanting an "I told you so," or having to rehash the whole incident, I kept it to myself, locked away in my room with me. She knew something was wrong, offered to talk, but ultimately gave me space.

Today, I stood at the bus stop, practically in tears. I was wearing my galaxy print leggings and a black crop top – I'd thought about going back to boy clothes, but that would be letting them win. They weren't going to fucking win this, no matter what. My legs bounced as soon as I took my seat and all the way to school, where I exited the bus and was immediately greeted by Theo and Alex. Monica's pushback on Theo's suspension had gotten them one less week, but that also meant that Kyle was back. I wasn't in the place to deal with him, and I think Theo knew that, the way they were guarding me – all the way to my classroom, even though we passed theirs. We didn't see Kyle, but we all knew he'd turn up like the cockroach he was.

I sat at the computer in Clare's room – the photos were all done, and I'd formatted the words of the responses artfully. The only thing I had left was my own response, and there was no way I could do that now. After staring at a blank document for twenty minutes, I got up and walked to Clare's desk.

"Is it okay if I go see Quinn?"

"Of course, is everything okay?"

"Fine, I just need to talk." I felt bad lying to her, but I felt like I'd only be able to talk about this once today, and she wasn't the person I needed to tell.

I took a deep breath as I knocked on Quinn's door, and it opened a minute later. She gave me a weak smile and ushered me inside, closing the door behind me.

"I assume you're here to talk about what I think?"

I squinted. "What do you think?"

"About the incident in the bathroom last week."

How did she know? I glanced around the room as my anxiety rose just at the mention of this. Maybe I wasn't ready.

"I spoke with Monica last week. She couldn't get through to the principal. Phee, I'm so sorry that happened. It never should have, you didn't deserve it."

Tears started to sting at my eyes as I sat down, dropping my backpack on the floor and leaning forward, putting my head in my hands. "I can't stop seeing it. I can't focus on anything else. I hate being here."

Quinn sighed sadly, tapping her fingers on her desk. "I wish there was more I could do."

I lifted my head from my hands to look up at her. "What do you mean?"

"The principal won't do anything on just your word of mouth, I already had a pretty long argument with her. She said you were 'prone to making things up' which, please don't think I believe that. I know it's real. I know it happened. But she won't listen to me."

"Are you *fucking kidding me?*" I slammed my hands on the desk, anger overtaking me, "How fucking *useless*—"

I was stopped short by a knock on the door. I looked at Quinn, tears streaking down my face, and she gestured for me to sit as she walked to the door and opened it, just a crack, "I'm sorry, hun, can you come back later? I'm with someone else."

"Please, miss? It's really important." I couldn't figure out where it was from, but I knew that voice.

"I'm sorry, I really can't—"

"It's about something I saw last week. In the bathroom."

Quinn turned her head to me so fast I thought she'd get

whiplash. I nodded, and she opened the door, revealing a very guilty-looking boy.

I stood up from the chair and backed into the desk so quickly I almost fell over it. It was the boy that had asked for my number at the skatepark, Chris. Now that I was seeing him, I remembered. He was there that day. He didn't put his hands on me, but he stood there while that shit happened.

"Get out," I hissed.

"Phee, let's hear him out—"

"GET OUT!" I screamed, and Chris held his hands up in defense.

"I'm so sorry I didn't do anything. I want to make it right."

"You can't fucking make it right. No one can. Maybe if you'd *stopped* them—"

"You think I could've stopped them? Look at me, I'm scrawny as fuck. But I got this." He held up his phone, which, at first I didn't even look at, but then I recognized the tile of the bathroom.

It was me. Being held down over the sink, a boy's hands on my hips, about to pull my leggings down. You could see the desperation on my face, the blood on my lip, the crack in the mirror. Everything.

And you could see every. Single. Face. Laughter on them all.

I sat back down in the chair, covering my face with my hands as tears flowed freely. Chris showed the picture to Quinn, who gasped and dropped the phone on her desk at first, but then I heard the squeak of her chair as she sat down.

"Phee, I know this is hard to see, but this means something. We *got* them."

"Fucking *how?!* The principal didn't do shit when we had a literal video of Theo getting knocked out. You think she'll care about this? No one fucking cares! No one's going to help us!" I was so done, angry at everything, tired of being swept under the rug.

"The principal might not, but I will."

I looked up, realizing that Chris was now sitting in the chair next to me.

"Phee, bring me the folder you brought the principal. If I'm going to go over her head, I may as well do it with everything. Chris, you'll back up Phee's story?"

Chris glanced at me, then back at Quinn. "Every word."

I rummaged through my bag and dropped a manilla folder on Quinn's desk. I'd kept a copy, just in case.

She flipped through it quickly, then looked up at me. "Every single one of these boys are going to get consequences, you hear me? This shit's gone unpunished long enough." Quinn's eyes were on fire. She was on a mission now, "Chris, why don't you come by after lunch and we'll have a chat, let Phee and I talk for a bit."

Chris nodded solemnly, then stood up from the chair. He stopped with his hand on the doorknob, then turned to look at me again. "I'm really sorry, Phee, I wish I'd done more. I'm really glad you got away."

I gave him a slight tip of the head, then turned around as he left. Quinn had her hand on the folder, while pulling something up on her computer with the other before looking back at me. "If you'd like to talk, Phee, we can talk."

I wasn't ready.

I shook my head, standing up from the chair. "Just get these fucking assholes."

She gave me a weak smile before nodding and focusing all her attention on the computer and picking up her phone as I left the office.

CHAPTER NINETEEN

I sat cross-legged in my room, photos strewn all over my floor and a stack of mats next to me. I was framing all of my photos for my senior project, avoiding doing my response to the questions. Maybe I'd just leave myself out. There wasn't anything I could find that I liked about myself anyway. I felt disgusting. I was unfocused, lost in a sea of thoughts that overwhelmed me. Mom cutting my hair. Plates thrown against a wall. Theo's panic attack. The boys in the bathroom. One trauma to the next.

I jumped as the music I'd been playing on my phone stopped and it started vibrating. Picking up the phone, I stared at the screen briefly before answering. Alex.

I accepted the call and didn't even have a chance to speak before the urgency in her voice spilled out. "Look at the school's website."

"What?"

"The school's website, Phee, I'm serious."

"Okay, okay." I pulled my laptop from my backpack and opened it, letting out an audible gasp when the site loaded up.

The normal homepage was gone, replaced with a white background and a message in bold red letters: "This school condones assault, hate crimes, and rapists. Show your support to keep students safe, join the walk-out protest, this Friday." I scrolled down, and below the initial message in a slightly smaller font was "Call for principal Lewis' termination."

"Shit."

"Click on the words."

I squinted, scrolling back up and hovering the cursor over the words, realizing the words "assault", "hate crimes", and "rapists" were linked. I clicked on assault, which led to a page with the video of Theo getting knocked out. Going back, I clicked on "hate crimes", and it led me to a page filled with the photos I'd taken of our injuries over the years. Hovering over "rapists" I took a deep breath, praying it wasn't what I thought it would be.

But it was.

The picture of me in the boy's bathroom.

"Did you do this?" My tone was sharp as I quickly clicked off the page and slammed my laptop shut.

"Phee, outside of social media I barely know how to use a computer, you think I'm going to hack the school's website? And I would've asked before posting that picture."

"I'm guessing Theo didn't either."

"I don't know who did this. I know you probably didn't want that picture up, but whoever this is, I think they're on our side."

"I don't want—"

"Phee, come out here!" I was interrupted by my mom shouting from the living room.

"I gotta go, Alex." I hung up the phone before she could respond, rushing into the living room.

I froze as soon as I crossed the threshold.

This picture would haunt me to my grave.

My mom had a local news station on, a reporter's words muffled by the ringing in my ears as my vision tunneled on the screen. It was flashing through all of the pictures, but kept coming back to mine.

"My baby, when did this happen?" My mom's wavering voice broke me free.

I blinked and shook my head, trying to come back to the present.

"What did those boys do to you? Is that why you missed school last week?"

Still stunned, I stared at her, mouth working but refusing to make words.

She got up from the couch, putting her hands gently on my cheeks. "Why didn't you tell me?"

Tears started to fall as I grasped my mom's arms. I felt so exposed, so dirty. Now everyone knew. I'd never escape this image of myself. Everyone would think I was disgusting.

My mom pulled me into a hug as I cried and even over the ringing in my ears, I heard her words clear as day. "We'll make them pay."

––––––––––

Walking into the school the next day, I'd never wished more that I was invisible. Everyone was staring at me, and I tried to shrink myself into nothing.

Theo and Alex caught up to me as quickly as they could, Alex giving me a sympathetic look while Theo placed a hand gently on my shoulder. "You okay, Phee?"

I shrugged, attention still on everyone gawking at me.

And then I saw them. Kyle, his friends, everyone that had made our lives a living hell, gathered in front of our lockers, ready to bombard us. I stopped short, I couldn't do this today.

When suddenly, it looked like I wouldn't have to.

Everyone in the hallway froze, attention no longer on me. We all stared at the glass doors as police officers walked through them, headed straight for the group. Theo bristled, even though they weren't headed for us, and Alex rested a hand on their shoulder to bring them down a little. My mouth fell open as they stomped up to the group of boys, and each of them turned to face them. Immediately, fear lit up in all of their eyes. The boy who had put his hands on my back bolted away, and an officer took off after him, quickly outpacing him, tackling him to the ground, and roughly cuffing his hands.

The rest remained frozen until Kyle blinked quickly and he put on his facade of cluelessness. "Can I help you with something, officer?"

"Can it," the officer barked, pushing Kyle away and cuffing the majority of the rest of the group.

The boys were escorted from the school, and we stood there dumbfounded, wondering why they didn't take Kyle, too. It hit me as the faces walked past me, it was every boy that was seen in the picture with me. One of the officers split from the group and started walking towards us. Quickly, I glanced at Theo, whose face had gone sheet-white and whose muscles had begun to twitch as if they were using all of their willpower to not bolt as the guilty boy had.

"You're not in trouble," the officer said, less gruff than he had been with the boys, "but we'd like you to come have a chat with us."

Instinctively, Theo had stepped in front of me to protect me, and I placed a hand on their shoulder as if to say that it was okay. They gave me a wary look, taking a step back, but kept their eyes trained on me as the officer led me away. He took me to a small conference room near the principal's office and gestured for me to sit down as he took a chair across from me.

I wrung my hands together, eyes darting around the room.

"What do you need from me?"

"I'd like to have a chat with you about the incident that happened in the bathroom, take down the details. Your mother got in contact with us to press charges. We've taken the boys in for questioning and they will be detained until we do so, but we don't have any proof aside from that picture that's been going around. It's a good start, but we need more."

I swallowed, closing my eyes and taking a deep breath. There was this thing Theo always said when I asked them things and they dodged the topic: "Talking about it makes it real."

I hadn't made it real yet. Only the picture had. I'd said what I said to Theo, but this felt so much more official, and I wasn't ready for this.

"Let's start with some easy questions. What's your name?"

"Phee."

The officer squinted. "Your mother gave us the name Jeremy."

"I'm called Phee."

The officer took a deep breath as he looked me up and down, and there was a realization in his eyes. His whole demeanor changed. He'd been sympathetic before, at least a little. Now his face was cold, and he suddenly seemed to care a lot less.

"Okay, *Phee*, what happened on that day, in the bathroom?"

My throat felt like it was closing, I didn't want to do this. Charges meant a court case – I'd have to stand up in front of an entire courtroom and tell everyone what they did, only for the jury to decide I'd deserved it because I was trans.

"Spit it out, kid." The officer was almost as gruff as he'd been with the boys.

"They…" Tears started to well up in my eyes, and I took a deep breath. If we were going to get any kind of justice in this place, it needed to start somewhere. In order for our voices to be heard, we needed to speak. I took a deep breath, then tried my best to distance myself as I was talking. "I had to pee. So I went in the girl's bathroom because I thought it would be safer. A group of girls cornered me and made me stay there until the boys showed up, then the boys dragged me into the boy's bathroom, and threw me against the mirror. The mirror broke and I fell, but then they dragged me up and bent me over the counter. They pulled my pants down, and I heard a boy unzip his pants. They said they were going to 'Make me feel like a girl.'"

I hadn't made eye contact the whole time, but when I was done I looked up for a split second to see the officer's blank, uncaring eyes.

He scribbled something down in a notepad, then gestured towards my face. "That's how you got those bruises?"

"Yes."

"Do you have any other marks on you?"

I pulled up my sleeves and showed him the now darkened bruises on my arms. He took a few photos of them and my face, then turned towards the door. "That's all I need."

I sat there, alone, as my ears started to ring again. I dropped my head onto the table, silent tears falling. I was too tired for the sobs that wanted to make their way out of my body, and instead closed my eyes and felt waves of emotions take me over. Grief, anger, disgust, fear. They kept going and going.

I jumped at a hand on my shoulder, picking my head up so swiftly that I saw stars. Theo and Alex were sitting on either side of me, Alex with her hand resting gently on my shoulder.

"You okay?" Alex asked, wiping some of the tears from my face.

"Not really," I muttered

"Do you wanna go see Quinn?" Theo asked.

"No."

"What do you need from us?" Alex's voice was soft.

"I don't know." I leaned forward on the table again, letting my head fall with a thud. Placing my hands over the top of my head, I tried to breathe, to escape, go anywhere but here.

The door opened with a slam.

"My office." The familiar, uncaring voice of the principal made me jump up once again.

Theo had it. They stood up, nearly knocking their chair over as they took a step towards the principal. The principal's eyes narrowed, and Alex called out to Theo, almost begging them to stop.

They weren't going to hit her, no. That would only hurt us, as vindicating as it might be. They stood inches from her, balling their hands into fists and unclenching them repeatedly. Shaking, their fury was about to bare itself in front of us all.

"Leave us the fuck alone."

The principal squinted, shocked at the gall that Theo had. She shouldn't have been. Even if she thought of Theo as an ingrate, she should've seen the passion that they fought with. "Be careful of the way you talk to me. What you've done to the website, it's open vandalism. It's illegal, it's defamation.

"We didn't do it." Theo's voice was a growl. "We never would've posted that picture of Phee, it's a violation of her privacy. But whoever did it, they're fucking right."

"How are they right? Breaking the law is never right."

"They were right in saying that this place supports criminals."

"Says the only one in the room with a criminal record."

Theo shook harder, the tips of their ears turning bright red. But still, they kept themself composed.

"Look at it however you want. We didn't do it, so leave us alone."

Huffing, the principal turned on her heels to leave, before

turning back for one final remark. "Get to class before I bring down detention on you all."

Thursday. One day before the walkout. The website might've rallied more participants, but it had also blown our cover and put us on a timeline. Theo and Alex had been scrambling, while I was just trying to keep it together.

That meant staying in the present. Right now, I was in the small gallery just outside the school that Clare had set up for me. I was putting up my senior project, carefully and meticulously trying to make sure each frame was straight and pristine.

The space was filled with beautiful and amazing people. People that I admired, who I wouldn't be the same without. People that knew themselves enough to answer my damn questions.

But I didn't.

As I took a step back from the wall, I stared at the photo of myself, no framed text to accompany it like the other pictures had. I just couldn't do it. As it was, I wanted to shred the picture, tear it to pieces and light it on fire, just how I felt like my life was. I couldn't see the beauty in the picture anymore, all I saw was a boy wearing the mask of a girl, too naive to see how foolish she looked. I wasn't beautiful, I never would be. It had been taken away from me by so many people in my life, and I wasn't strong enough to fight to get it back.

I didn't think I would ever get it back.

Friday morning didn't feel any different. I stared in the mirror after I'd pulled on some glittery leggings and a white frilly blouse. Tears kept coming to my eyes as I tried to do makeup, smudging it and ruining my futile attempts at making myself presentable. I sat down on the lid of the toilet, holding my head in my hands and sniffling, closing my eyes to this world, trying to escape.

I heard a small creak of the door which hadn't been completely shut, but didn't bother to look up. Just the wind, most likely. I was wrong though, as I found out when a pair of hands grasped mine. Lifting my head swiftly, I was met face to face with my mom, who wore a sympathetic look – her eyes glassy, almost as if she was about to cry herself.

"Phee, don't give up, my baby."

This was strange – the first time in a long time where I felt like she was the mother while I was the child. I'd been the parent for so long, I'd forgotten what this felt like.

My voice cracked as I squeaked out, "I'm so tired, I don't want to do this anymore."

My mom ran a hand through my hair and wiped away my tears. "Let me help you."

How was she going to help? How would this get any better?

She took a makeup wipe and wiped my face clean before pulling my makeup into her lap as she lifted my head up by my chin. She didn't have all the precision and speed that Alex had, but she was still better than me. Working on my face carefully, I tried to force back tears that threatened to ruin her work.

This was a gesture I couldn't handle. A gesture of acceptance, of love that I wasn't used to. I never thought I'd see the day where my mom did my makeup.

When she finished, she sat back and smiled. "There you go. Beautiful."

I jumped from the toilet seat and wrapped my arms around her. She returned the embrace, placing a hand on the back of my head as I heard a sniffle from both of us.

"No matter what happens, I'm always going to love you. I haven't always shown it, but I'm changing. I'm changing myself to be the mom you always deserved, okay? Don't let anyone break your spirit, it's what's gotten you this far."

We stayed there for a few minutes, in an embrace that was long overdue, until the alarm on my phone broke me from a place of love that I'd never had before. I let go, turning my alarm off as my mom stood up. She picked up my backpack from the hallway and led me to the door before handing it to me.

"You're going to change the world," she said with a smile, "Just like you've changed me."

The halls were quiet when we arrived. The principal had threatened detentions and suspensions on anyone who participated in the walk-out, and a somber air settled in the hallways. It almost felt like it wouldn't happen.

But we could see it — in the eyes of people passing us by, the slight nods tipped at us in the hallways. We were ready for this battle, all of us.

We stopped by our lockers, where Kyle was nowhere to be found, apparently he didn't have any guts with his whole crew missing. They hadn't been back at school since the officers escorted them out. We made our way to our classes, giving each other hugs before parting ways. We knew this was going to be hard, and had no idea how it would pan out, but it was going to happen. It was written in stone.

Everyone settled into their seats around me as the bell rang. I took a deep breath, glancing around the room to see what others were planning. Silence, even on the teacher's part, was deafening. As soon as the clock hit 8:15, I mustered up the strength to stand from my desk. Looking around for a second, my heart pounded as no one else moved a muscle. I bent down to pick up my backpack, waiting for the reprimand from the teacher, when to my surprise the words that came from her were, "Let's go."

The whole class stood up.

Staring in wonder as everyone started to file out of the classroom, I was so caught off guard that I practically had to pick my jaw up off the floor. The teacher was the last to leave, and at the door she turned back towards me. "You coming?"

I nodded, swiftly weaving around desks until I was right behind the teacher, when I was surprised once again. The hallway was buzzing with students and faculty, everyone headed in the same direction – the doors that led outside. Normally, the halls would be barren at this time, almost everyone in class. I let the sea of bodies take me out the doors and listened to the chatter all around me. There were *hundreds* of people out here, far beyond the scope of our little group. It wasn't just people from school either, there were reporters and camera crews everywhere. My heart started to race until my attention was brought to the middle of the crowd.

Theo stood on top of a picnic table, Alex at their back facing the opposite direction. Their shouts caused a hush from the crowd. "No more abuse! No more fear! We're here for queer rights!"

A roar erupted around them, cheers from all sides. Then, another person climbed up onto the picnic table with them – it was the person from the queer rights group that Alex had given all our information to.

They shouted alongside Theo. "We stand with the queer students! They deserve a safe school!"

Reporters swarmed around the table. I watched them part briefly before I felt a hand grab mine through the crowd. Alex pulled me along towards the table, and I hesitated as she started to climb on top of it, looking around as reporters shoved cameras in my face.

Alex paused, putting her other hand on my shoulder. "Come on, Phee. We worked so hard for this. We can't give up now."

Inhaling sharply, I climbed the picnic table with her. Theo put an arm around my shoulders, still shouting over the crowd as they began to chant. The chanting slowly died down, as a figure threw open the doors of the school.

The principal had finally gotten our message. She stood there, mouth agape as a few students peeked their heads out the door — Kyle among them, of course. The reporters swarmed her, then they suddenly turned around to hear a shout from my direction.

It was me. I was shouting. I hadn't intended to, but it was happening. "She has our blood on her hands! She knows about everything, she won't protect us!"

The principal's face reddened and she turned back inside the school, disappearing into the darkness of the building. Everyone continued to rally around the picnic table, Theo leading the crowd and urging everyone on.

Before long, cars began to pull up to the front of the school – student's parents, members of the school board, and police. She called the fucking *police*. Parents pushed their way through the crowd to get their kids that weren't participating. The board members spoke with some reporters briefly before disappearing inside of the school, and the police began to surround us. They stood, hands on their belts, but silent. They didn't touch us.

One officer made her way towards the picnic table and shouted from the ground, "Come down from there!"

Theo stomped up to the edge of the table. "Or what? This is a peaceful protest, we're not doing anything wrong."

The officer took a step back. "We just want to talk."

"Then talk from there! I'm not moving."

My anxiety was eating away at me by this point, and all the noise and people around me weren't helping. Breathing fast, I knelt down on the table, putting my hands over my ears.

Alex knelt down in front of me. "This is too much, isn't it?"

I nodded, and she took my hand again, guiding me down from the table and fighting her way through the crowd while pulling me after her. I had no idea where we were going, but I let her take me there anyway, closing my eyes as the shouts around me began to fade.

And then everything was muffled, and Alex stopped and put her hands on my shoulders. "Hey, we're here."

I opened my eyes slowly, and found myself in the gallery, surrounded by all of my pictures. As I sighed, my legs gave out beneath me, and I tried to take a few deep breaths. Remind myself that I was safe. After a minute, Alex pulled me up, and I blinked at her.

"I needed to show you something anyway." She led me across the gallery, to my final picture – the portrait of myself. I looked away quickly, and that's when I noticed. There was a framed bit of text next to my portrait now. I hadn't put it there. Gulping as I stepped forward, I tried to prepare myself for the nasty comments I expected to find written there.

They were anything but. They were all hand-written, some in writing I recognized – Theo, Alex, Seth. And some that I didn't. Bracing myself against the wall, I began reading.

"Phee isn't always fair to herself, but she's a beautiful person, inside and out."

"She has a light you can't extinguish, one that is a guide to us all."

"Phee's beauty is radiant, nowhere near as hard to find as she thinks it is. It's right there, in your face, all the time. So much that you can't look away."

"She loves with her whole self and has a passion that won't be deterred. Her beauty is in the life she breathes into everything she does."

"She is an ethereal goddess of a woman — no one can take that away."

"There is a spirit inside her that's going to change the world as we see it, she's going to make it as beautiful of a place as she is."

The last one was in my mom's handwriting.

"She is my love, my light, my everything. She's taken care of me through my dark times, and now it's my turn to support her in her journey. She will make this world a better place, one picture at a time."

EPILOGUE

I don't really have words for what we've accomplished. All I know is that we fought with passion, with a fierce spirit, and that's how you get things to change. That's how you survive. You surround yourself with the fighters, the people that support you and all your dreams, your true family.

Family hasn't always been something positive in my life. That is, until I realized that family goes beyond blood. The family you find, the one you create for yourself – those are your true companions in life. If you pick the right ones, they'll be there for you until the bitter end. They'll fight for your safety, to make your dreams come true. When things aren't fair, when they get hard, they'll be there to pick you up from the ground, dust you off, and build you back up.

I'm very fortunate to have found this family, and I wouldn't trade it for the world. This family is the reason I'm alive, fighting. I love them with all my heart and soul. And they love me, they're not afraid to show it, even when it's hard for them. People show love differently, but if you're willing to receive it, it'll be there in whatever form it comes. Don't forget to love them back, ever. They'll come through for you in ways you'd never imagined. They'll help you through this journey of life, until you're off your feet, flying.

It took me a while to find them, but in the end I had the best family I could've asked for. Don't ever forget – if I made it, my messy, worn-down self, then so will you. You'll find your people, it doesn't matter what point in life, you *will* find them, and they'll lift you up as it was always meant to be. You'll fly one day, don't let your clipped wings stop you. They'll grow back, and you'll experience freedom like never before.